In Her Words

By
J.S Ellis

In Her Words
All copyright © 2019 Joanne Saccasan
All right reserved. No part of this book may be used or reproduced in any way without permission except in the case of quotations or book reviews. This book is a work of fiction. Name, characters, businesses, organizations, places, events, locales, and incidents are either the product of the author's imagination or used in a fictitious manner. Any resemblance to an actual person, living or dead, or actual events or locals is entirely coincidental.
For information contact:
Black Cat Ink Press
https://blackcatinkpress.com/
J.S Ellis
https://joannewritesbooks.com/

Cover Design by: German Creative
Edited and proofread by: Sharon Woodcock & Doreen Muscat
ISBN: 978-99957-1-443-7 Paperback
978-99957-1-445-1 e-book

2nd January
Evening,
Dear Diary,

I'm in trouble.
To everyone else, I have it all: the handsome husband, prestigious apartment, successful career, and the designer clothes. What they don't know is, I'm the saddest person I know. I've lost touch with who I used to be. I'm the same person I was at 11:59, and as I was at 12:01. No new me, no difference, no New Year's resolutions. It's bullshit, we are what we are. If we want to change, we make it happen. I don't know what's what anymore. No-one realizes I'm a chain smoker, with a drinking habit. You wouldn't suspect it from my polished exterior.

An hour ago, I was lying on the bathroom floor with a bottle of whiskey. Hiding evidence of my drinking has become second nature to me. When we're sad, we drink to forget. When we're happy, we drink to celebrate. When nothing happens, we drink to make something happen. I drink to escape from the pain of life and to forget what happened.

I'm writing this at the kitchen table, with a glass of water, a box of aspirins, and an overflowing ashtray beside me. I haven't kept a diary since I was a teenager. Back then, I didn't write often. And now? I need to keep an account of my bad behavior before it catches up with me.

3rd January
Afternoon.
Diary,

It was busy walking to work this morning. I must have blended in with the horde of grey and black-suited corporates in my charcoal grey designer suit.

For some, London is a jaded city. It's not for everyone. Yet, as I looked up at all the Victorian buildings, I wondered what goes on behind closed doors. I love London: its lack of community and rudeness. I even like its weather. I caught a bloke giving me the eye as I walked past a cafe. It was either the click-clacking of my heels on the pavement that did it or my tight pencil skirt. Probably the latter, or both!

I work at *Miller & Miller*, a new accountancy firm in central London, which opened two years ago. I've been an accountant all of my life and used to work at one of the big four accountancy firms until I quit the stress of it all. At *Miller & Miller,* I take care of twenty big clients, with whatever worries they have-which can be a lot.

When I arrived at work, I freshened up my makeup and applied eye drops to hide the redness. I then gargled mouthwash and sprayed a little perfume. My usual routine to mask the smell of alcohol and cigarettes. As I walked out of the bathroom and into the corridor, Wendy, the secretary, stalked after me.

'Mr. Williams called. He wants you to call him back, it's urgent,' she gasped.

Everything's always urgent.

I plodded past Charles' office, the accounting manager. He's a short beefy man, going bald with thick glasses. He glanced at me and then carried on with his client.

'He said, they're going to investigate him. He received some nasty tax assessment,' Wendy continued.

I stopped and turned to face her, 'What?'

'You should call him, he wants you to defend him,' she said.

'I will but,' taking the paper from her, 'he's not the most organized of clients. Connect me to him.' I said, opening my office door.

I shut my eyes. The phone rang. Another day at the office.

5th January
Evening,
Diary,

I can hear the sound of sax and guitar again from one of the apartments down the street. I've been hearing it for the past three months. It's enchanting. I've been listening to it for the past hour. My hands are trembling as I write this. It's time for my fix, so I'm sitting by the window with a bottle of wine, smoking. The music keeps me company. Where does someone get the inspiration to write music like this? I love the sax. I wonder who's playing it? I'm picturing an African-American man standing by a window of a bar somewhere.

I'm alone in the apartment at the moment. Every time Richard goes away, the anxiety kicks in. He's in New York for business until the weekend. You can sense his importance when Richard walks into the room, with his tailored suits and bow ties. He's a remarkable man, and the vice president of an insurance firm, where he oversees their international division. He's worked there for thirty years. I worry about him. He's not taking it easy, as the doctors ordered. I hope he's taking his medication. I always have to remind him, except when he's at work, where his secretary tells him as well.

Richard had a major heart attack two years ago, resulting in bypass surgery. He takes beta-blockers to decrease his blood pressure and relax the heart muscle. Speaking of which, I'd better call him.

6th January
Evening,
Diary,

Just been talking to Richard on the phone - nothing new to report.

I'm sick of this apartment. It's like a crypt. The walls are closing in on me. I don't know why I feel this way, I used to love this apartment, with its bright lights and classic contemporary décor.

There's a vase of white lilies sitting on a red oak table in the middle of the living room. I like lilies better than roses. Roses are overrated. The floor is made of grey marble. The wallpaper is grey samphire, a delicate native seaweed. I picked it, but now I can't help thinking how boring it looks. There aren't many pictures of Richard and me. When I go to a dinner party at someone's house, the number of photos they have around overwhelm me. There are two photos of us, both in silver frames. One is from our wedding day. My twenty-five-year-old self-stares back at my older self. My hair was black when I got married, now it's chestnut brown. I like to think of myself as a beautiful woman. I put a lot of effort into my looks, and even more recently, to hide the strain drinking is putting on me. I look lost in my wedding photo, with my grey/blue eyes staring wide-eyed at the camera. My clam-shaped lips are slightly parted. I had a more defined jawline back then, but I've still got the same distinctive high cheekbones and heart-shaped face. And the dress! I look like a lemon meringue. My mother insisted I pick that one. Which reminds me, I must call her. I can't believe eleven years have passed since walking down the aisle.

The other photo, taken after we got married, is of Richard standing behind me, wearing his trademark bow tie and one of his many-tailored suits. I'm on the chair with my legs crossed, looking rather demure. We were happy back then, so in love.

7th January
Afternoon,
Diary,

    I scrubbed our maple kitchen until it's spotless, and made sure everything's nice and tidy for when Richard gets back, not that he will notice, but it makes me feel better.

    No music today. Just a sense of dread in the silence. Somehow, the music helps to fill the void. Makes me feel that everything will be alright.

    Is it though? Is everything going to be alright?

    This evening I went out to find where the music was coming from. As I walked through the streets, I had to cover my mouth with my scarf. After walking around for a while, past various bars and restaurants, a woman's voice stopped me in my tracks. I looked up and saw the sign, *Mau Mau*. Maybe this was the one, I thought. Inside, there was a band in front of a red curtain and a crowd of people watching. A black woman sat on the stage with braids. Her voice was husky and sensual. A guitarist, a bass player, a black drummer, and a blond, androgynous young man with a saxophone stood behind her. The singer stood up and continued to sing in her deep voice. I stared at the sax player. His face seems familiar, but I can't remember where I've seen him.

    And the sax… is the one I've been listening to all this time. I'm so glad I've found this little place, it's going to be great to hang out there. I must tell Sylvie.

10th January
Evening,
Diary,

The strangest thing happened at the grocery store today. I always pay by cash. I hardly ever pay by credit, since Richard checks my bank statements. I don't want to give him the satisfaction of knowing where my money goes, after all, I'm the accountant, not him. I took a basket and filled it with shower gel, deodorant, biscuits, bread, and cheese. I stopped by the wine section and, being careful with my choice, selected a nice bottle of Chablis. I heard fits of giggles, and then noticed three tall, young men a few yards away from me. Two of them had black hair and hats. They were both clutching a pack of beer each. The other one had a black suit on and a red scarf. He was stunning. His blond hair hung past his shoulders like gold silk. Something inside me stirred. I feel guilty for thinking it, but he was rather hot. I started to worry they were laughing at me. I think I've done well hiding my vices, but maybe people around here have started to notice my buying habits. I'm so paranoid. I must stop this. I recognized one of them - Evelyne Robinson's boyfriend. Evelyne is an art student. Her father is a wealthy man and owns a marketing company and many estates around the city. He seems to be buying up bits of London like he's taking part in a real-life Monopoly game. Her apartment is on one of his estates. I think she shares it with her boyfriend and his mates.

Anyway, as they were looking at me, I raised my eyebrows as if to challenge them. They looked away and started mumbling to one another. I'm pretty sure they were talking about me. One seemed to be trying hard to stop himself from laughing. I snatched another three bottles of wine from the shelf, paid and left. I couldn't wait to get out of there. What was so funny? Was it me? Oh, I don't know. I just feel weirded out by the whole thing.

11ᵗʰ January
Evening,
Diary,

'Sophie? Have you forgotten about me?' Sylvie asked

'No, of course not. I was going to call…' I said, as I clutched the phone with one hand, and scrubbed my dinner plate with the other

'What are you doing tonight?'

'Nothing much… Richard's away.'

'Perfect. It's been a while since we had a girly night out. Want to meet up for a drink?'

'Sure, but I can't stay late, Richard is coming home tomorrow morning.'

'Okay, I'll pick you up at 9 o'clock.'

Sylvie and I have been friends for fifteen years. She owns a modest boutique selling vintage clothes. I do her accounts, and in return, she pays me with old clothes. Sylvie is a beautiful woman with long, shiny black hair, blue eyes, and olive skin. She looks like an Arabian princess. She's recently been through a painful divorce. Her husband cheated on her, but she's now ready to mingle again.

I better go and get ready before she gets here. What on earth shall I wear?

12th January
Morning,
Diary,
Woke up this morning with Richard yelling at me, "What are you doing still in bed? This room stinks of alcohol." he said

I buried my face under the pillow.

'Leave me alone.' I cried.

'Come on, get up.' he said, tearing the pillow away from me.

'Don't shout, I have a headache.'

'Great welcome home Sophie. Cheers,' Richard growled, as he stormed out of the bedroom.

What did I do last night? I force my brain to remember, but I can't recall a thing. I dragged myself out of bed, and everything around me began to spin. My ears rang like church bells, and my left cheek throbbed like mad. My mouth tasted metallic and of blood.

I couldn't even remember getting into my pajamas. Did I change? Or did someone help me? My head felt like it was caving in. Everything hurt. As I got out of bed, I had to balance myself against the wall. Even my thighs ached. The worst hangover of my life!

I could smell something sweet and pungent, but I couldn't see where it was coming from. The buzzing in my ear got louder.

I managed to hobble down the corridor slowly to stop myself from being sick. Richard's suitcase was in the hall. He stood by the counter, studying the ashtray full of cigarette butts, and an empty bottle of wine on the floor. I've been so careful until now, how could I have been so stupid. He towered over me, waiting for an explanation. His brown eyes bore into mine. I collapsed into the armchair and pressed my hand to my head to try to ease the throbbing.

'What is this? Is this what you been doing while I was gone? Smoking and drinking?' he chided as he brushed his hand through his salt and pepper hair.

'Don't shout.' I said, pressing my fingers deeper into my temples.

'This is *my* apartment, I shout how I see fit.'

An intense sick feeling started to rise up. I placed my hand on my belly. Richard glared at me. I couldn't make it to the bathroom, it all poured out of me onto the living room floor, a grotesque puddle smelling like acid.

'Dear God. You're a walking disaster, there should be a fucking tornado named after you.'

'Please, don't.'

My stomach churned again, in pain.

'I can't be here and witness this, you better clean that up.'

The front door slammed and rattled through the room.

I've spent the last couple of hours racking my brain about last night. We went to a lounge bar called *The Yellow Bar*, a quirky hole Sylvie suggested. The decor was eclectic and charming. I remember a small fish tank, various chaise lounges, old vinyl LP's, and arty pictures on the walls.

'I need new experiences, new horizons, and new orgasms,' Sylvie said.

I sipped on my martini cocktail. My hands clutched to the glass as if someone was going snatch it away from me. It tasted that good.

'You're thirty-five, not twenty-five,' I said, as the cocktail sent a buzz through my body.

Sylvie flipped hair, 'It's not the age but how you feel. How is Richard?'

'Busy as usual. He's in New York.' I said.

It was then I noticed an old movie being projected onto a wall.

Sylvie narrowed her eyes at me, 'I hardly see you these days. We should go out more. Don't you think?'

A couple squeezed to our table to get through. It grew crowded and hot in there. 'I know, it's just my job, it's keeping me busy.'

'Is there a place I can find a decent man?' she asked.

We looked over at a group of blokes in their twenties drinking, shouting, and dancing - behaving like total wankers, and laughed.

'You're asking the wrong person. Though I doubt there are many good men left at our age,' I said.

Sylvie frowned and then raised her eyebrows at me, cheekily, 'Or, maybe, I should get myself a toy boy.'

I remember we sat there and chatted and giggled for quite a while, and had at least a few more cocktails, I felt damn good.

But that's all I remember. What happened next.

I'm so annoyed with myself. Every time Richard goes away, I lose control.

I think I may have done something stupid this time. But what? Or am I just being daft? I wonder if Richard will call me. I doubt it - he's probably cursing me right now, and booked me into rehab or even worse.

I hate my life.

Even Later,

I've racked my brain, but all I can remember is leaving *The Little Yellow Door* with Sylvie.

After that, there's a total blackout.

I've got bruises on my legs, a scratch on my forehead, and a red cheek, which looks like I've been slapped. It hurts to touch. Everything aches. I feel like I've been hit by a train.

What am I going to do?

Just checked out the black dress I wore last night. It's soiled and ripped from the shoulders. What happened? Did I cause this or did someone else? Was I in a fight? From the looks of the bruises, the soreness, and my red cheek, I could have been in a fight with a bear. Who changed my clothes? Sylvie? I have to call Sylvie.

I just found my phone in my bag. The battery's dead. Grrr! I'll call her once it's charged. Hopefully, she will fill in all the gaps. I want to scream. Maybe not, my head still hurts.

Even later,

Oh my god, I switched on the TV and can't believe what was on the news.

'A heated argument raged into a pub brawl last night, at a bar in Russell Gardens, Notting Hill.' The newscaster announced.

Was I involved in the fight? I'm going insane in here.

Richard is still not back. I'm going to take a couple of aspirins for my crashing headache and retrace my steps.

Evening,

Just came back from my stroll. What a strange experience. It was a beautiful evening, but I still felt rough so I couldn't appreciate it. I even had to wear my sunglasses to stop my eyes from hurting. I walked through the streets with a dazed zombie-like motion. My ears were still ringing, which was so annoying. A Jaguar drove past, and the smell of its exhaust made me want to puke again. I wobbled on the pavement with no idea where I was going. I kept going straight past all the houses.

I noticed a blond young man walking towards me, and a vision came to me. I was lying somewhere, maybe on the floor, faces around me, but they were blurry. Why was I lying on the floor?

I froze and then realized; he was looking straight over at me. It was one of Evelyne's roommates. He was lanky and skinny and staring directly at me. It was like I was looking at an angel. I felt sick, and couldn't breathe properly. My eyes traced his facial features: his blue eyes, and small straight nose, his bee-stung lips and full mouth, his sharp cheekbones, and laser-cut jawline, and his strawberry blond hair which cascaded to his chest. He wore a red jacket, black jeans, and a t-shirt, with something written on it. It wasn't in English. His fashion sense was like the teddy boy style from the fifties. He wore silver bangles on his wrists that jingled as he walked over to me. He also wore a snake ring on his index finger and a plain platinum ring on his middle finger. He was too colorful, and it hurt my eyes.

'Are you all right?' he asked in a soft-spoken voice.

I detected an accent.

'Yes, no, I don't know,' I mumbled.

'You were really drunk last night,' he said.

I stared at him, confused, 'Sorry? What do you mean?'

His eyes sliced through me, 'I'm Michael, you and your friend partied with us last night.'

'I did what?'

He blinked at me, 'you don't remember, do you?'

'No, I don't,' I gasped.

'I didn't think you would, you passed out.'

'Passed out.' I shouted in horror.

'Yeah, you blacked out or something,' he said.

'Oh, I err, sorry, I've got to go.' I said, walking away from him. I could feel his glare like he was judging me. I paced back up the street, with his face haunting my head, feeling like shit.

Once I got home, I rang Sylvie. According to her, we went to *Blagclub* after we left the *Yellow Door*. We had a drink at the bar, and some executives invited us over to their table. I didn't want to join in, but Sylvie insisted. They turned out to be boring. A young man came over and tried to burn one of the business men's hair with a lighter, as a joke. We left their table and joined the table of young men.

Sylvie was impressed by their sense of fashion and good looks. Apparently, I insisted I knew them, even though I'd never spoken a word to them before that night. She got on well with Nicky and nipped out with him for a while, leaving me alone with the other three boys. What happened between the time she left the club with Nicky, and when she returned, she can't say.

'Ask them,' she said, 'one of them didn't drink or smoke - the blond one.'

'I've already spoken to him,' I said.

'Really, when?' she said.

'I bumped into him in the street.'

'And what did he say?' she said, sounding surprised.

'He didn't say much only that I passed out.'

'Well, you can always ask him to be more specific.'

'As if I am going to knock on his door and ask him. It's too embarrassing.'

'You weren't drunk when I left. Well, you'd had around five drinks, like me. And I was fine, so…'

'So, you left me alone with three strange men, to go and have sex?'

'They weren't strange boys, they were cute.'

I thought of Michael and his angelic face, oh, he was cute all right.

'What happened then?'

'We took you home.'

'Who's "we"?'

'Me and the boys,' Sylvie added.

'You brought strangers to my home.' I snapped.

'It was only one of them.'

'Who?'

'Nicky.'

Why can't I remember any of this? I sighed, 'and then?'

'I took the keys from your bag, unlocked your door, and I made sure you were in bed and all.'

'How considerate. So, you're the one who undressed me?'

'Yes, and put on your pajamas.'

'Sylvie, my dress is covered in soil, and it's ripped from the shoulders.'

'You must have torn it when you fell.'

'And what about the bruises all over my leg, my swollen forehead, and the graze on my cheek? Are you sure I didn't get into a fight?'

'No, I don't think so. They said you hit the floor pretty hard.'

Sylvie started talking to someone in the background, and then returned to the phone, 'something's come up, and I have to go,' she said, 'it was a fun night we should do it again, without you passing out, of course.'

'That's not funny, Sylvie.'

14th January
Morning
Diary,

Richard came home late at night. I didn't know where he went. I didn't ask, and I didn't care. I was more concerned about what happened to me. I guessed he was at the golf club. I detected cigars and whiskey on him. He's not supposed to smoke or drink, but I wasn't going to tell him off, not after what I did.

Why do my thighs ache? Was I raped? Should I go to a GP or a gynecologist, or maybe the police? And tell them what, that I passed out and suspect I've been raped? What if I haven't? How stupid would I look then? They have better things to do with their time. What if I wasn't drunk, but drugged? And, who would do this? Michael? His friends?

Richard fiddled with his drink as we sat on the sofa opposite each other.

'I'm sorry I behaved appallingly,' I said.

He glared at me, 'you have.'

'I'm sorry.'

He sighed. 'When I married you everyone thought you were too young for me. I knew the risks, but for God's sake, is it so hard for you to behave?'

I stared at the floor.

'And can you put the cigarette out? You're like a chimney.'

'Sorry,' I said, putting the cigarette out.

Richard got up and went to the kitchen. 'Promise to cut down the drinking, we all need to blow up some steam, but you seem to be blowing a lot of it lately,' He said coming back into the room with a snack, 'where did you go?'

I laid on the sofa. 'For a drink with Sylvie. I lost track of time. It won't happen again.'

'Would you like a sandwich?'

'No, thanks. I needed a change of scenery, darling. All I see is figures and papers,' I said.

'I know you have a stressful job and I don't mind you going with Sylvie, but please take it easy.'

'Ok. I will. I'm going to bed. I need to get some rest.'

I laid on the bed staring at the ceiling for ages. My whole body still ached. Richard didn't come to bed, I could hear the TV blaring out for hours. I couldn't sleep at all. My brain was going haywire trying to remember what happened to me last night.

16th January
Afternoon,
Diary,

A client, whom I hadn't seen in a while, came into the office today, claiming his VAT had never been paid and was years overdue. This is the last thing I need. He sat across from me with his old suit and greying beard.

'I need to see the books,' I said to him.

'Books?' he asked.

'Yes, you do keep your accounting records, don't you?'

I knew what was coming, he didn't do any bookkeeping that year.

'No, I didn't. Can you fix this for me? I need this done this week.' He demanded.

Excellent, a man who didn't do his books and, by the scared look on his face, has no clue where that year's actual documents are and wants me to sort out his mess in less than four days. Why am I even in this business, again?

Evening,

I can't stop thinking about that night. What if I did something horrible? There is one last hope, to shamefully go and ask Michael. Maybe he can help me pick up the pieces. I don't want to see him. The prospect of being intimidated by someone so young is laughable, but there's something about him which is dangerous and sexy.

My mind's racing. What if they pulled a practical joke that went horribly wrong? I can't think of anything in particular. And how much did I have to drink? How much would I have needed to drink to fall over and pass out?

The truth is, diary, I thought my life would be so different from what it is right now. I had good grades and worked hard to get my ACCA. I thought being successful was everything. But I paid the price for this achievement and didn't put myself "out there" as the other girls did. Go out, party, and go on crazy one night stands. I was the girl who had long-term boyfriends, not escorts.

And now, what's become of me? I pass out at the age of thirty-seven in the company of twenty-year-olds. It's disgraceful and pathetic, a woman of my age allowing herself to get into this position. I'm living my life in reverse.

18th January
Afternoon
Diary,

I've done it, I left a note addressed to Michael in the mailbox.

I need to speak to you. There's a small coffee shop a few blocks away from here called Teas Me, can you meet me there on Tuesday around 5pm?
Sophie.

I hope he can make it.

19th January
Evening
Diary!

He was there all right, facing the door by the window, drinking a cup of coffee, looking bored. He saw me straight away and smiled.

The smell of coffee was overpowering. *Etta James* played in the background. I placed my bag on the stool and felt my cheeks flush. He looked me up and down. I wondered what he thought of me. His elbow rested on the table. His fingers curled his glorious hair, looking demure and serious.

'Hi,' I said.

'Hi,' he said.

'Thank you for coming.'

'I had nothing better to do, so…' he said with disinterest.

I ordered a double gin and tonic from the waiter. Michael flashed me a disapproving glance. I noticed him looking at my legs, his eyes followed the length of them. I looked away.

'Do you really need that, lady,' he said, looking at my drink.

'My name is Sophie.'

'I know.'

I felt my cheeks flush again.

'What do you want to know?' he asked, stirring his coffee.

'Anything you can remember would be helpful.'

'You don't remember anything?'

I shook my head. The waiter brought my gin. I let it sit there for a while, so I didn't show any signs of desperation. My mouth watered thinking about taking a sip. I began to tell Michael what Sylvie told me.

'After she left, you just sat there. You didn't join in the conversation, and my friend went to the bar, and you followed him. And then, you two were on the dance floor together.'

'Who is this friend of yours?'

'Sam.'

I grabbed the glass of gin and took a big gulp.

'And what happened?'

'Nothing, you just danced.'

'Well, that's a relief.'

I admired his full bottom lip. I wanted to reach out and run my finger ever so gently on those pillowy lips, and stare deeply into his eyes. It was ridiculous, I was there to gather information about that night, with bruises all over my body, and the suspicion that I was assault or raped, but instead, I was sick with desire for this boy. I bet girls won't leave him alone or maybe boys too.

'You two did slip, though,' he said.

'And?'

'When he tried to pick you up, you pulled him back on the floor.'

I started to think it was better not knowing.

'You weren't that bad…' Michael continued, 'you have nothing to worry about.'

'I am worried because I can't remember a bloody thing.'

'That's what you did. You danced. You slipped a few times, but you were having a good time. It looked like you just blacked out and collapsed on the floor. I think that's when your friend came back. I'm not sure. I had to leave because my friend Andy got into a fight.'

'Is that all?'

'Yes.'

I still sensed there was more, and blurted, 'My dress was ripped. There was soil all over it. Did I leave the club?'

'Not that I recall, maybe your dress ripped when you fell. You hit the floor quite hard.' He said looking at my scratch. I adjusted my hair to hide it.

'Are you sure there isn't more?'

'No.'

'I remember lying down.'

'Maybe you remember yourself lying on the floor of the club. Is that all you can recall?'

'Faces, but I can't make them out.'

I watched him playing with his bangles. I felt butterflies stir in my stomach. My heart beating fast against my chest. There was an uncomfortable silence. My breath rose and fell in rapid succession, unable to stop staring at this strange, but stunningly beautiful boy. I've grown so accustomed to Richard's body, the grey hairs on his chest, the scar from his surgery, and the softness of his body. Michael was like a newly hatched man in front of me. There were no grey hairs, nor a scar across his chest. Just a trim, tight body.

'It's amazing…' I blurt.

He stared at me. 'What is?'

He held my gaze, for the first time he looked at me properly. It was as if he could see me as a whole person. He studied my face. I haven't been looked at like that for ages. It's nice to be looked at by someone else who's not your husband. This sort of behavior is going to lead me into trouble. The more determined I am to be good, the more unsuccessful it's becoming.

'I know what I look like,' he said.

My eyes widened. Of course, he's aware of his beauty. He's confident, and sure of himself, and no doubt spends a long time in front of the mirror studying himself.

'That's a little vain, don't you think?'

'No, beauty is what's on the inside. I believe modesty is admirable, but everyone wants to look good. Why not admit it? Besides, I am a musician, I have to look good,' he said.

As much as I admired his confidence, I found him arrogant. 'That's most impressive... so you are the one who plays that music?'

He raised an eyebrow. 'You've been listening?'

'Hard not to. We don't live far from each other.'

'Oh yeah,' he said.

I was sure he didn't want to be there with me, in that coffee shop. I must have dragged him out of bed. How old was this boy anyway, nineteen, twenty?

'Where are you from? Your English is perfect, but you've got an accent... I'm not sure-'

'Sweden,' he said, inspecting his nails, 'I suppose you're English?'

'Yes, very.'

'From London?' he said without looking at me.

'Yes.'

He smiled, still not glancing at me.

'Are your friends Swedish too?'

'Yes, except Nicky, he's English. Sam and Andy are from Sweden too.'

'I see. What's your second name?'

'Frisk.'

'And how old are you, Michael Frisk?'

He sighed. 'Twenty-one.'

I smiled. He's still a baby. Oh, to be young again, I wanted to tell him to cherish those years, and you're only young once, but I didn't want to appear like I was lecturing him. He wasn't interested in what I had to say.

'That's a hell of a good age to be,' I said, and stood up to leave. 'It was nice talking to you, Michael, and thank you.'

'For what?'

'For taking your time to come here,' I said, taking out a five-pound note and placing it on the table. 'But before I go, may I ask…'

'Yes?'

'Do you play in a club? I don't recall the name of it.'

'*Mau Mau*, yes, I play there with my band.'

'I thought it was you…. anyway, I must go.'

'Take care,' he said.

Something isn't right. I know Michael's hiding something. He didn't tell me the whole truth. But, why?

20th January
Evening
Diary,

I haven't thrown the dress away, or washed it either in case it helps me to trigger something about that night. It's all still a blur. I've kept the dress hidden in my closet so Richard won't see it. I haven't mentioned anything about the night to him. I don't want to worry him. I've avoided sex, so he won't notice the bruises on my body and start to ask questions. I should go and see my gynecologist. There's got to be more to the story than Michael told me.

21st January
Afternoon,
Diary,

Just got off the phone with my gynecologist's secretary. It was an awkward call since I couldn't go through the details over the phone. 'Can it wait two weeks?' She asked.

'No, it can't, I need an appointment fast.'

The secretary sighed and flipped the pages of the diary. The only available space was a week from now. All I knew was, the longer it took, the more difficult it would be to tell. I made the appointment anyway, despite how difficult it would be to tell now so much time has passed.

22nd January
Evening
Diary,

I'm shaking here. WTF? I've just checked the mailbox, and there was a note inside with these words:

Be careful, nothing is what it seems.

It was typewritten. Was it really intended for me? Who would post such a thing? It must be a practical joke. Kids taking the piss. Anyway, I'm going to throw it in the bin. Kids pull these kinds of pranks all the time, don't they?

24th January
Evening
Diary,

Ugh! Last night, Richard and I went to an opera, *Tosca*. It made me cry. Operas have that effect on me. When we got home, Richard unzipped my dress. I wasn't in the mood for sex, not after what happened. Or didn't happen? Oh, I don't know.

'I was thinking, we should go away somewhere,' he said, caressing my back.

He brushed my hair away from my neck and kissed it. 'I'm tired, Richard.'

Richard sighed and pulled away.

'Did you take your medication, darling?'

'I'll take them now,' he said.

I threw my hands into the air. 'Richard!'

'I know, I know, Sophie don't worry, I'll take them now.'

25th January
Evening,
Diary,

This morning, Wendy barged in on me while taking a sip of Gin & Tonic in the ladies toilet. I almost died. I don't know how long this can go on before I get caught and get sacked.

Every day, I fill a small, empty bottle of water, and take it in my bag with me to work. Canned tonic tastes better than bottled, and, yes, I'm well aware of how stupid this is. I must try to be good.

The bruises are slowly healing. Richard is growing suspicious, and I can't avoid sex any longer. He'll be home soon. I've brushed my teeth, gargled with mouthwash, and scrubbed my nails to remove the nicotine smell.

Later

I can hear the sax playing again. I've circled the living room several times, smoking a cigarette and drinking a bottle of Chablis, which has worked its magic - I can feel the room spinning. Shit. I have to cook dinner before he comes and finds me like this. I MUST be good this year. I don't want Richard to drag me to rehab.

Where's the chewing gum?

26th January
Morning
Diary,

Last night, dinner with Richard went okay. He took off his coat and left his briefcase by the door, as he always does.

'Smells good,' he said. 'What's for dinner?'

'Shepherd's pie.'

'Mmm, a nice hearty meal,' he said, and kissed me on the cheek.

'Why don't you go freshen up, I'll call you when it's ready.'

He left the room. I shut my eyes, in bliss, listening to the sound of the sax.

During dinner, Richard talked about a boy who crashed his car, and how the firm has to pay.

'People die, we pay. People crash cars, we pay. People burn down their houses, we pay,' he said.

I laughed, 'You should add that into your brochure,'

Richard glared at me. 'It's not funny, Sophie. You should know better.' He took a sip of water.

'Yes, darling, you're right, I'm sorry.'

I continued to laugh.

'Oh for goodness' sake. I can't have a discussion with my wife.'

'Sometimes it's better to laugh about it. Take me, for example,' I said, pausing to eat a forkful of Shepherd's pie. I washed it down with a mouthful of white wine, and continued, 'my clients ask me how their business is going. You know what it's like?'

'Yes.'

'I make their balance sheets, profit and loss, consult with them, and give them advice.'

'I know your job pretty well, sweetheart.'

'Do they appreciate what I do? No, they don't, and they don't pay on time either.'

He took my hand and kissed it. 'They're making you work too hard.'

'I'm not complaining. Actually, I enjoy it.'

He poured me more wine. 'You need to take days off too.'

'I have to say the same for you,' I said.

'I am an important man with an important job.'

'Isn't my job important?'

'Of course, it is, how about we take that vacation? Where do you want to go? Not a city please, I need somewhere quiet, not surrounded by noise.'

'Oh Richard, we live in the most multicultural inspiring city in the world.'

'I need some peace… how about Tuscany or South of France?'

'I don't mind, we can go wherever you want.'

I rubbed Richard's chest with essential oils to help him relax. I kissed the scar across his chest, then laid my head on him and listened to his heart beating. I almost lost him once. I HAVE to be good for his sake.

28th January
Evening
Diary,

I've just got back from the gynecologist. I had a few drinks before I went to see her, to build up my courage to face her. Dr. Williams is about my age. Her office was dull, with a desk and chairs, and an examination chair at the end of the room. No photographs. She had an iPad on her desk with a blue pen and a notepad. It was difficult to sit across from her and explain what happened. She must have thought here is a woman pushing forty behaving like a twenty-year-old. I had to tell her the truth. I asked her if she could run some tests.

'What kind of tests?' she asked.

I stared at the wall behind her, while I told her what I remembered. I didn't tell her about the part where I woke up with aching thighs, and bruises all over my body. I couldn't put it into the words.

'Are you alright?' she asked concerned.

'If you run tests…' I paused to clear my throat, 'would you be able to tell if a person had been… sexually assaulted or not?'

She leaned forward. 'Have you been sexually assaulted?'

'I'm not sure, I can't remember,' I said, feeling my cheeks flush.

'No need to be embarrassed, I can run some tests, to see if there are any tears or infections. Is that what you want?' she asked.

I nodded.

'Did you report any of this to the police?' she asked.

'No.'

'Since it happened some weeks ago, any evidence, such as sperm or DNA will now be destroyed. You should have gone to the police as soon as possible.'

'I know, but I couldn't remember anything at the time. I was in such shock, and I don't want my husband to know.'

She ran some tests and told me to come back to see her in a week. It was such an uncomfortable and humiliating experience.

30th January
Afternoon,
Diary.

Back from the grocery store. I'm so ashamed, diary. I'm such a stupid, ridiculous woman. Everyone was looking at me. I knew what they were thinking - 'Look at her, pretending to be posh. She's just a drunk, so much for prim and proper.' Their eyes burned a hole in me, whispering to one another. I think I heard laughter. Even the clerk was looking at me funnily. I left the store without picking up the change. Even in the street, eyes were on me. I was shaking and sweating. In the apartment, my heart hammered. I placed my hand on my chest. I had left my rubber gloves on, no wonder people were staring at me.

31st January
Afternoon,
Diary,

When I got back home, Richard glanced up from his newspaper.

'I've made reservations at *Marcus*,' he said.

'For when?'

'Tonight- I booked it two weeks ago, thought I'd surprise you, and spend an intimate evening with my queen.'

'Oh, you did, did you?' I said.

I don't know why he thinks of it as a surprise when going out for meals is such a regular event.

'Why? Do you have plans?'

'No.'

If a man told his wife, he's taking her to one of the most expensive restaurants in the city, she would be thrilled, but I can't help but find this a drag. Posh restaurants are not my thing. Having to doll myself up is exhausting. I didn't want to wear high heels that make my feet hate me, or do my hair and makeup. I wanted to stay home with my husband, order a pizza, watch a movie, or talk instead. Embrace the simple joys of the world that don't come with a price tag.

'How nice,' I said, bending over, and kissed him on the lips, 'What time is the reservation?'

'Eight.'

I didn't need much time to get ready, only forty-five minutes, so I finished off some work on my laptop first. I then carefully picked an outfit that symbolizes a date with my husband. If he said he was taking me to McDonald's, and I could throw on some jeans and a top, it would be more exciting than this fancy fluffy stuff. Going to posh restaurants that serve lobster tail on a large plate is just a means to show off, to impress.

I leave hungry every time Richard takes me to those places. The host showed us to our table and handed us the menus. Richard ordered a bottle of *1989 Chateau Palmer*. We ordered our food and some ketchup for me. I don't care if it's a posh restaurant, I love ketchup. I have it on everything, Richard raised his eyebrow at me.

'Ah Sophie,' he said taking my hand. 'What I am going to do with you?'

Ever since Richard had his bypass, things changed even in the bedroom. He can't get too excited because of his heart. I ate slowly and sipped my wine, being careful how much I drank. I admired the people in the restaurant, comparing the couples that are at the beginning of a relationship, to the ones who looked like they'd been together for years. The new couples barely touched their food. They focused on each other, both knowing the evening will end in bed. The other couples ate their food quietly. One or two seemed like they were having heated debates, and I wondered if their evenings would end up in bed, minus the sex, or not.

Richard and I met twelve years ago, at a dinner party, a friend of a friend was hosting. We sat next to each other. I thought he was handsome, intelligent, and well dressed. We talked about finance, history, and politics. He thought I was the most beautiful thing he'd ever seen. He loved my high cheekbones, my defined jawline, and my eyes. He fussed about the way I looked and told me I looked like a porcelain doll. We exchanged phone numbers and met again for dinner. We dated for about a year, and then he proposed while we were on holiday in Rome.

We ate and drank our wine quietly. We touched hands to show some kind of intimacy. When the waiter cleared away our plates, Richard took out a box from his breast pocket and placed it in front of me.

'What is this?' I asked.

'Open it, and you'll see,' he said.

Another piece of jewelry, a bracelet judging from the size of the red velvet box. It was a pearl bracelet. Great. More things, I don't care for. I want Richard, the man I married, not the man who buys me gifts. He is my investment, my asset, not things. I kissed him on the lips and told him the bracelet was beautiful.

After dinner, we went home to bed and made love. I do it as a form of obligation, a sense of duty as a wife, to keep my husband satisfied sexually. It's quick and easy. We're good at it because we've been doing for years. I guided and pushed his penis into me, and I lay under him, groaning softly until he came. I watched him empty himself out, and then roll off me, without allowing me to orgasm. I've forgotten what it feels like to have an orgasm. Sometimes, I fantasize about having the kind of sex where my head is banging against the headboard. Volcanic sex, as I like to call it. It's not going to happen with Richard, or he'll have a heart attack.

I passed him tissues to wipe himself and the sheets, and I cleaned myself up as he washed at the bathroom sink. Richard joined me back in bed, pleased with himself. We both read in silence, apart from the *flup, flup* of pages from time to time. I wasn't reading, I was questioning myself. What have we become? Who are we? What have we done to each other? I closed the book, placed it on the bedside table, and switched off the lamp on my side.

    'Good night,' I said.
    'Good night,' he said.
    'Switch off the light when you're done.'
    'Will do.'
    'Did you take your medication?'
    'Damn, I forgot…'

3rd February
Evening,
Diary,

Back from the gynecologist to discuss the results. The tests came back normal. No signs of tears or infections. But, although that's great and exactly what I hoped for, I can't help feeling uneasy, I can't rest. Something happened that night, or I did something. One of the two. The bruises came from more than a fall in the club. Maybe I was assaulted. Nothing adds up. The smell. The blurry faces. The ripped and soiled dress. The note. Something happened, I know it.

5th February
Evening
Diary,

I don't know what came over me today. I felt like a woman possessed. I went to a meeting with a client in Camden.

'It's better you prepare me the bank statements every month so I can keep track of everything.' I said to the client in frustration.

I hope she didn't notice, but I'm tired of chasing after clients.

At noon, I went to a nearby café, sat by the window, and ordered a half bottle of white wine and tuna salad. As I was about to pay the bill, I heard a squeak and then a *bang*. An Audi and Ford Fiesta had crashed outside the restaurant. The Audi driver stomped over to the young man and pushed him. Someone crossed the street to break them up. I paid the bill and left a generous tip. As I peered out through the window at the arguing drivers, I saw Michael watching them too from the roadside. He was dressed in a red teddy jacket, a black ruffled shirt, and jeans, which were so tight, I wondered how he got in them. I took the last gulp of wine and rushed out of the café.

By the time I got outside, he was walking up the street, so I followed him. I know it seems crazy, but I wanted to create an opportunity to speak with him and get any clues to what happened.

I kept my distance so he wouldn't spot me. He stepped into a music store. I fiddled with my phone outside as I watched him talk to the salesman behind the counter. When he left the store, I spun around to face a display of leather jackets in the next door shop window. I could see his reflection as he strolled past with his hands in his jacket pockets. I realized it was almost 1:30pm. I should have been back in the office, not following Michael. I called Wendy and told her I would be a little late back from lunch, not taking my eyes off him. I followed him to a record store - does he still buy CDs? He came out a few moments later, empty-handed. He went into a jewelry store, again left empty-handed. My heels were killing my feet. What if he had noticed me and was browsing the stores on purpose? He met with a few friends, and at one point, his head turned to my direction. My heart dropped into my stomach.

'Good afternoon,' the sales assistant said, as I rushed into the store.

'Good morn—I mean afternoon.' I said.

I pretended to look at the punkish clothes. I hoofed to the window to see if he was still there. What if he *did* see me, what if he comes in here? My heart raced, and my feet ached.

'May I help you?' the sales assistant asked.

I'm sure she didn't expect a woman dressed in smart plum dress to come in this store.

'I'm just looking, thank you.' I said.

I peered out of the window again. The sales assistant arched her penciled eyebrow at me. He wasn't there, damn! I rushed out of the store and frantically scanned the street. He vanished. Did he see me?

8th February
Afternoon
Diary,

What if Richard finds this diary and reads it, what would he think? I have a monster in me that wants to come out. If it does, bad things will happen. Did the monster come out that night? Did my other persona take over, and I can't remember? Was I raped? Was I drugged? Did I have too much to drink? What's the smell and music I hear sometimes? Do they have a connection with that night? It's killing me not knowing. Imagine Richard reading about all of this, the woman his wife turned out to be.

That's why I need to keep you hidden, diary. Somewhere he won't find you. What if one day I forget to hide you? What will happen then?

13th February
Evening,
Diary,

I saw Michael again today, this time in the neighborhood. What was he doing in Camden? I went to the laundry to pick up Richard's suit, and there he was putting his arms around a girl, in a *Mills and Boons* sort of way, with a big fat smile on his face. They looked so happy. I wanted to punch them right in the face. Ah, young love. I'm sure he has high standards when it comes to women. He's open to the world. It's his oyster. To be at an age where nothing matters, to party, drink, smoke pot, and have lots of sex. I'm sure he fucks many women. At his age, I was already in a serious relationship for three years. I didn't sleep around. I was in love, or at least I thought I was. My life has always been dull- work hard, find a well-paying job, and steady relationships. What's the point to study, work hard, and have stable relationships? When you've done nothing dangerous or exciting in your life? I wasted my youth on studying. He looked at me as though he could see through my soul. This time I let him see me, before walking away, questioning if he knew I had followed him the other day.

Later

I switched on my laptop, logged into Facebook, and searched for Michael Frisk. I didn't find him. But what if I did, then what would I do? Send him a friend request? This is all too silly to comprehend, even writing about it makes my face bleed with shame.

15ᵗʰ February
Evening,
Diary,

On Valentine's Day, we didn't do anything special. We don't believe in it. Cherished everyday love should be not just for one day. I cooked dinner for us. We watched a romantic comedy and Richard slept halfway through. I curled up on the sofa and drank a full bottle of wine. With each sip, the wine sent tingles through me.

Tonight, Richard went out for a business dinner. He wanted me to go along, but I didn't feel like it. I didn't want to sit in another expensive restaurant and talk to people. I can't stand it.

I had a long bath, where I spent ages cleaning my nicotine-stained fingers. I'm ruining everything, including myself. At some point, I fell asleep, and my head slipped under the water. I could have drowned.

16th February
Morning,
Diary,

I felt troubled and unsettled all morning. I circled around the office, shifting in my seat as though I was sitting on pins.

I've been going over last night in my head.

I went out to the club on my own, the one Michael plays at. It wasn't crowded. I even dressed up for the occasion - green dress, opaque tights, high heels and make up applied immaculately. I'm a grown woman but feel like I'm behaving like a teenage girl. As I entered the bar, the band was playing, but Michael wasn't there. I ordered Bells, no ice. I watched the band, the drums, piano, and trumpet. The group is so good, I'm sure they could be famous one day, but then I wouldn't be able to appreciate them like this. They wouldn't perform at this little club anymore. The music would become an echo of the past. I drank the whiskey, ordered another, and drained it. When I ordered my third, the barman leaned over the counter. He was handsome with olive skin, and short, black, gelled back hair, brown eyes, and muscular arms.

'That's your third one,' he warned.

'Who are you, my mother?'

'Fine,' he said, 'your funeral, lady.'

A waitress stopped at my side to clear away my napkins, I grabbed them before she could.

'These are mine,' I said.

'I was just going to take them out of your way,' she said.

'I didn't ask you to move them, did I?'

'Whatever,' the waitress said.

'I'm sick of people touching my stuff,' I mumbled.

The barman placed my refill and a bowl of peanuts in front of me. 'Eat something,' he said.

'You eat something.'

I sighed, reaching for the fresh glass of whiskey, and noticed Michael two stools away, leaning against the counter. His blue eyes burned into me. I didn't know for how long he had been standing there, but he had a look of total disapproval. He's twenty-one for crying out loud, doesn't he drink?

'Oh, don't look at me like that,' I said, taking a sip of my whiskey that set my throat on fire.

'Like what?' he said.

'You know what I mean.'

He moved to sit next to me. 'Whenever I see you, you're either buying alcohol or consuming it… you should slow down.'

'You came here to tell me this?'

'No.'

'Are you working?' I asked.

'No, I just came here to pick up some stuff. Why?'

'How about a drink, I owe you one?'

'I don't think it would be a good idea,' he said.

'Why not?'

He noticed the wedding ring.

'Oh, I see, I said, looking down at my ring. 'And that should stop me from talking with you?'

He smiled, and ordered a bottle of beer.

'Have you got a girlfriend?'

His eyes looked me up and down. I felt myself blushing or was it my body? 'No,' he replied.

'Oh,' I said, remembering the girl I'd seen him smitten with, 'I see.'

We sat in silence for a while, watching the band and taking sips of our drinks.

'Is this what you do?' I asked.

'What do you mean?'

'A musician, is this what you do for a living?'

'Yes'

'From where do you get the inspiration to write such wonderful music?' I asked.

He reached for the beer. 'I will get it from the landlady every month.'

I laughed hard. 'But you live with Evelyne.'

'Yes, but I am renting a place of my own, it's getting too crowded over there, and I need my privacy.'

'You're moving out?' I asked, and signaled the barman for a refill. Is that why he was in Camden to look for an apartment?

'Soon, how about you don't refill that drink,' he said, putting the bottle of beer down.

'And if I don't, what happens then?'

'I guess there's only one way to find out,' he said smiling.

Michael tapped his hand against the counter, abandoning his beer. 'I'm out of here.

'See you later, mate.' The barman said.

Michael stood in front of me, hands in his jacket pocket. 'What do you do?'

'I'm an accountant.'

'Are you keeping your whiskey receipts?'
'I am.' I laughed
'Were you always an accountant?'
We began to walk. 'Yes... so you have no other interest besides being a musician?'
'You sound like my mother.'
'Sorry.'
'Where did you learn to play?'
'I learned to play the flute at music school, and then switched to sax... how long you been living here in Notting Hill?' he asked.
'Eleven years, right after I got married.'
'You've been married for eleven years?'
'Yes... why so shocked?'
'You married young.'
'I was a fool in love.'
He stopped walking. 'Are you still a fool in love?'
I laughed. 'You ever been in love?'
'Yeah...' he said.

I thought of the brunette with him the other day. Was she the lucky lady? But he said he doesn't have a girlfriend. Maybe he has more than one girlfriend, so what?

It felt like he was flirting with me, and I was flirting right back. Going to bed and waking up with the same man can be a little boring after all. I'm not complaining, as far as I'm concerned, despite the drinking. I have been a good wife. Loyal, dutiful, and caring. I've stood behind Richard through the good times and the bad. After the operation, I took time off from work and nursed him, making sure he was comfortable. I never complained. I did what I had to do as a wife, through sickness and health. I took those vows seriously.

To be looked at by someone new, a stranger. It felt good. I shouldn't have gone to the club. He must think I'm leading him on.

'I saw you the other day,' he said.
My heart stopped. 'When?'
'You know. When I was with that girl.'
'Oh.'
'You were looking.'
By this time, he'd walked me to my street.
'Yes, I. Erm, was walking back to work?'
What does he want from me?
'I find you... interesting.'

I sniggered, 'Really? I don't know why.'

We stopped in front of my apartment. Why would Michael notice someone like me? I stood on the step. He was on the pavement, with both hands in his trousers pocket. A man marched past and looked at us suspiciously, then kept on going to wherever he was heading. How must we have looked in the eyes of strangers - the colorful, glamorous blond, and the dull corporate potato of a woman?

'My husband might be home,' I said.

'I'll leave you to it.'

'It's sweet of you to walk me home.'

'It's a pleasure.'

Why am I so nervous? Why have I been circling around the room trying to reassure myself that it is? Innocent situations don't need to be labeled as such.

Later,

I didn't feel any better during the day. I went to a seminar at the Hilton. I arrived there early, located the bar, and ordered a Black Velvet. The taste of whiskey sung wonders in my mouth. I drained the glass in one go and asked the barman for another.

I thought about Michael. Does he sense I crave affection? I emptied the glass and ordered another.

'Madam,' the barman said, 'are you all right?

'You are not a priest, you're a bartender, so just pour.'

He refilled my glass and kept staring at me. 'Thanks,' I said.

God, I can be such a bitch sometimes.

I mustn't do anything like that ever again. Going to the club where Michael works is a ridiculous thing to do.

17th February
Afternoon
Diary,

I ran into Michael again on my way out to the grocery store. I'd bought a bottle of gin, half a dozen cans of tonic, two lighters, and cigarettes. I felt my cheeks flush.

We made small talk about our day. It was a friendly, neighborly chat, nothing out of the ordinary. When he was about to walk away, he turned again and caught me gawping at him. I lowered my head as if I were a naughty child who had done something she shouldn't.

'Don't take this the wrong way,' he said, 'but you're a beautiful woman. You have no idea how beautiful you are, and you're throwing it all away. Gordons is not your friend, the same goes for the Marlboros.'

My chest caved as I stared blankly at him. I wanted to drop the bags and cry.

'Take care of yourself, will you?' he said.

His eyes begged me to do so.

I wanted to reach out and hug him, but instead, I watched him swagger away from me, with no care in the world.

What did I do, diary? Opened the bottle of Gordons that's what I did and smoked. I sat at the kitchen table with my feet up and cried until I couldn't cry anymore. Afterward, I ran a bath and laid there with a cigarette tingling between my fingers, and a large glass of gin.

In the bedroom, I inspected my face in front of the mirror. My hair needed trimming and color. Was that another fine line on my face?

25th February
Afternoon
Diary,

Ran into Michael, again. Listen to me raving about a boy because he's gorgeous. I stopped at the grocery store to purchase cigarettes. I lit one and took a deep drag. Michael and his friends were sitting outside a pub, smoking cigarettes and chatting. His friends are dark, tall, and beautiful, dressed in strange clothes as if they dropped from another planet. Michael appeared to be having an in-depth, intense discussion with one of them, gesturing with his hands. He saw me, said something to his friend, and then came over to speak to me.

'Who are your friends?' I asked.

Michael turned to face his friends, I didn't like the way they were looking at me, especially the one with the hat.

'The wavy-haired one is Sam' Michael said softly.

I couldn't see Sam properly, but the way he looked at me, it was so strange God knows, what was going on his head. All I saw was a mess of fluffy black hair. He waved at his friends, and they waved back at him. He's such a happy, carefree boy, with the world at his feet. I envy him.

'Andy's, the one with the hat, and Nicky's the one with the long hair,' he added.

I looked at them both. Andy looked like he could be of gypsy origin. Michael gazed at me, warmly.

'Can I see you, again?' he asked.

It cracked out of me '*ha, ha, ha.*'

He stared at me without blinking.

'What, why?' I said, alarmed.

'I like talking to you.'

'I don't think that's a good idea.'

'Why not?'

I gazed at my shoes, smiling, 'Michael, you're beautiful and sweet, you're amazing, but I'm a married woman.'

'You never said happily married.'

This reply made me uneasy. So, he assumes I'm unhappily married because I didn't introduce myself with, 'Hello, I am Sophie Knight, and I'm happily married.' My marriage is nobody's business, except Richard, and mine.

'It's none of your business,' I said.

'What?' he whispered.

'How happy I am. Anyway, it's a bad idea.'

'Is it, though?'

Of course, it is. I wanted to yell, but I didn't. Why the sudden interest in me. Did he pity me? Is this what this is all about?

He moved closer, 'I think you shouldn't be wearing that.'

I gazed down at my navy skirt suit. 'What are you talking about? It's just a suit.'

Sam yelled from across the street, 'Come on, man.'

Michael signaled for him to wait. Andy rolled his eyes. Michael returned his gaze to me as if I were a precious ointment on display. I threw a disapproving glance at him.

'I'm not referring to your outfit,' he said slowly.

'That's enough.' I said in a firm tone.

I moved past him.

'Catch you later, Sophie,' he said, smiling and looking me up and down.

I don't understand how men think, but mostly it's with their cocks. Boys like him-at such tender age, they want to experiment, learn, and gain the experience. At their age, they focus on their pleasure rather than on their partners, they want to get on with it and move on to something else. But, for a split second, as I hurried away from him, I imagined what it would be like to lay beneath him. To have his hands on my body, that mouth on my neck and on my breasts. Teaching him what he didn't learn in school. I shivered, what's wrong with me? What is happening to me? What is this? I looked over my shoulder. He lingered on the pavement watching me. The drinking is bad enough, but Michael tempting me into being disloyal to my husband is monstrous. I poured myself a large glass of gin, which danced in my mouth.

After eleven years of marriage, I never thought about what I'll look like in the eyes of other men, especially younger men. My main concern is what I look like in the eyes of my husband. He doesn't say much, he doesn't have to remind me he loves me, and he's aware of how I feel about him. I have shown my love, and I have proved it. I've been there for him every step of the way.

Because we've had a faithful marriage, I haven't thought about what it might feel like to be kissed by someone other than my husband. To feel the pressure of another man's mouth pressed against mine. To feel his foreign touch on my body, not until now. Things fall asleep after marriage. It's natural that sexual alertness dies down.

I am grateful to be married. I don't have to put myself out there ever again. I don't have to sit across from someone and prove I am the right candidate. Dating is a form of a job interview for me, at least it was. That's why I only had a string of long-term relationships. Dating just wasn't for me. In fact, when I got married, I was relieved I didn't have to kiss or stand naked in front of strangers ever again.

The few dates I had were friendly meetings that sometimes ended in bed. I had forgotten how it feels, and how exhilarating it can be, and yet the buzz of it all, to be a little scared. Today, with Michael, it came back in an instant, the high of it all. How could I have gone on without it all of these years? Did I sleepwalk through them?

27th February
Evening,
Diary,

You wouldn't believe what happened today. Even I'm still having a hard time grasping all of this.

I checked the mail before I went up to the apartment. I dumped the mail on the kitchen table and switched on the kettle. I opened the letters, which were mostly bills and junk mail. Did I want my eyebrows tattooed? My carpets cleaned? There was also an envelope addressed to me, without a stamp or return address. I swallowed the lump in my throat, wondering if it was another of those notes. I studied the words. This one wasn't typed, but written in neat handwriting.

Meet me tomorrow at noon.
M x

Underneath was an address and a mobile number. I got up from the chair, removed the kettle from the cooker, and poured myself a glass of whiskey. I stared at the note again until the words began to smudge. What is it with him? There I was thinking Michael wouldn't take a second look at me, and now he's asking me to see him at his flat. I shouldn't have gone to ask for his help regarding that night. I should have let it all pass as one of those crazy nights that go unremembered.

Shall I tell Richard? Tell him what exactly? That a sexy, young saxophonist is hitting on me? I'd be shooting myself in the foot. I don't want conflicts between Richard and me, but leave it as it is, a secret. The thing about secrets is they are dangerous, and they can be seductive. I allowed Michael into my consciousness. He's undiscovered, unfamiliar, and the unknown. When the Devil presents himself to you, he's alluring and beautiful. He seduces you and tempts you into the wilderness. Puts you in a state of trance where you hardly recognize yourself or the world around you. Lures you into his trap and before you know it, you have sinned.

I touched the note as if there was a trace of him on it, shaking my head in disbelief. I opened the pedal bin with my foot, and threw the note inside. While preparing the evening meal, I slammed pots and pans, and slipping into a terrified murmured, *oh no, no, no, what am I doing? What am I thinking?* Trying to convince myself that, somehow, I am blameless.

Couldn't I be? There is the address of another man in the bin. Shall I remove it? It's unlikely Richard will go through the rubbish.

I've done nothing wrong. I admit, I find Michael positively beautiful, and I've flirted a bit, but I'm sure he gets it a lot from both women and men. He's a talented musician. It's his job to create a certain allure, but luring me into seeing him in his apartment? The danger of being with him in a room alone. How suffocating the whole experience would be. I have a fairy tale image in my head of the goblin leading the princess to his lair.

I stopped cooking and caught my reflection in the living room window, surprised how flushed I appeared. The streets were empty except a few people walking by. Does Richard have plans tomorrow? He told me something, but I can't remember. Everything he says is a blur. I'm sure he has to go golfing. Michael has conquered my eyes. Why have I allowed him into my imagination? I have a healthy marriage, not ideal or a perfect one, but I accept it for what it is. I get lonely, but I'm not alone. I have Richard. I get bored too sometimes because of the routine, but that's marriage. I never thought of it as a sport. If I did, I would have thrown in the towel a long time ago.

Did Michael sense something, or give him the impression I'm trapped in an unhappy marriage? Even so, the logical thing to do is not get involved with another man's wife. I took vows that Michael is breaking. I can't say I'm a fabulous wife, or Richard is a fantastic husband, but we've managed all these years. He's older than I am, and uses his authority and superiority which makes me feel inferior to him, but I don't dwell on the petty stuff. I've learned to ignore him.

I inspected my wedding ring, which I've never removed since Richard slipped it on my finger. My life commitment, forever. But forever is such a long time. How did I get myself into this mess? *Oh no, no, no, what I am going to do?*

I moved closer to the window. I saw a figure in a black coat and a hat across the street, looking up at my window. A chill ran through me. It was Michael's friend, Sam. What the hell was he doing here? What was he doing that for?

28th February
Midnight.
Diary,

Richard is snoring in the bedroom, so I've come out to the kitchen to write this. I'm still not over why Sam was looking at my window last night. I'm still a bit freaked out. Was he just passing by and saw me at the window. Did he even know it was me?

By seven this morning, I was already out of bed. I hardly slept at all. I laid on the bed and stared at the ceiling in the dark. My brain refused to sleep. As I made breakfast, I felt a serenity in me I haven't felt in years. Richard woke up, and we ate breakfast together. I drifted into my inner thoughts. Of course, I wasn't going to see Michael, why should I? He has nothing to offer except chaos. I'm not going to make a mess of my life. He's so young, and this is ridiculous and foolish. Somehow, I was trying to convince myself it wasn't. Richard placed his hand on my thigh.

'You are quiet, this morning. Are you feeling alright?'

No! 'Yes, darling, I'm fine.'

'You seem miles away.' He said, spreading Marmite on his toast.

I reached for the spoon. The thought of food made me want to throw up.

'I'm thinking about a problem at work?'

'Leave work where it belongs.' Richards said. Taking a bite of his toast and washing it down with tea.

I placed my hand on his. 'Would you like to go somewhere?'

'I have golf this morning.'

After Richard went golfing, I took my laptop to the kitchen table along with a set of clients' accounts and sunk myself into work. I poured myself a large glass of gin and tonic, my first one of the day. I cleared the table and threw away my rough workings of T accounts in the bin.

I took a long bath with Maria Callas playing in the background, emptying my mind. I put on a black long-sleeved skater dress, but as I inspected myself in the mirror, it seemed too provocative. I didn't want to send the wrong message, so I changed into a different dress that wasn't so short. I applied too much makeup which made me look like a tart, so I removed it and started again. My hands trembled as I drew on my eyeliner. I drank a glass of wine and took several drags of my cig to steady my nerves.

I went outside and hailed a taxi. I must have been out of my mind. The cabbie kept looking at me through the rear view mirror. I bet he knew what I was up to, or maybe not. I probably looked like a corporate woman heading for a meeting with a client.

I almost told the cabbie to turn around, but when I opened my mouth, nothing came out. *Mama* by Phil Collins was playing on the radio. Here I was on my way to meet a kid, who had seen me at my worst, if not at my most degrading. It wasn't too late to change my mind. However, I didn't change my mind when I paid and tipped the cabbie. I didn't change my mind when I scanned the block of flats and rang the bell. I didn't change my mind as I plodded along the corridor adjusting the hem of my dress.

When I arrived, Michael was leaning against the doorframe, waiting for me looking flawless in black, with long earrings dangling from his ears. I like how well dressed he is, unlike those boys who wear jeans under their buttocks - they make me want to pull them up for them. He led the way. It was too late to change my mind now.

He shut the door. I smiled, and he smiled back. With the back of my hand, I ran it across his cheek feeling the softness of his skin. A sexual wave built in my groin, I moved close enough that my lips almost brush against his. I was intoxicated by his beauty, his talent, his strangeness. It was so forbidden and sexy. The flat was small and gloomy, people shouted from outside, cars rumbled past.

Three saxophones sat on the grey velvet sofa, one gold, one silver, and one red. I wondered what the difference was between them. I don't know anything about saxophones. I scanned the room. There were two purple cushions on the floor, and red and blue scarves on the coffee table, books piled on top of each other, amps, large speakers and a beatbox stacked in the corner, various comic books and paraphernalia, and a poster of Marilyn Monroe on the wall along with a hand fan and Japanese artwork. Has he been to Japan? There was another poster of *A Clockwork Orange* on the other wall. I wonder which version he liked the best. The book, or movie? There were several photos glued to the wall. His flat was intriguing in the same way a foreign country is fascinating when you first visit it.

'You look nice,' he said.

'Just nice? I said. Laughing. I handed him my coat, and he placed it on the sofa.

'You've got killer legs,' he said, gazing down at them. Was he visualizing how he would fit between them, perhaps?

I laughed.

'So, what can I get you? I have a beer, wine…' he said, walking towards the kitchen. I followed him. I expected to find dirty dishes and pizza boxes, but it was clean. I leaned against the doorframe as he opened the fridge, 'or maybe I shouldn't offer you any booze.'

'I'm not going to get drunk.' I said offended.

'I'll keep an eye on you.'

'I want both on me.'

'As yours are on me.'

We stared at each other.

'That's a nice touch leaving the note in my mailbox, inviting me to come here. Did you consider my husband might have opened the mail and read it?'

'Does your husband open your mail?'

'No…'

'Then you had nothing to worry about.'

I felt jittery. Had I really, nearly kissed him a few minutes before?

'Did anyone see you?'

'Where?'

'Mailing me the note.'

'No, I was careful.'

'Can I smoke?' I asked.

'Sure.'

I nearly ran to the window to get away from him. Being so close to him was strange. I shouldn't have gone there. I can't trust myself around him. He handed me the beer, I took a sip, and he kept watching me as if I was doing something remarkable.

'What?'

Michael looked away. 'Nothing.'

'You are thinking of something,' I said.

'It's strange…'

'Strange?'

'I thought you were going to chicken out…' he paused, 'you look like you can make men kiss the ground you walk on.'

I puffed on my cigarette. 'Make men kiss the ground I walk on, huh?'

He frowned. 'Sorry, I didn't mean—'

'No please, I'm enjoying this, go on.' I encouraged.

'I thought you might.'

'What?'

'You know what I mean…. I've seen the way men look at you.'

'Have you now? As you were looking?'

He blushed. 'By looking, I don't mean it creepily. I do look at you… it's just that…' he shrugged, 'you are nice to look at.'

'Is it ok if I call you, Mike?'

'Sure.'

The room fell silent. I noticed music from the apartment next-door and waited for him to continue, but he didn't. He sipped on his beer contemplating, perhaps realizing this was a bad idea and was having second thoughts.

'What is it?' I asked.

'Nothing…'

'I am an older woman, not a girl, say what you have to say.'

'You're not that old.'

I threw the cigarette out of the window 'I said older, not old.'

'How old are you? 'I think he felt uncomfortable and added quickly, 'you don't have to tell me.'

'Thirty-seven.'

This hung in the air. Michael opened the blinds and gazed out. I watched him as he looked out with an intensity you see in children caught in the wonder of the moment.

'But you are aware,' he said, without looking at me.

I jumped at the sound of his voice. 'Aware of what?'

'Of the effect you have on men.'

I opened my mouth, but no words came out. I couldn't move. I wondered what was going to happen. Was he going to possess me? Did he know I was already seduced? Did he see how dazzled I was by him? How I couldn't think of much else. Did he know how hooked I was and how I hated myself for it? I despised myself for being there. Each time I looked at him, I felt a mix of panic and excitement. I was enchanted, enslaved, and at his mercy.

'I'm sorry,' he said, 'I didn't mean to make you uncomfortable.'

'You're not. Why did you want to see me?' I asked.

'I enjoy your company.'

'But it's not just the company, is it? Tell me, what is it? Do I excite you, because I am older? Because I'm all over the place? Which one is it?'

He glared at me. 'You had a choice not to come. I didn't put a gun to your head and force you, you came willingly.'

'True... I enjoy your company too, although, I hardly know you,' I said.

He arched his eyebrow. 'More than your husband's?'

'I enjoy his company too.'

'But you're here.'

'Indeed...'

'You could have gone anywhere with any man,' he said, leaning against the sofa.

'I can't say... I've never done anything like this before. And you're a boy.'

He seemed hurt by this statement, 'I'm not a boy.'

'Oh, so you think you're a man?'

'Everything about you is dramatic.'

'Cheers.'

'Sorry.'

'How many dramatic women have you met in your life?'

'A few.'

'You've been with lots of women?'

He looked at me in horror. 'I'm only twenty-one.'

'You be surprised how many boys your age have been around.'

'Would you like it if I had been with lots of women?'

'I like what makes you, *you*.'

'But you wanted me to be older, didn't you?'

I pulled a face, 'No, I didn't want anything.'

He lowered his eyes.

'Have you ever been with an older woman?' I asked.

'Why are you asking?'

'Curious I guess.'

'Yes,' he replied.

I was intrigued. 'You've been with an older woman?'

'Yes.'

'How old was she?'

What I wanted to ask was, was she beautiful?

'About thirty,' he said, holding my gaze. 'Do I make you curious?'

I paced around the room. My heels clicked on the wooden floor. I stopped opposite the shelf full of LPs, by artists that ranged from Black Sabbath to Adele. It was refreshing for someone so young to own LPs. Nowadays it's either iTunes or Spotify for music and Kindles instead of actual books. You have to go through someone's playlist to find out what music they listen to or what books they read. It's not sentimental at all. It's better to hold an actual CD or a book in your hand than downloading it. There was a record player made of pine and acrylic. It looked expensive. I scanned the photos on the wall. One was with his friends sitting on a leather sofa. They looked candid and happy. There was a photo of him posing by the wall and another playing sax on stage. A stand of earrings caught my eye. I placed my index finger on a silver skeleton earring.

'Maybe,' I said, dipping at him over my shoulder.

'Is it because of the way I look?'

'You look different, but no, there's nothing wrong with the way you look.'

'No,' he agreed, running his hand through his hair. His bracelets jiggled.

I sat on the sofa. On the coffee table were stacks of books. Biographies. The one on top was of Little Richard. There was also an ashtray with a few spliffs in it, and a lighter and rolling paper beside it.

I ran my finger along one of the saxophones beside me. 'Why in all the instruments in the world you picked the sax?'

'It's not the only instrument I play,' he said.

'What else do you play?'

'Flute, guitar, bass, piano, drums. Do you play anything?'

'I took guitar lessons when I was little. I played until I was sixteen, and then, I don't know… I stopped.'

'Would you like to give it a shot? I have a guitar.'

'No, I can't,' I said horrified.

'Why?'

'Not today.'

I didn't want to admit. I wasn't good at playing the guitar, in fact, I sucked. He stopped and inspected himself in the mirror. The narcissistic behavior was off-putting. He didn't have to be so full of himself. I stood up and lit another cigarette.

'Don't worry, you look great,' I said, sarcastically.

'I just like the way I look,' he said.

Boy, he's arrogant. He was doing so well, why did he have to spoil it? The conversation shifted from movies to books, and then to music. He opened a bottle of wine and poured me a glass. I gulped it down as he watched me, wide-eyed. He sat on the sofa. I sat on the floor by his legs as if he was the king and I was his slave. I didn't know what time it was, and I didn't care. I thought of Richard golfing while I was in Camden, a place he wouldn't be caught dead in.

'You haven't told me,' I said.

'I haven't told you what?' Michael asked sharply.

'Where do you get the inspiration to write music like that?'

'From making love,' he said quietly, staring at me.

I smiled.

'Are you sad?' Michael asked.

His question threw me off guard. 'What makes you think I'm sad?'

'The drinking, something must trigger it...' he shook his head, 'I'm sorry it's none of my business.'

'I don't drink much,' I said.

'You don't drink much? You're like a sponge. Did something happen to you... sorry.'

'Yes,' I paused, 'and then my husband had a heart attack. I had to look after him. I knew what I was getting myself into when I married him, the age difference I mean. When you spend so much time living with someone, it's natural, it becomes a routine. You end up becoming more like a brother and sister.'

'But it doesn't have to be like that.'

'What?'

'A routine and treating each other like siblings.'

'Marriage is hard work. Do you want to get married?'

'Someday.'

I laid on the floor, his eyes penetrating me, tracing each shape and curve of my body.

'The thing that happened to you-you don't have to tell me, but was it bad?' he asked.

'... Yes.'

'So you started to drink afterward?'

'In a way...'

'Does he know about your...' he trailed off.

'He makes remarks but, as I said, I don't drink much.'

He stared at me. 'Why are you telling me this?'

'I need to be honest. It's funny that the only person I can be honest is with you.'

'Don't you think you should be honest with your husband instead of with me?'

'You invited me here, and I came. I told you how things are... or maybe because of the music.'

'The music?' he asked, confused.

'I listened to you for months. I'd light a cigarette, pour myself a glass of wine and sit by the window, wondering who it might be playing. It kept me company.'

'Glad I could be of service.'

'Thank you.'

He smiled at me, 'He doesn't know about you blacking out?'

I sighed, 'No, he doesn't. I don't want him to worry.'

'So, I'm the only one who knows about this secret of yours.'

'I already told you, *yes*.'

'Are you angry at me?'

'Oh Mike, you're the last person I would be angry with.'

'You're angry at him, aren't you?'

'No, I'm not angry at my husband.'

'But you're bored.'

I laughed.

'I know you are,' he said after I stopped laughing. Does he find my boredom erotic?

Michael listened to my every word, as if he wanted to savor my words for later. I laid my head on his lap, and the room fell silent. I listened to the sounds of the city rise and fall outside the flat.

'How long you've been in England?' I asked.

'Two years, almost.'

'Why did you leave Sweden?'

'It's not for me. I left my mother when I was eighteen, and I got by on my own, did odd jobs, saved up, and came here. I always wanted to come to England. I like London better than Sweden, there's nothing for me there except my parents... but you—the Brits are so loud and obnoxious.'

I giggled. 'So you plan to stay here or move somewhere else?'

'New York seems a possibility.'

'I've been to New York.'

'What's it like?'

'Like London, but bigger. If you like noise and crowds, it would be perfect for you.'

I closed my eyes to rest them for a bit. I woke up surprised to find myself still on his lap with his arms around me. I had no idea what time it was. I glanced at his lips - pink and tempting me, wanting to press mine against his. I longed to kiss and lick every bit of him, to taste all of his different tastes, and to smell him like a curious wild animal. It was time for me to go. Going there and exposing myself to him was idiotic.

'We could get into trouble,' I said, looking into his eyes.

He studied my face. 'You're such a beautiful woman.'

I stood up to go. 'I better go.'

'No, I mean it, you look amazing,' he said getting up.

I turned away from him, smiling. 'You're adorable, but you don't have to shower me with compliments.'

'I think you should be lavished with compliments every day... stay a bit longer, please?' he pleaded.

We lunged toward each other and kissed. His lips were like silk and tasted of beer and wine. I pulled away, and thought, what the hell am I doing? Coming here to talk is one thing, but kissing him is another. Panic and terror surged through me. I dragged my coat from the chair. The chair hit the floor. My heart raced, and my blood coiled. I had to leave as soon as possible before I ended up in his arms again. I got as far as the door, and something stopped me.

'I saw your friend yesterday,' I whispered.

'Which friend?' he asked, narrowing his eyes at me.

'Sam. It was weird, I saw him in my street looking at my window.'

He looked at the floor. 'Are you sure it was him?'

'Of course, I'm sure. What makes you think I'm not?'

'Had you been drinking?'

'I had a couple,' I admitted.

'So you might have mistaken him for someone else.'

I crossed my arms across my chest. 'I know what I saw. Please tell your friend not to creep around my neighborhood.'

'Why don't you tell him yourself when you see him.'

'What happened that night?'

He stood up. 'I already told you what happened.'

'I find it strange that I danced with your friend, and then he starts creeping around my neighborhood, staring at my window. The same day you left me that bloody note.'

'What do you want me to say?' he barked.

'How about the truth.' I snapped.

He glared. 'You're thirty-seven, you're responsible for your own life and actions. If you didn't drink yourself senseless, then you wouldn't be in this position now, would you? Where is your self-respect?'

'Why don't you go ahead and say it.'

'Say what?'

'Come on sweetheart, hit me with it. I'm a big girl. I can take it.'

'You said so yourself, you're an alcoholic. You're weak and pathetic, it's disgraceful the way you behave.'

'Boy, you're good-looking, but your mouth makes up for it.'

'For what? For telling the truth? You told me to say it, and now you're pissed off because I did. What's wrong with you?'

'I'm going to go now,' I said.

'You want to go, fine be my guest.'

I plodded towards the door. 'I don't understand what the fuck is going on?' he shouted 'first you are all over me, opening up your personal life to me and now you're pushing me away. Fucking drunk!'

'I wasn't all over you. Stop being a pompous prick. Let me break it to you, sunshine, look in that mirror, embrace it because this,' I pointed at my face, 'it's only temporary, enjoy it while it lasts.'

'Fuck you.'

'No, fuck you.' I shouted, pointing my finger at him, and then stomped towards the front door.

'Wait.' he shouted.

He picked up my bag from the floor and handed it to me. I took it and stared into his eyes. My heart beat fast against my chest, and my body shook. I opened the door, and he kicked it behind me.

The air bit my skin as I stomped down the street. I lit a cigarette and took a deep drag. It didn't calm me down. Who does he think he is? Nobody has spoken to me like that before, not even Richard. I hailed a taxi. I won't tolerate being spoken to like that, not by anyone, and especially by a twenty-one-year-old. What enraged me the most was not what he said or how he said it full of spite, but the way he kicked the door behind me. As I got in the taxi, the driver turned to me.

'Hey, lady, can't you read,' he said, pointing at the NO SMOKING sign.

Richard was in the living room, watching a talk show.

'Successful day?' he asked.

It's a habit of his whenever I go somewhere, he always asks me... Successful trip? Successful meeting? Successful seminar?

'Yes, how was golfing?'

'Golfing was good, you know who I saw today?'

I took off my coat. 'Who?'

'Hector Walsh bought his granddaughter with him today. She's sixteen.'

I don't remember Hector Walsh. I must have met him once or twice, but Richard's friends are a blur to me. When Richard introduces me to them, I don't see their faces. When I'm around them, there's no real me, just an abstraction. I'm just not there, perhaps I never was.

'Lovely girl, bright. She wants to go to Oxford to study journalism. Girls like her give me hope. She wants to do something with her life. She has ambitions and goals, not just taking pictures of herself and posting them on social media.'

'Hmm...' I murmured, 'I'm going to take a shower. We'll talk about it later, darling.'

I jumped in the shower and shampooed my hair furiously, still worked up about how Michael treated me. He was so immature and disrespectful, but what should I expect? He's still a boy for Christ's sake. I washed the whole day off me. Mozart's *Lacrimosa* started to play. How stagy!

I prepared a small meal, and hardly ate any of it, I wasn't hungry. I spent the afternoon with a bratty, spoiled musician and kissed him as if I were a lover, and then had to sit across from my husband, having dinner with him as though it was just another Saturday night in. It was surreal. How could I do this? Thank God, I left on time. I almost let my desire cloud my judgment. I am supposed to be good this year, not the opposite. What's wrong with me? I heard the music again in my head, this time it was a beat. Am I going insane?

'Are you alright?' Richard asked.

'Yes, why?' I said, taking a sip of water.

'You look pale.'

'I'm always pale.'

I mean, more than usual.'

'I'm fine, just a little tired?'

My mobile went off and Michael's number flashed on the screen. I ignored it.

'What do you want to do tomorrow?' Richard asked.

'Tomorrow?'

'Yes, it's a Sunday. Let's have lunch. I can call Judy and Patrick.'

Judy and Patrick are Richard's friends. He's a lawyer in real estate, I think, but could be wrong. His wife, Judy, hosts fundraisers, and charity events. An obnoxious woman. The last thing I needed was to spend a Sunday afternoon with a snobbish, uptight couple who bore me senseless.

'Or we can go watch a movie,' I suggested, pushing the plate away.

'Movie? What movie do you want to see?'

'Whatever's showing.'

He frowned at me like I was mad.

My phone lit up again. Richard took a sip of water. 'Aren't you going to get that?'

'No,' I replied.

'Who's calling you at this hour?'

'A client. You know how these people are, no consideration of the time or day.'

Why is he calling me? What did Michael want? He knows I'm home and Richard is here. We said what we had to say, there's nothing more to add.

'Or bowling?' I suggested.

'Bowling?' he asked. His eyes looked as if they were going to pop out of their sockets.

'Why not?'

'Sophie, I am a middle-aged man, bowling is for children.'

'Adults go bowling, there is nothing wrong in playing once in a while. Let your guard down.'

'Don't be ridiculous, darling.'

'I don't want to have lunch with Judy and Patrick,' I responded. The mobile lit up once more. Richard sighed. I rejected the call and switched off my mobile.

'Are you sure you're feeling alright?' Richard asked.

'I'm tired.'

He got up, and leaned over and kissed my cheek. I couldn't bear to look at him.

'Why don't you go and lay down. I'll wash these for you. Tomorrow, I'll take you for lunch at *Dinner*. They might set up a table for us,' he said, reaching for my hand and kissing it.

Great another luxurious restaurant.

'Whatever you like, Richard.'

1st March
Evening
Diary,

I woke up with the sounds of the clatter of pots and pans and groaned. My head was pounding. I placed the pillow over my head and tried to block out the noise, but it was of no use. I was never going to get back to sleep.

Richard used to love making me breakfast in bed until he eventually stopped. Now, if he wakes up before I do, he makes it just for himself. Where did it all go? The sweet gestures, the staying in bed longer to snuggle? What happened to all of that?

As I walked into the kitchen, the smell of glazed onion and garlic filled my nostrils. It didn't smell like breakfast, plus there were pans and pots all over the counter.

'Richard, darling, what are you doing?'

'Good morning dear, I assume the goddess wants coffee,' he said, pouring coffee into two mugs.

I glanced around the kitchen. On the table was a chopping board with potato skins, and carrots cut in thick circles. He wasn't making breakfast.

'I'm cooking,' he said, pouring the milk into the coffee.

He handed me a mug and took a sip. 'I can see that, what for?'

'This afternoon.'

'This afternoon?' I asked, confused.

He had marinated the beef, which was for more than just two people. 'I thought you made a reservation at *Dinner*?'

'I changed my mind, we're staying in.'

'Ok.'

I sipped more coffee, as relief washed over me. I preferred to have a quiet Sunday in, rather than going out to a restaurant that serves fancy food.

He hummed a song to himself. I ambled over to the counter, and placed a couple of crumpets into the toaster, and had a nosy at what he was doing. Richard rarely cooks. I am the cook in the house.

'That's a lot of beef for just two people.'

'I invited friends over. You don't mind, do you?'

'Who?' I snapped.

'Jody, Patrick, Hector and Mary, they're joining us for lunch.'

'Without consulting with me first?'

The last thing I needed after Michael yelled at me and kicked the door after me, was to have to spend my fucking Sunday afternoon with uptight, snobbish farts.

'It'll be fun.'

Fun? Is this his idea of fun? All I saw was old. I am thirty-seven going on ninety-seven. We have become Mr. and Mrs. Old.

'You wanted excitement, isn't that what you said?' he asked placing the cooked onions on a plate and setting them aside.

'We have different ideas of what excitement is, Richard,' I said, buttering my crumpets.

I slammed the innocent plateful of crumpets onto the table and sat down.

'Problem?' he asked.

'I wish you told me…'

'Don't worry, I'll clean it all up,' Richard said.

'You better,' I warned him.

I suddenly had a brainwave. Invite Sylvie for lunch. He invited his friends without my permission, so I thought I'd do the same. Thankfully, she accepted my offer.

Richard stared at me as I hung up. 'What?'

'Nothing…' he said.

Hector and his wife Mary were the first to arrive. I'm sure I've seen them before, but I'm not sure.

'Ah Sophie,' he said, 'looking beautiful as always.'

'Thank you.'

He seemed to know me, but I had no clue who he even was.

Richard ushered them to the living room. They sat on the sofa and chatted. I went to the kitchen and checked on the food, and added more salt to the gravy.

'Sophie!' Richard called out.

'Yes?'

'Pour us some drinks will you? A martini, and two whiskeys,' Richard commanded.

What am I? A waitress? I took a deep breath and made them the bloody drinks. As I was about to sit down, the doorbell went. Jodie stood before me with a long face. She has long brown hair, hazel eyes, and high cheekbones. For her age, she's still an attractive woman.

'Sophie…' she said, taking off her cream coat. She handed it to me and slipped past me.

'Jodie!'

'Richard, darling!'

I hung her pesky coat on the hanger. Patrick came in.

'Sophie,' he said, giving me a warm hug and kissing me on both cheeks, 'whenever I see you, you always look younger.'

'Oh, thank you.'

'Such a stunner,' he said, ogling me. *Dirty old man.*

'Patrick!' his wife called out.

She was sitting on the sofa. 'Come here,' she said, as if I had the plague.

I wondered where Sylvie was and what is taking her so long?

'Sophie, be a darling, make a gin and tonic and a whiskey,' Richard said.

Can't he do them himself? They are his guests. After I made their drinks and poured myself a large glass of gin and tonic, I sat on the armchair, not paying attention to what they were saying. They mumbled words, naming people I didn't know, or I do, but I don't remember. I lit a cigarette and took a large sip of gin. Jody scowled at me.

'Still smoking I see,' she said.

'Aha…'

She rolled her eyes. The doorbell rang. Sylvie at last. I took a deep drag from my cigarette. Richard eyed me and proceeded with his conversation. Sylvie was casually dressed in jeans, a t-shirt, and a grey coat. Sylvie and I exchanged hugs, and I introduced her to Richard's friends.

'Sophie, I wasn't aware you have such beautiful friends. Richard, you should invite me here more often,' Patrick said.

Jodie gave me a nasty glare. I poured a glass of gin and tonic for Sylvie and me. I got my phone from the kitchen table and sat back in the armchair. Sylvie moved a chair next to me. She didn't look impressed by Richard's friends.

'Thank you for coming, you saved my life,' I whispered.

'Hey, that's what friends are for,' she said, leaning in closer to me, 'did you manage to gather something about that night?'

I shook my head.

'Did you speak to the lads?' she asked.

I nodded.

'Did you tell him?'

Who?'

'Richard…' she whispered.

'No… I intend to keep it that way.'

'And what about-'

'I don't want to talk about it this now.'

After lunch, Richard and his crew retreated to his study, while Sylvie and I stayed in the kitchen. She helped me wash the dishes, and then we smoked cigarettes and drank brandy in the living room. We heard laughter coming from the study.

'Happy bunch,' Sylvie said.

'They're such assholes.'

Sylvie giggled. The phone rang.

'I'll get it.' Richard shouted from his study.

'Hello, Richard speaking?' he shouted happily. 'Hello? Are you there? He paused for a while, then continued, 'who is this?' he said, exasperated.

'Whoever it was hung up,' he said to the others.

I swiped the screen of my phone and opened Michael's text. *I'm sorry, let's sort this out…*

He sent it right after I switched off my phone last night. I shifted on my seat, there was nothing to sort out. He accused me of being drunk when I know what I saw. I'm not crazy. It was so creepy to see Sam lingering in the street, staring at my window. The phone rang again it made me jump. Richard picked it up, again.

'Richard Knight… hello? …I can't hear you.'

He slammed the phone back down. 'Someone taking the piss.'

'I met someone,' Sylvie said.

'Great news. Who is he?'

'His name Tim. He's an engineer, divorced, no kids.'

'Where did you meet him?'

'At a friend's party.

'And what's he like?'

'He's amazing… in and out of bed.'

'Oh…' I said, spluttering on my brandy.

She giggled. 'Last time we made love, I told him I was sore, and he took it as a compliment. He said that means he's doing something right.'

As Sylvie spoke about her sexual escapades, my mind drifted back to yesterday. Why was it so important to him for us to "sort things out." There was nothing to sort out, but I did make it worse by kissing him. How could I be so stupid? I have come across attractive men before, and I didn't go around kissing them. But Michael, he's what exactly? My body prickles every time I think of him, his fire, his enthusiasm, his passion, his unapologetic attitude. So seductive, yet so arrogant.

Mike, there is nothing to "sort out" you made your point as I made mine. It's best we leave this behind us and move on.

S.

I took Sylvie's half-finished brandy from her hand and refilled our glasses. The phone rang again. I picked up it on the first ring.

'Hello?'

Breathing. A bell ringing.

'Hello?'

Silence answered me back. Shaking my head, I placed the phone down and sat back on the sofa.

My phone beeped.

Yes, there is, and you know it too. I can make myself available to you whenever you want me.

M X

My mouth gaped open like a fish. What makes Michael think I want to see him again? Wasn't I clear in the text? Which part of moving on does he not understand? I like a confident young man, but who does he think he is?

'Are you there, Sophie?' Sylvie asked.

I raised my head. 'Yes?'

'Did you hear what I just said?'

'I'm sorry… I…'

'You seem distracted…'

'I—'

She leaned forward, looking at me skeptically. 'There's an affair written all over you.'

What made her say such a thing? 'What an outlandish comment.'

'I hope you don't do anything foolish. I know Richard can be… challenging but he's a good man,' she said, getting up from her chair.

'You're leaving?' I said unable to hide the panic.

I didn't want to be alone with Richard friends.

'Yes, I have to meet Tim,' she checked her watch, 'in half an hour, thanks for lunch. Will you say bye to Richard for me?' She gave me a hug. 'I love you.'

'I love you too.'

'If you need to talk, call okay?'

'Yes, same here.'

The phone rang again. I heard footsteps behind me. I turned to see Jodie removing her earring and picking up the phone.

'Knight Residence…. speak up. Hello?'

She placed the receiver back down.

'Whoever it was hung up on me, how rude. Be a doll and fetch me a gin and tonic,' she said.

'You have hands, why don't you fetch it yourself, doll,' I snapped.

I reread his text again. *I can make myself available to you* - what a tempting offer. I deleted the message and his number from my contacts. There wasn't any point in erasing it though because I already remember it. I left the mobile on the bedside table. My phone beeped again. I stared at it as if it was the most dangerous object in the room.

I'm outside. M

What does he mean, he's outside? Outside this apartment? Is he out of his mind.

I opened the bedroom door and strolled past Richard's office. They were all talking and drinking, sat on the sofa or in armchairs, with Richard behind his desk. I made it to the living room and opened the curtain. Michael stood on the pavement across the street. My jaw muscles tightened. What excuse am I going to tell Richard?

I dragged the garbage bag out and plodded down the street, without looking at Michael. I stopped around the corner. He came over to me.

'What do you think you're doing?' I said.

'I wanted to see you.'

'What are you doing calling and sending me those bloody texts invading my space. My husband is in there with his guests, he could easily have seen you.'

'So? He doesn't know me.'

'Yes, but there's a good chance he saw me.' I said, almost raising my voice.

He took a step closer. I jumped. 'Come and see me again.'

If I were another girl, she would do it in a heartbeat. However, I wasn't any other girl.

This can't be happening, I shouldn't have gone to his place, I shouldn't have kissed him.

'Why?'

'Think about it,' he said, placing his hand on my cheek. I tensed and pulled away. 'Remember, I meant every word in that text.'

He walked away. I watched until he had disappeared around the corner.

When I got back in the apartment and paced past the study, Richard's desk was empty. Jodie was sitting in one the armchairs playing with her hair. I couldn't see Mary or their husbands. I hoped Richard hadn't left me alone with these cows.

'She's doesn't socialize with us, she's always been distant. I told Richard he was crazy to marry such a young woman,' Jodie said.

Yes, she's not one of us, how can she? She's young.' Mary said.

'She's a gorgeous girl,' Jodie said.

'She's beautiful, but the smoking is just vile.'

'Yes, totally… '

'You think she's had work done?'

'Of course, she has, her arse is in exactly the same place as it was ten years ago.'

'Well, I need names.'

How ridiculous, I have never considered plastic surgery.

'Richard could have done better,' Jody fumed, 'he married her to make himself look good.'

'Richard's a handsome man. He hardly needs a pretty girl to make him more appealing.'

'You know how it is… she didn't even give him any children, except miscarriages. Useless girl, all she cares about is to look pretty and smoke.'

I ran to the bedroom in tears. How dare she come into my house, eat my food, drink my booze, and say something like that. Is this what that cow thought of me? What a dreadful thing to say. Where is her shame? What did I do to her to cause such contempt? After what I did for Richard, they should get down on their knees and thank me. I was there for him, not them. They didn't even come and visit him, so much for friends. Doesn't she realize how the miscarriages affected me? I've never recovered from the grief.

The front door opened, and I heard laughter and talking. Was Richard outside? What if he'd seen me?

The phone rang. 'Bloody phone,' Richard said.

'Richard Knight…. Malcolm, how are you? Good, good no, I haven't forgotten about tomorrow, yes I see, good day to you too.'

2nd March,
Late at night,
Diary,

It's official, I'm the shittiest person that ever walked on this earth. You are my only confidant. No-one must find you, and I mean *no one*. You hold a dangerous secret now.

I haven't told Richard, what I overhead Jodie say about me. He would defend her, so what's the point? So, I suffer in silence. I spent the day, trying to recall, when I was an ordinary woman, before the drinking, and everything else that happened. The first time I got pregnant, was a year after we got married. Oh, the joy of having a baby. I always wanted to be a mother. For me, it's life's greatest achievement. I was careful about what to eat and not to stress myself. I never knew that kind of happiness. I didn't want to know the sex of the baby. I wanted it to be a surprise. We set up the nursery and had everything ready to welcome the baby. We were happy. Richard proudly placed his hand on my growing tummy. We came up with names - Grace if it was a girl, Tommy if it was a boy. However, there wasn't any baby. The doctor didn't give me a reason.

'It happens,' he said.

I stayed at home, staring at the walls. I didn't want to talk, or go to work. I refused to do anything. It was like I'd lost the will to live. Richard friend's wife was going to have a baby. Of course, there was a baby shower.

We were invited, but I didn't go. I urged him to go. I thought to myself, how could she have a baby when I didn't. What have I done wrong? We were scared of trying. Seven years passed, and I got pregnant again. This time, I wanted to do everything right. I stayed in bed from the moment I found out. We didn't think about what we'd name our child or make a nursery.

Again, before the three months, there was another miscarriage. It threw me over the edge. That's what triggered the smoking and the drinking, and it's got worse over the years. Then there was Richard's heart attack. He was doing a seminar when it happened. I was working late on an audit when I got the call. Before the operation, he told me to call his solicitor, to change his will. I wanted to hear nothing of it.

'You're not going to die, you hear me, you are not going to die,' I cried.

After the operation, he stayed home, so I wasn't just his wife, I was his nurse too. I made sure he took his pills, made sure he was comfortable, and I cooked and cleaned. I didn't mind. We never tried for a baby again. It died right after Richard's heart attack. Last year, I brought up the option of having a surrogate, or an adoption. Richard said no, point blank.

I never got over the cruel response, *no*. I am an island. Now I smoke and drink, to forget the pain. The pain that my own husband caused me. I only wanted one thing from him, and he didn't give it to me.

I paced from room to room, with my hands clenched. I didn't want to be in this tomb of a place. I went down to the club. Nobody was playing, yet. *Sade* pumped out from the speakers. I ordered a double Chivas. The liquid sang in my mouth. I scanned the room, a few people were drinking, talking, and laughing, having a jolly wonderful time. Michael was sitting on the stage, dressed in a white jacket with a black collar, leather pants, a purple shirt, and a red scarf around his neck. He wasn't alone, there was another man with him. He was having an in-depth discussion and took no notice of me. Seeing him, even just a glimpse, has become the high point of my day, everything is downhill from there.

Michael chatted with his friend and brushed his hand through his golden hair. I finished my drink, tempted to order another, but wanted to be sober for once.

Michael glanced at me, and so did his friend. Michael said something to him, and they looked away.

I got up to leave and stepped out of the club. My eyes filled with tears. I turned to see that he had followed me out.

Thwack.

I slapped him because of that night, for not knowing what happened. I slapped him for the way he talked to me at his flat, and for kissing him. I slapped him for sending me the texts and the barrage of phone calls. I slapped him for showing up outside my apartment.

His flared his nostrils and held his cheek. He pulled me against the wall. He smelled of aftershave, weed, and beer.

'Don't you ever slap me again!' he roared, studying my face. He frowned and backed away, 'sorry…' He placed his hand back onto his slapped cheek.

'Do you think you can manage to get away for a few hours?' I asked him.

'What?'

'Can you?'

'Now?'

He glanced down at the ground, 'Yeah, I suppose... sure why not?'

'Good.'

'Fine... give me a minute, okay?' he snapped.

He disappeared into the club. I scanned the street to make sure no one I know was passing by while I waited. Richard was at a business dinner with Malcolm, and those dinners always take a long time.

Michael came out glaring at me. I stared at him adoringly. Is that why he showed up outside my apartment asking me to see him again? I was about to make it easy and straightforward for him. I threw my cigarette to the ground, moved away from the wall and hailed an approaching taxi.

'Hey, can you tell me what this is all about?' he shouted.

'You know what this is about.'

'Do I?' he asked in bewilderment. I didn't reply, the fewer words spoken, the better. The taxi stopped, 'oh I get it. You're still mad about Saturday. Or is it about yesterday? Is this why you came all the way to slap me? Fine, I deserve it.'

I opened the car door, 'It's not just about that.'

That text, that bloody text, I wanted to tell him, but instead, I kept quiet.

'Are you drunk?' he asked.

'No, I'm not bloody drunk.'

'You look odd.'

'I'm having a bad day.' I said getting in the taxi.

'Is that supposed to be my problem?'

'Get in the car.'

We traveled in silence. My hands were shaking. He looked out of the window, deep in thought. I placed my hand on the leather interior; it felt cold against my sweaty palms. I stole a sideways glance at him. I could see he was looking at my legs, tracing them up and down. I looked away. My heart was palpitating.

Rain beat fast against the taxi windows. What would my parents say if they saw me right now? What would they think? This is not how they raised their daughter. I'm not as close to them as I used to be. Since I married Richard, our relationship became strained. My mom thinks Richard is condescending. We'd have dinner together as a family and hardly say a word. Richard looking as if he didn't want to be there. We should have gone to couples' therapy, instead of playing hide and seek with our feelings, pretending we were fine, that the miscarriages and his heart attack were part of the past. But the past is affecting our future and my drinking. I did consider couples' therapy once, Richard disapproved of the idea, he said it's a waste of money. He said we would solve our own problems, and not address them with strangers. Did we address them? No. I still want a baby. It's the only thing I want in my shitty life. Richard tries to avoid this as much as he can. So, there I was seeking solace with a kid. It's absurd, or is it though?

I paid for the fare and followed him into the flat. I knew that once I went in, my life wouldn't be the same again, that it would change drastically. The flat was messier than the last time, with packets of biscuits, milkshake glasses, an empty pizza box, and comic books strewn on the floor. I sniffed the chilled air. He slammed the door shut, but didn't switch on the lights. He put the keys on a sad-looking cabinet by the doorway.

I took off my coat and let it drop to the floor. I glanced into the bedroom. The bed was unmade with grey sheets, and a book lying face down on it. There was a Les Paul in the corner, an amp, various other musical equipment, and a leopard-skin jacket placed on the chair. He shut the door. I walked over to the window and looked out at a group of young people in the street. I stared at the darkness of the sky, and the heavy rain beating against the window. A thunderbolt shook the whole room, followed by a lightning flash. I swung around to see Michael. I told myself, why fight something that's there? Why hold back? Why restrict yourself, when both of you know it's going to happen either way? I could almost hear him thinking too. I wished he would do anything, instead of just stand there, like he's never been in a bedroom with a woman before. I wondered how to make myself sensual for him, and if to start undressing while he watched, or if I should walk up to him and kiss him.

'You've done my brain in,' I said, and looked down.

I walked over to him and started to unbutton his shirt, while he stood still, watching me.

I didn't know him or his body, and yet, there I was undressing him, feeling both excitement and fear.

As I made my way down to the last button, I admired his smooth, fair chest, and his flat stomach, and the beauty in front of me. What has he done to me? I've never been like this. It was like a dream. Like I was under his spell. I pulled my blouse from the waistband of my skirt and took it off. I trembled as his eyes inspected my white lace bra. I slipped off his jacket. We kissed hard, and moved to the bed, hitting my toe on something. I yelped but kept on going, dropping onto the bed. I traced his perfect features with my fingers, so beautiful just like an angel. He wanted to take control, and I allowed it. He was so eager to please me, and he didn't have to work too hard.

It felt like all this time, I've been asleep, and now I'm finally awakening. It was painless, easy, urgent, a thing of hunger, of instinct. Looking back, I'm overwhelmed how confident I was as if I'd done this before—but nothing like this has ever happened to me. I was sure of myself and of my body. I wanted it, I needed it, and now it would be something I would do for myself. My secret.

What I've done hasn't sunk in yet. Nor how easily I could destroy everything. It didn't feel wrong. It felt right like I had become myself.

'Are you all right?' he asked.

'I'm fine...'

'You seem upset? Is it me? Did I hurt you?'

I smiled. 'No, no, not at all. Can I ask you something?'

'Yeah...'

'Err... how to say this... do people make remarks about the way you look?'

'All the time, but I don't give a shit what people think of me, why? Did someone say something hurtful to you?'

'Well-

The phone rang.

'Yeah... I know... yes...' He stared back at me. 'I got held up with um... something... yes... I don't know... start off... without me.'

'It's incredibly important we keep it secret, no-one and I mean *no one* should know what happened tonight,' I said, after he hung up.

'I already told my friends you are here,' he said.

Blood drained from my face, and my jaw dropped open. He barked with laughter. 'If you could see your face. I'm joking nobody knows you're here, you can relax.'

'I'm serious.' I said.

'I was kidding, nobody knows, I promise.'

'I better go,' I announced, gathering my clothes piled on the floor.

'Wait...' he said.

'What?' I said.

'Don't you want to do it, again?'

Afterward, flushed, and burning, and feeling like a masterpiece, a whore, and so ashamed, I ran out of there.

I didn't know how I could go home to Richard without confessing my sin. I thought I would dissolve in tears, but when I got back, I was surprised how calm I felt as if nothing happened. Richard was laying on the sofa, watching a TV show.

'Where have you been?' he asked.

Couldn't he tell? I stood in the middle of the room, my body stinking of another man. His eyes moved back to the TV.

I took off my coat. 'I had to meet a client. I thought I told you.'

He frowned. 'I don't know, maybe you did, and I forgot.'

'How did the business dinner go?' I asked.

'Swell.'

'Did you take your medication?'

'Not yet.'

I grabbed his pills and a glass of water and took them over to him. I watched him popping the three tiny pills into his mouth and wash them down with water.

'Sophie, have you been drinking?'

'Had a few drinks, yes,' I said.

'Again?'

'I'm stressed.'

'Quit your job, I make enough money to sustain both of us. There's no point for us both to work. There are no mortgages or any lavish expenses, nothing I can't manage. '

'Don't be ridiculous, I like being independent, and I've worked too hard to quit now.'

Had my third shower of the day. How could I have had sex with him? How could I do something like this?

He's so beautiful.

He was all mine, for a while.

He didn't ask to see me again anyway. I don't want to have to fit him into my timetable. I cried, and then slapped my cheek. What were you thinking you foolish, stupid, ridiculous woman?

Anyway, as I was lying there in our bedroom, thinking about how stupid I've behaved, Richard came in. I closed my eyes and pretended to be asleep.

'Sophie,' he whispered.

He kissed my cheek. 'I love you. I don't know what I do if I lost you. Please think about that.'

Quit my job? I've already lost half of my identity for this man. My job is what gets me out of bed in the morning. I've worked hard to make it this far, and my husband wants me to quit? Why doesn't he quit? He's the sick man, not me. Why do women have to make all the sacrifices? It's not going to happen. I'll be damned to stay at home while Richard runs the show. Well, this marriage is already a one-man show. If I leave my job, I'm sure I'd do something even more stupid than I already have.

5th March,
Evening,
Diary,

Richard was right, there should be a tornado named after me, I am a walking disaster. I don't want to open this diary in years to come and read about how I became a whore, a bad wife, and a terrible human being. I tried to put that evening behind me and get on with the familiarity of my life. Today, I worked on journal entries. At 3:00pm I had a meeting at the office. Afterward, I made a few phone calls. I left the office at around 18:30, took the tube home and headed to the grocery store. I bought ingredients for supper. I turned to the wine section and browsed the wines, tempted to buy each and every one of them. I opted for a bottle of Merlot. As I was about to leave the section, I nearly hit someone with my basket.

'Sorr—'

My jaw dropped.

'It's all right,' Sam said.

His beauty differs from Michael's. He's still good-looking, with black and fluffy waves falling over his face, partially covering his blue eyes, fair skin, high cheekbones, and full lips.

'Oh, it's you,' I said, 'I saw you the other night, you were looking up at my window.'

He looked me up and down. 'Just admiring.'

'You what?'

'I didn't mean to scare you. I-' he blurted.

'What do you want?'

'... It's hard to explain.'

'What's hard to explain?'

'Well...'

'Maybe you can explain this and what happened that other night... The night-'

'... Nothing happened, we danced. We were having a good time, and then we slipped on the dance-floor, and then you fainted.'

I got a distinct impression that Michael and Sam had agreed to tell the same story. In case I ask questions.

'Are you sure no-one hit me?' I asked.

I couldn't make out a reaction. 'No, we just fell, that's all.'

'It must have been a pretty big fall, I had bruises all over my body.'

'Look, lady, I don't know what you want me to say,' he said, looking into my basket, 'but you need to take it easy with the booze.'

I sighed. He turned to face me, wide-eyed.

'You should look on Facebook a little more, you might find something of interest to you.'

'What?'

He didn't answer. He went over and paid for things, not looking back.

Are there photos of me from that night on Facebook? Guh. I paid for my things and rushed home.

I checked the mailbox when I got home. There was another note. This time typewritten like the first one.

You naughty minx. I know what you're up to.

Who's sending these notes? Maybe I should notify the police and show them? But wait… a note that says I'm a naughty minx and someone knows what I'm up too? I'd be a laughing stock. I crumpled the paper into a tight ball and threw it into the nearest bin. That's where the notes belong.

Richard wasn't home yet. I logged onto my Facebook and searched for Sam, but nothing. I searched for Evelyne Robinson. Her profile is public. Someone needs to show her how to change her privacy settings. The last time she uploaded a photo, a selfie of herself with another girl, was three hours ago. Evelyne's a pretty girl, in her early twenties, with long blonde hair, green eyes, low cheekbones, and cupid-shaped lips. She pulls off the boho style beautifully. The daughter of a rich man, with a privileged life who studies, art and takes selfies. I don't understand the concept of uploading every photo on social media, it's like you're seeking approval from society. Look at how great my life is. I don't get it, and perhaps I never will. Richard stomped in. I closed the laptop.

'What are you doing?'

'I'm writing an email to a client.'

7th March
Afternoon,
 Diary,

I never heard from Michael, probably it's for the best. I served my purpose. That's how it is with men his age. They lay off and fuck off. I have no plans for this to be an ongoing thing…

10th March
Evening
Diary,
Can I see you? M xx

I stared at Michael's text on my way to work, I didn't reply though. I entered my office building and took the lift with the other black suits. I pushed the glass door open into the reception. 8:00am and already the phones were ringing, and the printers whirring and jamming. This is my life.

Wendy stopped typing as I approached her desk.

'Good morning, these are for you?' she said, and handed me notes from clients who have called.

'Thanks, put me through to Mr. Williams. I need to speak to him regarding the profit margins.'

In my office, I sat at my desk and switched on my laptop. My phone beeped -another text from Michael. I switched it off. If clients wanted me, they could reach me at my office. I got on with my papers and figures. It's been brought to my attention that I forgot a deadline for a VAT return. I had to explain to the client, and he has to pay a fine. I must pay more attention. Charles wasn't happy.

'Pay it from your own pocket,' he said when he came to my office to tell me about the mishap, 'it's mistakes like these that make us look stupid in front of our clients. Are you stupid?'

'No.'

'Do you want to look stupid?'

'No.'

'You're making so many mistakes lately, and it's making me question your ability to concentrate, Sophie. You have twenty-four hours to fix this.'

Maybe I should quit this fucking job. I pictured it, marching to Charles' office with my notice and telling him to stop talking to me as if I am dirt stuck under the sole of his shoe.

I left the office at 6:00pm to work from home. I stopped dead as the blood drained from my face. Michael was across the street, waiting. How long had he been there? I told him where I work, but I didn't expect him to show up there. My colleagues know Richard, so there's a chance someone might tell him if they started to suspect something.

I dropped the plastic bottle, and the gin poured out onto the ground, I didn't screw the tab properly. It splashed all over my legs. I wanted the floor to open up and swallow me. I picked up the bottle and chucked it in my bag. Michael didn't move. I didn't want him to. I couldn't have him spoil everything for me. I crossed the street and plodded past him, feeling his eyes burning a hole in me. I stopped at the corner, six blocks away from the firm. I fired up a cigarette and waited for Michael. He lumbered casually towards me as if he was on an evening stroll around the city on a cloudy evening.

'You can't show up at my work, people can see us together. I can't be seen in public with you, do you understand?' I said.

'You gave me no choice,' he said softly.

'What?'

'Why you didn't reply to my texts… you were not coming to see me again, were you?'

I ran my hands through my hair. 'What happened that night… it was…'

It was what? Wonderful? A roller coaster? It's going to fuck up my life?

'… It was wrong.'

'I know but it was great, wasn't it?'

'That's beside the point…'

'I missed you.'

'That's sweet, Mike.'

He kissed me passionately on the lips. I grabbed the collar of his shirt to push him away, my brain yelling at me *you're in public*. A rush of anger spiraled into me. I pulled him away, wanting to scream in outrage.

'Come with me,' he whispered.

'I can't do this,' I said, studying his beautiful face. I lingered at his lips, *but I could*.

I have no relationship with Michael, there is no *we* or *us*. Still, he arouses emotions in me, ones I have no control over. He gave me an innocent glance, and my heart melted. Maybe just one more time I told myself, just like my drinking, I always say one more time. That *one more* led to more drinks until I was drunk. This is the same, I knew it, and he knew it.

'Bollocks,' I said.

He smiled at me, and stepped out in the pavement, and whistled at the passing taxi. A few heads turned. I shut my eyes. Which part of discretion doesn't he get? I threw my cigarette to the ground and scanned the area to make sure no one from work was around, although in the rush hour crowds it was hard to tell.

'How did you learn to whistle like that?' I asked as we stood side by side.

'It's easy,' he chirped, opening the car door for me, 'I'll teach you.'

He gave his address to the driver. The cabbie stared at us from the rear-view mirror, how odd, and strange we must look in his eyes. This thought made me smile. My eyes went to the passing streets and thought, I'm at it again. The taxi stopped at the traffic lights. I placed my hand on the handle and noticed both Michael and the driver watching me. I needed a drink. I couldn't go through it without any. I searched for my plastic bottle and found there was a bit of gin left. Even a tiny drop helped. Michael swiped the bottle from me.

'You have a serious problem, do you drink on the job as well?' he whispered.

The driver could have easily overheard our conversation.

'I have my drinking under control. I only carry a bottle of water with me.'

He raised an eyebrow at me. 'You're a terrible liar.'

'Just give me the damn bottle,' I said, trying to snatch it away.

'I'm not stupid,' he said.

As we got out of the taxi, he threw my plastic bottle in the bin and stomped past me, inside the flats.

Music blared out from one of the apartments. He took out a set of keys from his jacket pocket and opened the door. I felt unsteady, as though I was walking on jelly. Once inside, I began to unbutton my coat.

'No, please, let me,' he said softly.

I stared at his hands, as he unbuttoned my coat. He smelt of soap and sweat.

We need to have boundaries. I can't have Michael showing up at my work. *We* again, I have to remind myself there is no *we*. With Richard, there is *we* and *us*, but in that flat there was nothing, I wasn't myself, I was possessed. In that room, the past, the present, and future were erased. Nothing made sense. Next, he removed the belt from my waist and unbuttoned my dress at the front, taking his time. He stared at my black lace bra. Did he like lace underwear? What sort of man is he? What does he like? He felt the curve of my breasts with his hand. I shivered slightly. They were cold. Someone from outside shouted,

'I'm going to get you, you cunt!'

A bottle dropped on the ground, glass shattered followed by more swearing. Michael sighed.

'This is so wrong,' I said.

'Nobody has to know…' he said, kissing my neck and my chest. He then knelt down and kissed my stomach, as I ran my fingers through his hair.

I shut my eyes and gazed dumbly at the ceiling. He removed my tights, and I put my hands on his shoulders to avoid toppling over. I moaned in his mouth.

He nuzzled my neck, as he slipped off my dress. *I can do this*, I thought, as I removed his jacket and let it drop to the floor. I unbuttoned his shirt and yanked it off with force. My hands were all over him. Of course, I can do this, it was so easy. This will be our secret. Sliding further down, welcoming myself to the rest of him, his neck, his chest, his stomach, I unzipped his trousers, and tasted him salty in my mouth. This will tear me apart. How could I go through life without this passion? How could I think that studying and having a successful job is more important?

Afterward, I dressed and collected my bag. Michael stood shirtless by the coffee table, as I shut the door closed behind me. I shut my eyes in discontent outside his door. We didn't even set up our next date….or should I say…meeting of sex. This is not a proud moment for me. What are we even doing? What is this?

14th March
Midnight
Diary,

The only thing familiar about my life is my job. I can say words such as 'trial balance,' 'assets,' and 'liabilities.' while I am sitting on a bomb waiting for it to self-destruct.

I went to see Michael tonight. I knocked and knocked, but no answer. I waited for half an hour sitting by his door, but he didn't show. I ended up nipping to the pub across the street and ordered a shot of vodka. I drowned three in a row. A middle-aged man sat on the stool looking at me adoringly.

'Nice legs,' he said.

'Excuse me?'

'I said you have nice legs. What's a beautiful woman like yourself doing drinking on her own? Would you like some company?'

'I'm waiting for someone,' I said, moving away from the bar. I found a sofa by the window and sat down.

From time to time, I peered out of the window, hoping I'd catch Michael on the street. I opened my third packet of cigarettes for the day. I waited another fifteen minutes, then I gave up.

'Where have you been?' Richard asked when I arrived home.

'Had to meet a client.'

'Hmmm,' he said and continued reading his paper, 'how about we go out for dinner tonight?'

'Sure, let me have a shower first.'

'Sophie?'

'Yes, darling,' I said.

Richard studied me with hard eyes 'Did you consider what we discussed?'

'About?'

'Your job.'

'We didn't discuss it, Richard. You were suggesting, and no, I will not quit my job. I like what I do.'

'I will support you on whatever you decide,' he said.

The chicken tasted like cardboard in my mouth. I asked for ketchup and took a sip of wine. All I could hear was the sound of forks and knives hitting the plates, and a cacophony of voices, which made me drift off to my escapade with Michael. Each act of love slapping me on the face. Michael pounding me against the wall and wrapping my legs around him. My nails sinking into his skin.

No amount of food or wine will wash off his taste in my mouth. Each time, he touches me, he takes a part of me with him. The drinking, the chain-smoking it can come out in the open, but nobody has to know about this. Do I want an affair? Do I want to ruin everything I've worked so hard to achieve? Where did Michael go this evening? Why wasn't he there? I shouldn't get high hopes of him sitting in his flat waiting for me to show up. He has his own life, friends to meet, a job to go to, girls to shag. Was he with a girl? *Don't even go there* my brain whispered to me.

Richard stared at me eating, and I smiled nervously at him. I promised myself, I have to be good for him. Each time, I betray him with Michael, I kill a bit of my husband. Slowly, little by little, I will kill him. He can't find out about this, it will break his heart.

'You're eating like a pig,' said Richard.

'I'm starving,' I said.

'You seem preoccupied.'

'I'm getting over something.'

'You seem preoccupied a lot these days.'

'I have lots to do at work.'

'We're having dinner, relax,' he said, moving closer to me.

For a moment, I wanted to confess everything, and capture his humiliated expression. If anyone looked, they would have seen a respectable couple having dinner, but what they didn't know was, I longed for another man, and was figuring out more excuses to go and see him again.

20th March
Evening,
Diary,

Charles came out of his office when he saw me walking past.
'Sophie?' he called.
'Yes?'
'Where are you going?' he asked, checking his watch.
Shit!
Think of something quick. Is he monitoring my moves?
'I'm meeting a client,' I said.
'How come I didn't know about this meeting?' he asked.
Fuck! Fuck! Fuck!
'It's a last-minute thing. He called to set up a meeting,' I said, turning away.
'Wait a minute,' he said.
I froze.
'Who is this client?' Charles asked.

If I said a client's name, there was a possibility that Charles would call the client to confirm. I was so screwed.

'Charles, something is wrong with this thing?' The clerk said, trying to free paper jammed in the printer.

He removed his glasses and wiped them with his jacket. He put them back on and attended to the printer. I think printers smell fear, the busier you are, the more it is likely to jam. Today, the printer saved my life.

I rang the buzzer. I expected another disappointment and was so relieved to hear the 'bzzz' to let me in.

I climbed up to the second floor. There was pop music playing, again. Michael stood by his door, waiting for me, dressed in a red shirt with ruffles and skinny black trousers. I smiled.

'Hi,' he said, gazing down at me.
'Hi… who keeps playing the loud music?'
'A neighbor, she likes her music loud, like I do, but I don't like this kind of music,' he said.
'We need to talk…'
'I know, come in.'

I didn't take off my coat. I scanned the flat. There were more scarves on the coffee table - black, purple, yellow, and silver bracelets.

'I came over looking for you the other day, but you weren't in.'
'When?'
'Monday, around six.'

'I was out with Sam. Why didn't you text me, I gave you my number to use it.'

'It didn't cross my mind.'

He rammed me against the wall, kissed me hard on the lips, and undid my coat slowly, button by button. He lifted my skirt to my waist.

'No, we have to talk.'

'Right, of course,' he said, taking a step back.

He went into the kitchen. I adjusted my skirt, and sat down. He returned with two beers. He hesitated about giving it to me. The beer was too mild for my craving, but I took it and gulped it down.

'What are we doing?' I asked rubbing my hands together.

'I don't know,' he said, 'I'd rather not think about it.'

I glared at him. He blinked at me. 'Doesn't it bother you?' I asked.

'I don't see it as an accomplishment if that's what you mean.'

'You're too young, you don't want to go through this. I'm playing a part in the most important years of your life…'

'I can't explain it…'

'Does it excite you that I am older, or that I'm a hot mess? Which one is it, or is it both?'

He frowned at me, 'I don't like your drinking, that's for sure.'

'So it's because I'm older. You want the experience and the thrill of it all. There's something sexy about an older woman and a younger man, don't you think? God, I'm a walking cliché.'

He sat beside me and placed his hand on my thigh. 'You do excite the hell out of me, and I don't think you are a cliché.'

'What do you think of me?'

'What do you mean?'

'Well… you must have an opinion of me?'

'*Me*! I like your grey, blue eyes, your lips, those high pouty cheekbones of yours, your wide face. I like the way your face crinkles up when you smile. I also like that you're classy, elegant, and stunning.' He said as his hand moved up to my inner thigh.

I stood up, shaking my head in disbelief, and lit a cigarette. He's in it for the sex, for the experience, to turn his sexual fantasies into reality. I can't deprive him of that, but why me? Why do it with a drunk married woman when he can do it with any woman he wants? It doesn't make sense to me. He doesn't need the drama. He's got nothing to lose and is selfish, maybe that's why. We're all selfish, it's in our nature.

'I can't do this to you. I'm a drunk. Now, I'm drunk on something I can barely understand. It's like I'm on a runaway train, and I'm on a high from the delirious speed. Maybe I want to run away from it all, and that's why I'm here, to escape.' I took a deep drag from my cigarette.

The neighbor played *Radiohead Creep*. I forgot how much I love this song.

He stood up. 'What are you running from?'

'I don't want to talk about it.'

I stroked his cheek, traced his lips with my fingers, and ran my hand over his hair. My hand descended to his chest. He stared at me as if to challenge me to go on, alluring me deeper into his web. I stopped and took a swig of the beer.

'What I am going to do with you? You're in my mind all the time. You're in my brain before I open my eyes. You're the last thing I think about before I close my eyes. Do you have any idea what you've done to me? I can't even think straight,' I said.

I finished my cigarette and lit another.

He sighed heavily. 'As I said it will be our secret. Put it out and come here.'

What an explosive secret to keep. 'Are you going to fuck me now?'

'Or we can talk like we are doing now.'

'Sure, we can talk.'

'You want to go through with it then?' he asked.

I dropped my head and nodded.

He nodded too. We listened to the rain and the thunder rumbling.

'Why? Why would you want to do this? You know what this means, don't you? You're the other man, you're cheating with me. I took vows that I broke, and you're breaking them with me.'

I stood by the window, and watched a man's umbrella blow inside out, and giggled. Michael was sitting gracefully on the sofa, his hand resting on his chin, pouting as if he were a model ready for his close up.

'There's going to be a lot of sneaking around. We can't be seen together in public, and you're going to spend weekends and holidays alone. It will be a relationship based on lies and shame, everything in secret. I'm sure you don't want that.' I paused, hoping for a response, but he sat there waiting for me to elaborate.

'You're very young, so it's best I'm upfront and honest with you. I worked hard to get where I am. I have built a good life for myself-'

'Is that why you drink and smoke because your life is so fucking fabulous? Who do you think you're bullshitting?' he said.

I shut my eyes. 'Don't you have any vices?'

He looked away, without giving me a reply.

'Maybe we should call it a day and nobody will get hurt?' I asked.

'If we end it now, I'll get hurt... or maybe, we'll get fed up with each other and it will end anyway.'

'God, I hope I get fed up with you.'

He stared at me for a long time, silent.

'Where did you meet your friends?' I asked.

'Andy and I met when we were about fourteen or fifteen... a friend of a friend introduced us, and we hit it off.'

'In Sweden?' I asked.

'Yes.'

'What about the good-looking one?'

'Who?'

'Sam.'

His raised an eyebrow. 'You think Sam is good looking?'

He sounded amused.

'Well... err...'

'Do you want him too?'

'No, of course not.'

He grinned. 'Sam's a friend of Andy's. He's a year younger than I am. He didn't like me at first.'

'Why?'

'He told me after we became friends, that he thought I was a gay.'

I reached for the glass of wine. 'Oh.'

'We're blood brothers Sam and me. We were separated by birth.'

'What about the other guy?'

'Which one?'

'Nicky.'

'Nicky's a friend of ours,' he said as if it explained everything.

He got up and came over to me. He took the wine glass from my hand, and drank from the same spot I drank from.

'Enough about my friends. What are you thinking? What's going on in that head?'

'I'm thinking… How I've spent these past days thinking how to come here to see you.'

He took my hand, and positioned me on the table, as if I were a dummy,

Afterward, we laid side by side on the floor, my cheeks raw, and breathing heavily. Michael lit a joint. 'Where does your husband think you are right now?'

I placed my hands on my hot cheeks. 'At work.'

'Do you work late?'

'I used to when I worked for a big company.'

'How late?'

'Very late.' I snatched his joint, and took a puff. I coughed. He laughed at me, 'and on weekends, when there's a deadline, until two in the morning.'

'And you got paid?'

'No.'

'Why not?'

'I don't want to bore you about the details of my job. It's tedious.'

'No, I want to know, I want to know everything about you. Is it stressful, what you do?'

'Yes, very.'

'Why?'

'People always have a problem, and you have to solve it for them. All I see are papers and figures. It's a puzzle. I do their accounts, making sure they don't exceed their deadlines. I do VAT returns, and Tax Returns. That's the worst period, Tax returns.'

'I'm sorry, but if you drink so much, how did you manage to sustain your job, it requires a lot of attention. Have you ever screwed up?'

'I try to keep my drinking at bay when I'm at work.'

I hated myself for lying to him and to myself, given all the mistakes I've been making lately.

'How do you manage?'

'You don't want to know…'

'I do…'

'Mike!'

'Okay, okay, I'll stop now.'

We split the joint, listening to the sounds outside, footsteps, a dog barking, his neighbor yelling at her husband. Apparently, she caught him with the blonde again.

'Do you do drugs?' I asked.

'Sometimes…'

'You hardly drink or smoke, but you do drugs.'

'I said, sometimes, not all the time. There's a difference… unlike the others, all they want to do is party every night, they're such clichés.'

'They're young.'

'I'm young, but I'm not like them… well, I'm no angel but…'

'Were you addicted?'

'No…'

His mouth tasted of weed and wine. I caressed his cheek. 'God… you are going to be the death of me.'

25ᵗʰ March
Evening,
Diary,
You're making a huge mistake. Look around you and you'll find the truth.

Okay, now this is getting creepy. This person has nothing better to do with his/her life, sending crap to people's mailboxes. How childish! How nasty! I'm keeping this note, just in case I need to go to the police.

This is becoming a habit, I don't know how I can go on without being caught. I'm lying more than I have ever done in my life. I invent all the fictional appointments, meetings, and seminars. I write down to whom I tell the lies to keep track of them and hide the paper in the filing cabinet. It's humongous, but I keep on doing it so I can lead my secret life with Michael.

Why am I doing this? How had a drunken night out led me to do such a thing? Those few hours I spend with him, are an escape from the reality of life. I can be whoever I want to be, not Sophie Knight, the accountant with a drinking problem. A shambles of a woman. I can detach myself from the stress of my job, and a sick husband. I go there for a few hours, leave, and go back to my life as if nothing happened. How much longer before the affair, becomes part of my reality? What then?

27th March
Evening,
Oh, Diary,

Twice in one week. Oh, how could I? I'm such a shit. I'm a cheating dirtbag!

'I need to see you. I said to him over the phone with a voice full of desperation. As if my life depended on it.

This is an ego booster for him, or is it for me? I have a toy boy. *A toy boy* what a dreadful way to put it. I don't see him like that though.

'Of course,' he said, 'I'd love to see you too. I've got some errands to run… meet me around 1:00pm at my place. Can't wait to see you.'

There are important things to attend to, like taking my coats to the dry cleaners, vacuum the carpets, renew my passport, but no, there I was, on my way to Camden in high heels, and my hair in a messy bun. I didn't go to him right away. I nipped into the pub first. It wasn't busy. There was a young couple at a table in the corner, and a middle-aged man on the stool sipping on a pint. The TV was showing a replay of a football game. I ordered a neat whiskey from a barmaid with blue hair. I haven't seen her before. She looked like she didn't want to be there. I glimpsed down at my hands and noticed how terrible my hands are. It's the one thing I'd change about my body. They're not long and elegant, they're bony and thin. I bite my nails too. I have to stop biting them, it's not an attractive look.

I drained a couple of whiskies, and each sip danced in my mouth. As I went to order another, the pub door opened, and in walked Michael. He ambled over to me, scowling at the fresh glass of whiskey the blue-haired barmaid placed in front of me.

'Oh Sophie, Sophie,' he said.

'Hi Mike,' the barmaid said, betting her eyelashes at him.

She knows him? Does she know who I am? Has he slept with her too? I have to find a new pub.

'Hey,' he said without looking at her, keeping his eyes focused on me.

The barmaid rolled her eyes, and refreshed the middle-aged man's pint. 'Oh knock it!' he shouted at the TV.

'What are you doing here? I thought I was going to meet you at the flat as we agreed.'

'You're one firecracker aren't you? Don't be irresponsible, it's this kind of attitude that can lead us into trouble.'

'You're here getting drunk, and you're telling me I am irresponsible?'

'How did you know I was here?'

'I saw you coming in. I knew what you were up too. Come on we're going,' he commanded.

'Let me finish this first.'

As I lifted the glass, he took it from my hand and slammed it down. The liquid splashed on the counter.

I felt eyes upon us and, for a split of a second, the bar fell quiet.

'Is this faggot bothering you?' the middle-aged man asked.

Michael gracefully turned his head to the man. 'Why don't you bring your wife over here, and I'll show you.'

The man slammed the glass and stood up. The last thing I needed was a scene. He shouldn't have come here. I didn't need this.

I rushed to the man. 'Please sir, don't mind him. I don't want any trouble.'

'He has a big gob your boy,' he said, sitting back on the stool. He reached for his pint and looked up at me up and down. 'You like em' young, don't you?' he said.

I grabbed my bag, while Michael placed a few notes on the counter.

'See you around,' Michael said to the barmaid.

'Bye Mike,' she said, checking him out as he made it to the door.

'Don't do that again.' I snapped at him once we're outside.

'That guy insulted me, you expect me to keep quiet?'

'You shouldn't have come down here in the first place.'

I lit a cigarette and lurched away from him, it was rather difficult to walk fast in high heels.

'Where are you going?'

'Away from you.'

'Don't be dramatic,' he said, chasing after me.

He dragged me to a corner. 'I thought we're going to spend some time together, not waste time arguing.'

'I'm such a shit.'

'Sophie, you're not a shit. Stop the drinking.' He took my cigarette, and threw it on the ground, 'and then you'd be perfect.'

Like a woman adrift, I wrapped my arms around him. It was primitive. Why am I doing this? Why not do it with a man of my age? Why someone so young? I parted myself from him, my hair in a mess. I followed him to the flat. I sat on the sofa looking at the beautiful collection of scarves and jewelry. I took out a compact from my bag and inspected the damage. My hair looked like a nest. I let it down and brushed it with my fingers. He got a bottle of Sprite from the fridge and offered me one. I declined. He leaned his shoulder against the wall, watching me adjust myself.

'Are you hungry?' he asked.

We ate pizza together in his kitchen. He watched me eat, as though intrigued by something he'd never seen me do before.

'Is there a place you have to be?' he asked, standing up and taking out two Sprites.

'I have a seminar at three, why?'

He placed a bottle in front of me. 'No reason.'

I gazed at the bottle, and then at him. 'God, you're so beautiful, it's breathtaking,'

'You see me that way because I'm unusual to you,' he said, sitting beside me.

'No, it's not that. You know what I like about you?'

'What?'

'You're different from everyone I know. You don't carry a uniform of keys, briefcases, umbrellas. You are who you want to be, I admire that.'

'The problem with most people is, they hide behind the mask society expects of them. What is this seminar you have to go to?'

I shrugged. 'It's boring... it's about corporate turnarounds.'

He frowned. 'What's that?'

'It's about a business that's making a loss, and turning it around, getting it up and running again.'

He took my hand. 'If it's so boring, why don't you stay here instead?'

'Don't tempt me.'

'You'd rather go to a seminar than be here with me?' he said. He let go of my hand and stood.

I crossed my arms. 'Mike, please.'

He leaned against the kitchen counter. 'I like you, that's all.'

I uncrossed my arms and ran my hand through my hair. 'I like you too.'

'Do you like what you do?' he asked.

I took a sip of Sprite. 'It pays the bills.'

He narrowed his eyes. 'You mean it pays for the alcohol?'

'Wanker!'

He smiled. 'You want more?'

I regarded the pizza box. 'No, I'm full.'

'I'm not referring to the food.' He grinned.

I ended up not going to the seminar after all. It was dark when I left. This affair is going to consume me more than the drinking, it will be the end of me. The more I see him, the more I want him.

2nd April
Morning,
Diary,

Last night, I dreamt someone was cutting off my legs with a saw. I don't know who was doing it to me, but I didn't try to stop them. I just laid there, motionless, as the saw sunk deeper into the bone, and the blood spilled onto the sheets. I didn't scream, I laid there relaxed until my legs were completely sawn off my body. I woke up sweating, breathing heavily, and confused. It felt so real. I ended up inspecting my legs when I woke up to see if they were still there. It took a few minutes to calm myself. Richard was snoring beside me, with his mouth open. I wonder what the dream meant? Maybe, it was about punishment - for all the bad I'm doing. That's why I didn't fight back, because I knew I deserved it.

10th April
Evening,
Diary,

Went round to Michael's. He was in a strange mood. He didn't greet me with a kiss, or ask me how I was, or how my day was, as he usually does. I liked that about him. He showed interest in me, not just my body.

I sat on the sofa. The flat was really murky, with clothes on the floor, and blue plastic cups on the coffee table. He was polishing a silver saxophone, wearing a black fishtail coat with red cuffs. How odd he wears fishtails in the afternoon, during the week. It's not like he was going to a wedding or playing at one. He gently placed the sax on the sofa, got up, and looked straight at me. 'You're a drunk, you should attend an AA meeting.' He paced up and down. 'What the hell am I doing with you? You're married. This is bullshit. I don't want to see you anymore, you should leave,' he went on, thinking aloud to himself.

It would make sense for him to meet someone his own age, someone fun and pretty. I'm just someone to play around with in the meantime.

'It's like a different day with the same bullshit. You were right, I can't go through this. I'm too young. I could break up a marriage. It will be my fault. I can't carry that burden,' he added turning around and staring at me.

I shook my head. I wanted him to stop him and plead to him. I opened my mouth, but nothing came out.

'It's too much, and I deserve better,' he continued.

I felt a deep aching pain in my heart. I couldn't breathe.

'You have issues you need to resolve, and I have to stay away from you. It's the most perverted thing that's ever happened to me. It makes me sick.' he said, lowering his eyes to the floor.

Why argue with him when he had already made up his mind? What more could I say? I couldn't make any promises. I am the married one, and I'm the one that leaves.

He glared at me. 'Well say something.'

'I understand, thanks for clearing it up,' I said.

'Clear what up?'

'That I'm a sick and disgusting person.'

'*Sophie!*'

Once outside, I hailed for a taxi, looking over my shoulder thinking he would chase after me, but he didn't. In the taxi, I watched life go by as I fought back the tears. I felt used and disposable. He saw me as the right candidate to fool around with until he had enough. He took advantage of me, and my vulnerability.

'No smoking.' said the cabbie, pointing at the sign.

At home, tears smeared down my face. I made myself a Bloody Mary and smoked. I never thought it would hurt this much. It wasn't just a fling. It's much deeper than that. I'm in love with him. I'm the one who got hurt in the end. I crawled into a ball on the kitchen floor and sobbed. I was there for ages until I remembered Richard would be home soon. I picked myself up and poured the Bloody Mary into the sink. I had a shower to try and make myself look normal again before he got home.

15th April
Afternoon,
Diary,

I should be relieved it's over, it's the end of the lies, the sneaking around, and the faking, but I'm not. I messed up. Both of us were in the wrong, but what I did was so wrong on so many levels. It's for the best - he ended it before we got caught. Imagine the trouble I'd be in? I could have lost everything.

I'm sluggish, but not suicidal, not yet, but I will be. The day will come when I stop caring altogether, and when I drink and smoke myself to death.

17th April
Evening
Diary,

Today was one of those days where I wanted to shoot myself. My drinking is spinning out of control, and it's affecting my job. I lost an important client's file. I put it somewhere, but can't remember where. I didn't do any backups because I forgot. Charles wasn't pleased. I tore the office apart looking for it. Charles also told me off because the balance sheet didn't make any sense. He shook his head and sighed.

'Are you having problems at home?' he asked.

'No.'

He removed his thick glasses with his meaty hands. 'Jesus Christ, Sophie, Mistakes like this make us look bad in front of clients. Do you know what this means?'

'Yes.'

'Your eyes are bloodshot, there are dark circles under your eyes, and you're behaving strangely lately. You're leaving the office at odd hours or don't come back at all. You hardly socialize with us anymore. I've looked the other way, but now…'

I was hot all over. 'Are you firing me?'

'No, but you should go on leave, resolve your issues, and come back when you've sorted yourself out.'

My hands started to shake. 'But I have so much work to do.'

'Don't worry about that, just go and bury your head in the sand somewhere.'

I didn't tell Richard what happened, if I did, he'd try to persuade me to quit. Instead, I told him I'm going to take some time off.

'Good idea, you been looking haggard lately' he said, taking out his wallet. He handed me a few notes, 'go relax, go to a spa, it's my treat.'

I took the money knowing exactly where I'm going to spend it, and it has nothing to do with spas or, any form of pampering.

'Are you sure you're alright?' Richard asked, putting his hand on my shoulder, 'you stink of whiskey. You've been drinking, again?'

'I went for a couple drinks, yes.'

'With who?'

'On my own.'

'Alone?'

'Yes, alone… what's so strange about it?'

'It's not you being alone that bothers me, it's more the fact you're drinking too often.'

'It's been a long a day,' I said.

'That's not what I meant,' Richard said, taking off his bow tie and jacket.

'I'm sorry,' I said.

I have a lot to apologize for. If only he knew the other half of it.

His face was serious and frank. 'What are you apologizing to me for? I think you've been drinking a lot these past few weeks. You need to sort yourself. Or else I will do something about it.'

20th April,
Afternoon,
Diary,

I haven't left the apartment today, not even to buy cigarettes and booze. I don't want to know what's happening out there. All I think about is Michael, I can't get him out of my system.

If I died, would anyone mourn for me? I bet nobody will come to my funeral. Michael wouldn't go for sure, but my parents would. My parents would be devastated and Richard too. He would die right after me from a broken heart. That's a comforting thought.

I cleaned the apartment until it was spotless, it kept me busy. I could do other things, like read a book, go for walks, or meet up with Sylvie, but I don't want to see anyone. I don't have the drive to leave the apartment. It has been two weeks since the affair ended. Two weeks of emptiness. Would Michael laugh at me if he could see me now drowning in self-pity? A month will pass, then six months, and then the years will fly by, and he'll become a memory. I feel useless sitting here doing nothing, staring at the walls, recalling each touch, each caress.

I have to go back to work. I'll be good, and control my drinking, I'll be careful. At least at work.

The fridge is almost empty. There's cheddar cheese, rotten tomatoes, milk, and a bottle of white wine. I threw the tomatoes away and ordered food in for tonight. I'll tell Richard I cooked it. I'm lying to him even about the cooking. I need to go to the supermarket. I'll ask Richard to come with me. I can't face the world alone.

21st April
Evening,
Diary,
'Would you like to come with me to Tesco?' I asked Richard.

'Don't be ridiculous, dear. I've got lots of things to do,' he said, opening the Financial Times, 'I bought us tickets by the way.'

It was like I'd asked him to take a trip with me to the moon. Why couldn't he just say he didn't want to come?

'Tickets for what?' I asked, masking my annoyance.

'Phantom of the Opera,' he replied.

How dramatic. On my way back from Tesco's, I unloaded the purchases from the car, and noticed Andy across the street, with a dark-haired young man, I've never seen.

As I slammed the car door shut, Andy turned in my direction. I glared at them and made my way into the flat. Has Michael told him about us? What has he said? Are they all laughing about me? Do they think I'm scum?

When I got inside the apartment, Richard was talking on the phone. I could hear the music again, the melody of sax flooding my ears and into my brain.

I dumped the bags on the table and peered out of the window. I couldn't believe it. Andy was staring up at the window. The other bloke said something to get his attention, and they both stomped off. Was it Andy sending me those notes? And what about when I saw Sam hanging around out there? Will it be Nicky next? Why are they doing this to me?

OMG, something has just come back to me. That night, there was a woman in a red dress with Andy and the boys. An argument erupted, and she stormed out. I remember someone followed her, but I can't remember who. I totally forgot about what Sam said about me taking a look more on Facebook, what with everything that's been going on with Michael. Who was the woman in the red dress? Was it Evelyne? I need to look at Facebook.

23rd April
Afternoon,
Diary,

Spent the day trawling Facebook. I checked out Evelyne's profile, hoping she'd taken photos of that night. There were lots of pictures of her and Andy, of Andy playing guitar, and of Andy with Sam. There's something about Sam, I can't put my finger on it. Not in a dangerous, or psychotic way, but in a weird way. Is he the reason why I got the bruises? I stumbled across a photo of Michael. He wasn't looking at the camera. Evelyne must have taken it when he wasn't paying attention. My heart thudded. He's so beautiful, and he was mine for a brief time. Men like him don't belong to anyone except to themselves. I shut my eyes and closed the tab. How many photos can one take of themselves and their loved ones? It's uncomfortably narcissistic and banal to share your whole life with the world.

Selfies.
Photos with friends.
Photos on holiday.
Photos of food.
Photos of cocktails.
More selfies.
Photos of the boys.
Photos of parties.
Photos of concerts.
Drawings.

It took longer than I expected. There were many pictures of Andy playing guitar on stage. I opened another window and typed his name on Facebook. He has a fan page, Andy is a rock music producer and an accomplished guitar player, and he's playing an event that's happening two weeks from now. I closed the tab and proceeded on with my other search.

I clicked on an album called "nights out." More selfies and photos with friends. I was about to close the window when a photo caught my eye. It was a selfie of Evelyne pouting at the camera, dressed in red. I spotted myself in the background, leaning against the wall, with Sam in front of me grinning at me. It looked like I'd been hit by a bus. Fucking Facebook. What if someone shows this to Richard? I'm hardly recognizable, but it could do loads of damage if anyone knew. Maybe, I should ask her to take it down. I carried the laptop to the study and plugged it into the printer. I studied the image looking for clues.

Evelyne was there, dressed in red. The photo proves it. Why didn't Sylvie and Michael tell me she was there? Sam wanted me to see this, but why? What's he playing at? What's it got to do with anything? Sylvie should have taken me home, and then none of this would have happened. If only she had been sensible enough to call a taxi.

'It was ages ago, Sophie. I think you should let it go,' Sylvie said.

'I can't. I'm sure something else happened. I just know it.'

It doesn't feel like ages ago, the night that started everything still remains a mystery to me, a missing piece of my life I might not retrieve back.

She sighed.

'Do you remember a girl with them? She was blonde, dressed in red, a girlfriend of one of the lads?'

'No, maybe she got there after I left.'

'Are you sure you don't remember anyone?'

'Yes, I'm sure. What does this have to do with anything?'

'I'd rather not say over the phone. Can we meet up and have a chat?'

'Sure, how does Thursday afternoon sound?'

24th April
Afternoon,
Diary,

I tracked down where Evelyne attends collage, *The Royal College of Arts* in Kensington Gore. It was easy to find because she has all the details plastered on her Facebook. The reason I tracked her down was to ask her about the photo, and anything that might be helpful about that night.

After an hour of waiting for her to show up, Evelyne came out of the college, dressed in knee-high boots and a grey cape. She was talking to a girl and a chap with a beard. She laughed, and let out a snorting sound. They took a few photos of each other in different poses. After what it seemed like the hundredth photo, Evelyne turned in my direction. Her face went white. She said something to her friends and fled. I followed her, but as I turned around the corner, she vanished from sight. I've never spoken to her before, but whenever I've seen her, I've smiled or nodded her way, and she'd always do the same.

Why would she run? It's obvious, she's hiding something. All of them are. What though? All of them lying to my face. Did I do something that night to upset her?

Oh no, it can't be. Oh God.

25ᵗʰ April
Afternoon,
Diary,

Met Sylvie in Mayfair at cafe *Fratelli*. She was already there when I arrived and was drinking a cup of coffee. We exchanged hugs.

'So, how are you?' she asked as I sat down.

'Tired.'

I ordered a black coffee from the waiter.

'You look like shit,' she said, flipping her hair.

'Thanks.'

'So, what's new with you?'

'I took some time off from work.'

I was embarrassed to tell her the truth that I'm close to getting the sack.

'But you never take time off, how come?'

'I'm trying to get to the bottom of it.'

'You're not going back to work until you figure it out?'

I sighed. 'I can't go back when I feel like this.'

She nodded. 'What's this thing about the girl?'

'She's the daughter of a rich man who owns several estates in the city. She lives in one of his properties with her boyfriend and the lads.'

'All three of them?'

I didn't want to tell her Michael moved out. She didn't know about us, and I want to keep it that way, especially now it's over. There's no point.'

'I think so. Anyway, I tracked Evelyne down at the college she goes to. I wanted to have a word with her about that night, but it was bizarre because as soon as she saw me, she ran off.'

'Are you sure she saw you?'

'Yes, it's strange. I don't know why she ran off like that.'

Sylvie frowned. 'But what could she possibly have against you?'

'Fuck knows.'

'Maybe she's mad you were talking to Sam?'

'I think she's mad about Andy.'

'Why would she get upset with you for talking to him?'

'Andy's her boyfriend.'

'Oh, I see.'

I covered my face with my hands. 'It's so frustrating, I can't think why she'd be mad at me. I looked at her Facebook, and there's a selfie of her from that night. She was definitely there.'

'You've been busy.'

'I remembered a woman in a red dress, and now I know for sure it's Evelyne. She stormed out the club, and someone slammed a glass on the table and went after her. I presume it was Andy.'

Sylvie put her hand on mine. 'Sophie.'

The waiter placed my coffee on the table. Sylvie removed her hand from mine. I stirred two sugars in my coffee. 'I think I should have a word with Andy.'

I took out the photo from my bag, and handed it to Sylvie. 'I appear in a photo.' Sylvie studied the picture carefully.

'I don't understand why girls do those ridiculous duck faces, they look stupid....' She took a sip of her coffee, and continued looking at the photo, 'what were you doing with Sam? He's so young. He must be what? Nineteen or twenty?'

I poured milk into my coffee. 'I don't know. According to what I was told, I danced with him and we fell on the dancefloor.'

'You're overthinking this. Why can't you just let it go?'

'What if there's more?'

She handed the photo back to me. 'If something bad happened, don't you think it's best not to know? I read somewhere the brain blocks events because they are too upsetting.'

I took a sip from my coffee. 'That's the reason, I *have* to know. If you'd taken me straight home, none of this would have happened. If it had been you, I'd have called you a cab and got you home.'

'Sophie, you didn't look that drunk when we went to the club.'

I stared at her. 'Are you sure?'

'You were tipsy, but not blind drunk, you weren't making a total fool of yourself. I think the fall made you black out everything out. Do you recall drinking more after I left?'

I shook my head. 'Do you think I was drugged?'

Sylvie looked at me horrified.

'It happens you know,' I continued.

'I know it happens, but I don't think they'd do that.'

'Why are you so sure?'

Sylvie shook her head. 'Are you saying they're rapists?'

'I woke up with bruises all over my body, and my dress ripped. Something happened, or maybe I got into a fight with someone.'

Sylvie jerked her head. 'With whom?'

'I don't know. It could have been anyone... did you ever hear from Nicky again?' I asked.

'No...'

'So, you had sex with him, and that's it?'

'I didn't have sex with him.'

I slapped my hand against my cheeks. 'And you're telling me this now.'

'I don't know what made you think I had sex with him.'

'Then why did you leave?'

'We went to smoke pot, and had a snog, that's all.'

We sipped our coffees silently.

'Sophie, is there something else bothering you?'

I glared at her. 'Why?'

'You seem… distant, preoccupied… how is your drinking?'

'What has my drinking got to do with anything?' I snapped.

'I've known you for fifteen years, I've seen the change in you.'

'My drinking is fine.'

She raised an eyebrow at me. 'Well, I'm pleased you're drinking coffee. Does Richard know?'

'Know what?' I ask.

'That you drink.'

'He makes remarks.'

'Just remarks?'

'What are you getting at?'

She raised her hands. 'Ok, ok I'm sorry, I'm pushing.'

'Yes, you are. I have to go.'

'But you just got here, come on stay a little longer.'

'Fine…'

27th April,
Evening,
Diary,

Last night was my birthday. Richard wanted to take me somewhere special, but I declined his generous offer and ordered Indian food instead. I didn't want to have to try and blend in. He gave me a pair of diamond stud earrings. We ate the Indian on china plates, and Richard opened a bottle of vintage Barolo to mark the occasion. He told me about work, and that he might get another account. The phone rang, he was expecting a foreign call.

'Hello?' he said into the receiver, 'hello? Can you hear me?' Richard grunted. 'Whoever it was put the phone down,' he said, returning to the kitchen.

We continued to eat in silence. I was dipping naan bread into my curry when the phone rang again.

'Who is bloody calling all the time?' Richard said.

I shivered, and put down my fork. 'I'll get it.' I closed my eyes as I picked up the receiver.

'Hello?' Silence. 'Hello…' I said again.

Was it Michael? I didn't give him my home number, so who could it be? Maybe it was a wrong number, but deep down I don't think it was. People are out there watching me, mocking me, sending me notes, making phone calls. I'm petrified.

30th April,
Morning,
Diary!

'Made reservations at *Andina*,' I said to Richard.

'For when?'

'Tonight.'

'Tonight?'

'Yes, darling. I told you about it,' I said.

'I must have forgotten.'

'Don't tell me, you've made plans? I want to go, it's supposed to be one of the hottest restaurants in the city.'

Richard frowned. 'It's all advertisement, dear. A new place opens and it's named the best in the city, an *it* place.'

I kissed his lips. 'I'll take out your navy suit. You look so handsome in it.'

When I came out of the bedroom, Richard was reading the newspaper. I tore it from his hands, and wrapped my arms around his neck. 'We still have time before dinner…'

We made love. Afterward, I told him I loved him, and he told me he loved me too. I wanted to say it over and over, to convince myself.

I scanned the place, and all the lovely, happy faces. Faces I'd never see again. The restaurant was small but cozy.

'Good evening,' I said to the host 'we have a table booked-'

What happened next was unbelievable. Michael was in the restaurant. WTF? His eyes fixated on me and looked me up and down. His lips parted as if to say something, but nothing came out. He looked different, with shorter, shoulder-length, peroxide blond hair. Of all the restaurants in London, he had to be in this one, as I'm about to have dinner with my husband.

I've thought of this scenario several times and wondered what would happen. All I felt was anger rushing through me, and wanted to slap that stunning face.

'Well, this is lovely,' Richard said, entering the restaurant, and admiring the sophisticated decor.

Michael and I looked at him. Richard eyed Michael. Michael passed a quick glance at me. How must we have seemed to Michael- the polished, immaculate, handsome couple, who everyone envies - I know people look at us, and think to themselves, I want to be like them, they seem like they have it all figured it out. A powerful, grounded couple. But, of course, Michael knows the irony behind the facade.

'I've seen you before. Don't you live with Evelyne?' Richard said.

'I used to,' Michael replied.

My heart lurched. This couldn't be happening, my husband and Michael conversing. Richard offered him his hand. Michael hesitated, and then shook his hand. I could have died. My heart thrummed against my chest. I could hardly breathe.

'Richard Knight.'

'Michael Frisk.'

'That's not an English surname...'

'It's Swedish.'

'Ah, Sweden, beautiful country.'

'You've been?'

'Yes, I have... twice, in fact, a long time ago...'

'You know Evelyne?' I spluttered, not able to contain my curiosity any longer.

Richard looked over at me and frowned. 'I know Evelyne's father, dear.'

'Ah, ok,' I said, feeling ridiculous and uncomfortable after my outburst.

Michael eyes darted to my face. 'How are you, Sophie?'

The nerve of him! How dare he ask me how I am in front of Richard? My legs trembled. I was speechless. Richard looked at Michael, and then at me.

'How do you two know each other?' Richard asked.

'From the neighborhood, he's a musician,' I said, nearly choking on my words.

Richard turned to Michael, 'A musician huh, impressive, what do you play?'

Why was Richard bothering himself to talk to him? This wasn't supposed to happen. They were never supposed to meet. They belong in separate worlds, alternate universes, where their paths should never cross.

'I play lots of instruments, the sax is one of them,' Michael said flatly.

'Richard, our table...' I reminded him, irritated beyond belief. Was Michael getting a kick out of this?

'Ok yes,' Richard turned to Michael, 'is the food, any good here?'

'I haven't tried the food yet, my friend has just texted he's not coming. I was just leaving.'

'Oh too bad, well it was nice talking with you, Michael.' Richard held out his hand once more. They shook hands.

'The same to you,' Michael said, and turned to face me. His eyes penetrated mine. He extended his hand to me. 'Sophie, always a pleasure.' He was enjoying this. I wanted to disappear.

Michael didn't smile at me, but the way he looked at me was the same as when we were together.

'Same,' I said, surprised I still had a voice and followed the host to the table.

Once at the table, the waitress handed us the menus. I was hot all over, my heart jumping out my chest.

'Nice chap. Don't you think he looks a bit like a girl.' Richard said, studying the wine list.

'I need to go to the bathroom. Be a darling, and order a black velvet on the rocks for me, will you?'

'Black velvet on the rocks?'

I rushed to the bathroom, without responding. In the cubical, I leaned against the wall and took deep breaths to calm myself. I almost died with the shock. I hate it that they met, and I hate the way he made me squirm and going to shake my hand like that. What was he playing at?

2nd May,
Afternoon,
Diary,

Called Charles today to let him know I've got myself together, and I'm ready to go back to work. We agreed I'd start a week from today. He sounded concerned I might not be ready, but I can't stay here forever.

After the call, I paced around the apartment smoking, unable to keep still. As Evelyne is avoiding me, I'm going to have to speak to Andy. Maybe he will tell me what happened. Maybe he will give me the answers I need to hear. What if he tells me and it's too much to bear? What if Sylvie was right about our unconscious minds blocking out painful memories, and that it's sometimes better not to know? To hell with that, that freaks me out more. Plus, I have a right to know what happened to me. I *have* to know.

The thought of going to see Andy makes my stomach turn. He's a gypsy. It would take a stupid person to trust or believe a word he says, and I'm not daft, although sometimes I question myself. I invent fictional appointments all the time to tell Richard, business meetings with a non-existent client, deadlines, and late-night meetings, or last-minute audits. What am I going to say to him this time?

4th May
Morning,
Diary,

My affair with Michael was dangerous and toxic. It's over, he made his choice. It's for the best, before one of us got caught or fell in love.

Went to the club. It was heaving with sweaty people. I didn't belong there, dressed in a blue polka-dot mini dress. I didn't want to get too dressed up and make Richard curious. I sat at the bar and did a few shots of vodka, watching all the faces in the crowd.

I spotted Andy by the wall, talking to someone, Evelyne wasn't with him. I knew it was a ridiculous idea. I should have stayed at home with my husband, and left that whole night firmly in the past. It's better not knowing.

I finished my drink and made my way to the exit. Andy did a double-take when he saw me. He said something to the couple and then came over to me.

He looked like a pirate dressed in a white Victorian shirt, a leather blazer, and a hat. Not conventionally good-looking, but there was something charismatic, dangerous, and sexy about him, with his glossy, dark, medium-length hair, his angular features, and high cheekbones. He too wears lots of jewelry, like Michael, and was wearing silver earrings, rings on every finger, and a set of bracelets.

'You can't stay out of trouble can you?' he said, 'what's a woman like you doing in the place like this?'

'You know why I am here.'

'Do I?'

'I'm here to talk to you.'

'I'm flattered.'

'I'm not here to flatter you.'

A girl threw herself at him. It's wasn't Evelyne, this one was skimpily dressed. Her boobs were about to come out of her dress. She whispered something in his ear.

'Don't be bitchy,' he said to her, in a fake English accent.

The girl moved along. He returned his attention to me and asked if we could go somewhere private, where we could talk more freely. He led me all the way to the back. I had a hard time squeezing through the crowd.

He opened a door and gestured for me to go in first.

It was an office. It felt like I was in one of those offices at the back of clubs, where drug deals take place. I sat down on sofa and looked around. There was an ashtray full of cigarettes butts, a few stacks of papers-invoices by the look of it-and a skull on an oak table. Andy sat on a large leather chair behind the desk and put his feet up. He lit a cigarette and offered me one, but I declined.

'You waited a long time...' he said, puffing circles of smoke in the air.

'For what?' I asked.

He jerked his head to one side. 'To come to me, of course. I was wondering when you'd come. I know you been through Mike and to Sam.'

'They told you?'

'We're very close,' he said.

My body went cold. I checked my watch.

'You seem like you're in a hurry,' he said.

'I am.'

He checked his watch. 'We best make it quick then.' He laughed. I hated the way laughed, he seemed to be mocking me.

'Come on, relax and have a drink with me. We both know how you love your booze,' he said, winking at me. He took out a bottle of whiskey and two glasses from a cupboard. He poured the whiskeys and handed one to me, 'let's make a toast first.'

'To what?' I snapped.

'To blackouts,' he said.

'That's sick,' I protested.

'Where's your sense of humor?'

'I'm an accountant... I have no sense of humor or imagination.'

'Oh, that's such a shame... to beauty.'

He raised his glass.

I took a large swig. 'Why is Evelyne angry at me?'

He moved in a little closer and stared right at me. 'Is she angry at you?'

'She seemed to be. She gave me daggers, and practically bolted when I went over to speak with her.'

I studied his reaction, but he didn't flinch. 'Perhaps she was in a hurry.... Evelyne's a moody bitch.'

'Really? That's not very nice.'

He puffed cigarette smoke at my face. 'What's not very nice?'

I waved the smoke away. 'Calling your girlfriend a bitch.'

'As she's my girlfriend, I can call her whatever pleases me, and a bitch is one of them,' he said. He drank down his whiskey and poured himself another glass.

'Is this what she has to put up with?'

He stubbed his cigarette out on an ashtray and lit another. 'If she doesn't like it, she knows what to do.'

'Charming, considering she's sheltering you and your friends,' I blurted, without even considering what I was saying. He was making me so mad. Smug little shit, 'what do you want from me?'

'You know why I'm here so let's keep this brief, and I'll be on my way.'

I sparked up a cigarette, and he topped up my drink without asking. 'Mike and Sam already told you, Nicky pulled a prank as he always does, and burned that bloke's hair for a laugh. You were sitting with them at first, and then you and your friend joined us at our table.' He paused, blowing circles of smoke into the air.

'Your friend was all over Nicky. They were getting on well, but then everyone likes Nicky. Sam went to get drinks at the bar, and you went after him. The next thing I knew, you two were both on the dance-floor, dancing away, and I don't know, you slipped or something. And then you got up and passed out. You were all over the place.'

It sounded too orchestrated. A similar version to the others, and as though they had practiced it in front of the mirror. All three of them, Michael, Sam, and Andy, telling me the same lies.

He sat back on the armchair. 'Satisfied?'

I wasn't. 'Evelyne was there, wasn't she?'

He froze, this was the most honest reaction I've had so far, 'Huh?'

'You heard me.'

'Yeah, she was, so?'

Andy started to stare at my bare legs.

'My face is right here,' I said.

'Well excuse me, but your legs are distracting me.'

I sighed. 'So anyway, back to what you were saying.'

'Evelyne arrived after your friend left with Nicky. She was nagging about my drinking, and we got into an argument. She stormed out, and I followed her. I then got into a fight with this punk. I don't want to go through the details with you.'

'Where was Michael?'

'Mike hardly drinks, but you already know that don't you?' he said, and laughed.

'I have no idea what you're talking about?'

'Anyway, he drank a bit that night.'

'I see…'

'He's good looking isn't he?'

'Who?'

'Mike…'

'He's ok.'

He smiled. 'Don't pay attention to my bird, she's weird.'

I wasn't getting anywhere, so I got up to leave.

'Why don't you stay a little longer?' he said.

I looked at him as if it was the most stupid idea. 'I don't think so,' I said, tossing my bag over my shoulder and making my way to the door.

'I'd love to look at those great legs of yours.'

'It must suck for you to sit there and watch them taking me out of here,' I said.

'Cock teaser!' he shouted.

8th May
Evening,
Diary,

Today was my first day back to work, so I made sure I was on my best behavior. I didn't even think about drinking.

There were no warm welcomes, not that I expected any in this business, everyone focuses on deadlines and money. I'm in the wrong career. I only wanted to become an accountant because I'm good with numbers. As a job; it sucks.

All I got was a hello, and a file placed in my hands to crack straight on.

I should quit this job and go into teaching accounts. I'd be good at that. I don't see why not? I'm well qualified for the job. I can tell Richard I'm ready to move out of the city. The poor man stayed in London because of me. He wanted to live in the country, far away from the madness and the noise.

I could quit my job, move and start to teach. We'd be able to start over again and put all of this behind us. I'd look back on it all and see it as a stupid thing I did while I was still young. I'm thirty-eight in two years, I'm forty, there will be no more growing up for me to do. I am not young anymore, and I better accept this. Michael represents youth, and I wanted to taste it again. The youth I'm fast leaving behind. No, that's not what triggered me into Michael's arms, but I did need to be honest with someone without having any shame. The stuff Michael said to me was awful, but it didn't make them less true.

10th May
Evening,
Diary,

I'm scared. I think someone was following me, but I can't be too sure. I could hear footsteps behind me, and when I stopped to look, the footsteps stopped. I couldn't see anyone, but as I quickened my pace, the footsteps behind me got faster too. I took off my heels and ended up running. I was only a block away from the apartment, so it didn't take me long, but I shit myself. Was someone actually following me? Or am I going mad? I ran inside the entrance hall to the apartments. Checking to see no-one followed me in, I noticed a figure appeared in front of me. I screamed and then breathed a sigh of relief to see it was my neighbor Mr. Smith.

'Sophie, are you all right?' he asked, concerned.

'Yes, I'm sorry for screaming… you scared me.'

'You seem awfully jumpy,' he said, 'are you sure you're alright?'

'Y-yes I'm fine. I'd better go, good night and thanks.'

When I went into the living room, Richard was on the sofa reading a newspaper. He was dressed in jeans and a red sweater. He checked his wristwatch, 'Where have you been, you're late.'

He noticed my bare feet and looked confused.

'My heels were hurting.' I said, placing my shoes by the door. I went into the kitchen and peered through the window.

All I could see was a couple strolling by, and orange streetlights glimmering through the street. Nothing suspicious, nothing out of the ordinary. Maybe my mind was playing tricks on me.

13th May
Evening,
Diary,

Had such a weird day. It's getting scary now. Maybe I should take action.

I arrived at the office with my head buzzing after a long business lunch with a client. All I wanted to do was to lock myself in the office. I made sure my makeup was immaculate, and everything was in place. When I passed by Wendy's desk, she told me who had called and left messages.

'Your cousin's waiting for you in your office,' she said.

I stared at her blankly *my cousin?* I don't have any. 'My cousin?'

'I'm so sorry, but he insisted on waiting for you there… I didn't know you had such eccentric family members,' she said with a smile. Who was in there?

'Thank you,' I said.

My jaw dropped, Andy was sitting with his feet up on my desk, smoking a cigarette. Goodness knows what my colleagues must have thought of this young man, dressed in a white shirt, black leather trousers, hat, waistcoat and scarf, and jewelry flying all over the place. Everyone who works here, and our clients, are conservative by comparison.

'Had a pleasant lunch?' he asked.

I shut the door behind me. 'What are you doing in my office?

He stretched his hands behind his back. 'Come on now let's not get dramatic, shall we?'

'If you don't get out now, I'll call security,' I said in a firm tone.

He puffed circles of smoke. 'Is this how you greet your clients? How rude.'

'You're not a client. Why did tell my secretary you are my cousin!'

'Nice office you have here. What's the word… swanky, or, is it posh… no, clean?'

'I like things clean.'

He laughed, 'Ironic,' he paused, 'for a woman who's so dirty.'

My mind went haywire. Andy must know about Michael and me, otherwise, why he would say such a thing.

'How dare you! Get out now!' I shouted.

He carried on smoking, staring straight at me. I glanced at my laptop, calculator, pens, and client confidential file, which he had swept to one side, and seethed with anger.

'You have no right to move my things.'

He laughed. My anger rose up a notch. 'This a non-smoking office,' I snapped.

'Says the smoker.'

'Put it out now!' I shouted, 'and get out!'

I imagined Wendy hearing me shouting, wondering what we were doing. Andy got up, tossed the cigarette onto the floor and crushed it under his shoe. 'Is this better?' He looked to see my reaction, enjoying every minute of his stupid game. 'There's something I forgot to mention the other night.'

'Go on.'

'Come down to the flat tonight, you know where I live.'

'No, I bloody will not. Tell me now!'

He ambled towards the door. 'The guys will be out. Evelyne is with her parents. Come whenever you want, I'll be there all night, waiting, impatiently.' He opened the door and winked at me. My legs were about to give in. I sat on the chair and buried my face in my hands.

Got home in a daze. Richard was already back, looking dapper in a tailored grey three-piece suit.

'Ah,' he said 'there you are. How was your day?' he asked.

'My day was peachy, what about yours?'

'There are conflicts in the New York office. I might have to fly out there.'

'Oh.'

'It's only for a few days.'

'Oh.'

'You sound disappointed.'

'I hate it when you go away. I don't like to be alone in this apartment.'

'But you love this apartment.'

'I do, but...'

'But what?' he asked.

'It's nothing, Richard. I'll cook us a nice dinner,' I said, going into the kitchen, 'I'm meeting Sylvie later tonight. She's having boyfriend troubles and needs my moral support.'

He reached for a book and read the back. 'Boyfriend troubles, again,' he said.

'Something like that.'

When you lie so much, the fictional excuses come out so freely you start to believe them yourself. I made roast pork for dinner. Richard watched me gorging down my food, dipping roasted potatoes in ketchup. He finds me repulsive.

My brain made calculations, I couldn't go to Andy. It's dangerous, and I don't trust him. He has an agenda. Why Evelyne's place anyway? Why has he waited until now to tell me whatever he has to say? Why couldn't he tell me another time, in another place? Maybe he wanted to assure discretion. I don't want to be alone with him or anywhere for that matter.

After dinner, Richard showered, while I got my things ready for tomorrow. I took out the dress I wore that night. Maybe Andy could provide the missing link or even a clue. I knocked on the bathroom door.

'Richard, I'm going. Don't wait up, okay? You know how Sylvie is.'

'Yes, try not to be too long.'

As I left the building, I peered up at the windows, at all the apartment lights, and wondered what kind of life everyone leads inside. Are their lives as fucked up as mine? The wind sung through the trees, a paper bag danced in the air.

I pressed the buzzer of Evelyne's apartment and waited. My shoulders were tight, and my breath burst in and out. No answer. I knocked on the door. My knees went weak. I waited. No response. And just as I was about to turn and leave, I heard a voice from behind the door. 'Coming, coming.' Andy opened the door, puffing on a cigarette, 'hello.'

'Hi'

'Come in,' he said, opening the door wider.

I expected the apartment to be in disarray but, to my surprise, it was neat. There were many beautiful, expensive guitars lying around from Les Paul, acoustics, to archtops. It was like a guitar store in there. I don't recall the last time I played one. There was a red sofa in the middle of the living room, fashionable, modern art hanging on the walls, a bar in the corner with a variety of booze, and a large curved TV, PlayStation, and video games on the floor. On the coffee table, there were music books and classic novels, a laptop and a hat, along with bracelets and rings.

The smell of burnt wood and vanilla gave the place a warm, cozy scent combined with a more pungent and distinct smell, similar to the aroma I recall from time to time.

Did Andy do something to me? Was this the smell I've been remembering? My heart thudded. Then I realized as he picked up a joint and started puffing on it, that the pungent smell was, in fact, weed. It made me high just by passively inhaling. He shut the door to the living room and circled around me like a shark.

'I thought you weren't coming,' he said softly, his shoes clicking under the parquet.

'I was busy,' I said, with beads of sweat surfacing on my forehead.

Andy poured two glass of cognac and handed me a glass. 'Drink, Sophie.'

I wanted him to stop calling my name as if he was mocking me. I looked down at the glass Andy gave me like it was a dangerous and tempting drug. He didn't take his eyes off me. I sipped the cognac, and the liquid warmed to my body temperature.

He offered me a cigarette and lit it with a zippo. The flip of the lid sounded familiar. I sat on the red sofa, while Andy remained on his feet, his eyes not leaving me. We smoked in silence. I felt myself shaking and shifted my body to hide it from him. He watched me as though I were a piece of fine art in a museum.

He smiled, and took a puff on his joint, blowing the smoke into the air. 'Your face is unique. There's nothing traditional about it. Your jaw is wide, your cheeks high and pouty, but beautiful just the same,' he said quietly.

'Do you tell this to all women?' I said.

'I have been with many beautiful women, but no, not to all.'

'I'm not here to listen to you go on about your women or to hear your compliments.'

'Always business-like, why don't loosen up and have fun occasionally? Who knows you might grow to like it. With you accountants, everything has to be serious and boring.'

'And what gives you the impression all accountants are boring?'

He laughed. 'Please.'

'What did you want to tell me?'

'You came here to find out about that night, and that's all right?'

'I can't think of any other reason why I should be here.'

'Fine, if that's how you want to play it. What Sam and Mike didn't tell you, and I don't hold it against them, is that you got in a fight.'

'With who?'

'Sam's girlfriend.'

I stared at him. 'I didn't know Sam has a girlfriend.'

'You do now... anyway, she came in and saw you two dancing, and she's not exactly the laid-back kind of gal... she wasn't happy and well, anyway, she pushed you and told you to fuck off. You left, but she wouldn't let it go, so she followed you out and slapped you. Sam and I had a bad feeling, Angie, Sam's girl was going to hurt you, so we followed you out. Boy, you women when you get angry, you become dangerous.'

'She slapped me?'

'Yea, she knocked you over, and you blacked out.'

I stared at him. Me, in a fight with Sam's girlfriend? It sounded preposterous, but I waited for him to go on.

'So you were out cold, then Mike came out and began to panic. Sam and Angie got into a big fight and left together. I got in an argument with Evelyne, and Mike stayed with you until your friend came back.'

I found this a little strange, why didn't he didn't tell me the truth right away. He wouldn't keep it from me because I got in a fight with someone's girlfriend. I remember, Evelyne in the red dress, arguing with Andy. If I blacked out before her outburst with Andy, why do I have a recollection of it? It doesn't make any sense.

He reached for the bottle of cognac and refilled my glass.

'Yes, I know Mike didn't tell you everything. We figured it was best you didn't know. I mean who wants to know they got into a fight because of some bloke like Sam. Mike was doing you a favor.'

'No, he wasn't, he lied.'

'No, he didn't lie to you, he kept things from you.'

'It's the same. You should have told me this from the start.'

'Mike's a good lad. He's the most sensible one among us. He told me he ran into you the next morning after your blackout, about how disoriented and horrified you were when you found out you'd passed out, so he decided to shut up and say no more.'

What about me? He can't decide for me. I have a say in this too. My mind raced as Andy watched me. My head spun. I emptied the glass. Andy refilled it, again.

'Is this Angie still in the picture?'

'No, they broke up soon after. Sam attracts these kinds of chicks.'

She's not in the picture because she doesn't even exist.

'What kind?' I asked.

'Psychotic types,' he replied.

'Charming.'

'Indeed.'

'Sam could have said something when I bumped into him.'

'Tell you what, his psycho ex-girlfriend wanted to gorge your eyes out. That's what Angie would have done if we hadn't followed her out.'

I took a sip from my cognac. 'I need to talk to him.'

He gave me a stern look. 'Why?'

I finished my cognac. Andy refilled it again. He seemed eager to get me drunk. I placed my hand on the glass to cover it.

'I don't know… to get his side of the story, I guess.'

'What good will that do? Just leave it behind you and move on. You can't stay in the past, let it be.'

My hands began to shake. I placed the glass on the coffee table. I paced the room, smoking, trying to recall something from that night, but nothing. He lit a cigarette with his Zippo. The grating sound of the flap made me jump. That sound, I'd heard it somewhere before. Andy placed his hands on my arms. 'You're jumping at every sound, what are you afraid of?'

'I'm not afraid, I'm just…'

My stomach lurched. He moved closer. I could feel the heat from his body. I had to leave. I'd heard enough porky pies.

My instinct told me this is not how it happened. I know it's not. I think Andy might have twisted the story, because I'm persistent, and to make me shut up and move on.

On my way out of the apartment, Sam and Nicky were on their way in. Their laughter stopped, wondering what the fuck I was doing there. I knew what they thinking, Andy alone, his girlfriend away. I didn't have to justify myself to anyone. I ran past them and hurried home to Richard, who was sound asleep in bed.

15th May
Evening,
Diary,

Richard's going away to New York again, to take care of the company's international customers. It's different this time. I want to fall to my knees and clutch hold of his leg like little girls do to their fathers, and beg him not to go. I don't want to be alone in this apartment.

'It's only for fifteen days,' he said.

'Fifteen days.' I cried.

God knows what might happen in fifteen days.

He searched my face. I bet he could tell. 'Is something the matter?'

I broke eye contact from him. 'No…'

I don't understand Richard sometimes. It's like he lives in his own bubble and shuts me out. When he came in today, he laid on the sofa with his bloody newspaper. Not saying a word. As if I wasn't even there. I don't expect him to be chatty all the time, and he needs his own space, but lately, I don't know, he seems troubled and distant. This fills me with anxiety and absolute dread. Is it work? Or does he suspect something and refuses to confront me about it because he fears he'll lose me?

20ᵗʰ May
Afternoon
Diary,

Richard left today to go to New York. The apartment feels like a prison cell. It feels like someone's watching me, wherever I am. I can feel a pair of eyes on me, playing hide and seek with me from the shadows. Maybe it's my imagination, or I'm growing paranoid. Am I losing my mind?

Andy told me I got into a fight with Sam's girlfriend, Angie, but I still don't believe him. There's more to that night, like the sound of a Zippo lid flipping, the music, and the smell. Did Andy do something to me? Or was he involved? Maybe, I should go and see a therapist to help me regain my memory. What disturbs me the most is, if I do manage-by some miracle-to remember, what then? What if it's too upsetting?

22nd May
Evening,
Diary,
I'm a weak, stupid woman.

    I spent a couple of hours cleaning the bedroom and ensuite. I washed the bath, changed the sheets, and dusted the bedroom. I wanted to take my mind off everything, but I ended up collapsing in a heap, craving wine, and cigarettes. I am trying to be good, but all this is driving me nuts.

    I went to the grocery store before it got dark. On my way out of the store, I saw Michael coming out of where Evelyne lives. He saw me and stopped dead in his tracks. I hurried inside the entrance to my apartment block and called for the lift. I could hear footsteps rushing towards the lift. I didn't know if it was him or not, because the lift doors closed. I imagined him running up the stairwell, and placed my hand on my chest, feeling my heart palpitating.

    I got my front door keys ready in my hand, and as soon as the lift doors opened, I bolted to my front door. I heard the stairwell door bang open and turned to see Michael walking over to me. I rammed the keys into the lock, tears falling down my cheeks. Why the hell was he doing this to me? Anyone could have seen him. Didn't he care how risky it was, how easily everything could come out into the open? Or consider that Richard might be here. It was like he knew Richard was away?

    I tried to close the door behind me, but he pushed it open. The door banged against the wall, and my shopping bag dropped from my hand. Red wine splattered all over the floor like blood.

    'How dare you? How dare you follow me in here?' I hissed.

    'I have… to talk… to… you,' Michael replied, catching his breath.

    'What is it?'

    I waited for him to recover, with my arms across my chest. He leaned against the wall, with the door still wide open. 'When I saw you just now, I--'

    'What!' I snapped.

    He moved away from the wall. 'I don't know. I can't explain it.'

    Mr. Smith came out of his apartment. I shut the front door before he could see him.

    'I know you're upset,' he said, reaching to touch me.

    Anger pumped through my veins. I grabbed his shirt and pushed him roughly against the wall repeatedly.

'Get out!' I shouted, 'get out of my life! You caused me nothing but pain.'

'You brought it on yourself,' he said.

He shook himself free and stared at me accusingly. 'Don't blame me, you already had issues before you met me.'

'Why?' I roared, slapping him hard across the cheek, 'why!'

He stared at me flinty. 'Don't do that.'

'Or you'll what?'

He sighed heavily.

'Why did you follow me here? What do you want?'

His eyes dropped to the floor. 'When I saw you in the restaurant, looking like a couple from a love story, I couldn't bear it, you with *him*.'

'He's my husband. What do you expect? What are you doing? Are you spying on me?'

'No! I was supposed to meet someone that night, but he didn't show up, and then I saw you with *him*.'

The way he said *him* full of hate, it was all sexual jealousy. He had to see me with my husband to realize he'd made a mistake. He wanted me back, to have me all to himself. He couldn't bear the thought of me going home with Richard, where we could go to bed, and wake up together. Is this what triggered this childish, immature behavior?

He came up here to see the home I share with Richard, to see the way we live, to look at our things for clues about our lives. I was supposed to be the woman who came and left, invisible, and forgettable. He couldn't see this. In his eyes, this is real, this is my life, and this is what defines me. There is a past, a present, and a future. There is a history, a story, comfort, a sense of security, and stability. With me, Michael had none of this. We'd be together for a few hours, and then there would be a blank space between us.

'I see, so you got jealous. Is that what you're trying to tell me? Is that why you're here?' I paced the room, 'I can't believe this, and I don't owe you anything. I told you I'm married, I told you what it was going to be like. I made no promises to you. We went to bed, what? Eight, ten times? It wasn't memorable enough to leave him. There's a seventeen-year age difference, you're just a kid. A boy!' I screamed at him. 'You were a mistake.'

I moved away from him and lit a cig. Behind me, there was a crashing sound. I spun around. Michael was standing by the hall table, and my three hundred quid porcelain vase was in pieces on the floor. I imagined having to explain to Richard why the vase is not there, and making up a story about how it broke.

'Do you have any idea how much that vase cost?'

'I don't give a flying fuck about your ridiculous vase, you poisonous bitch,' he snapped.

I sunk on the sofa, taking a deep drag from my cigarette. It polluted my lungs, and I watched the smoke glide through the air, and disappear.

'It hurt, didn't it, seeing me with him?'

Michael sat on the floor. 'Of course, it hurt.'

'You assumed I have the ideal marriage because you saw me with my husband. You're naïve.' I hid my face from him, as tears fell down my face, 'no marriage is perfect.'

'No, I know you don't have the perfect marriage. But I still hated seeing you with him.'

I wiped the tears away with my fingertips. 'So you chased me down the street, hoping we'd pick things up where we left off? You made it clear what you thought of me.'

His eyes dropped to the floor. I took a deep breath as if all of my anger might evaporate.

'I'm going to make myself a drink, you made your choice, and it's all for the best. Forget my name, forget I live here, and forget you know me.'

I poured myself a glass of whiskey. The back of my throat hurt. I lifted the glass to my lips then stopped.

'Why are you still here?' I shouted.

'I'm not going anywhere.'

'Oh for fuck's sake.'

A hot wave flashed through me, I slammed the glass on the counter and pushed him against the wall.

'Are you nuts?' he protested.

He restrained my hands above my head. 'What is wrong with you? Are you insane?'

'Let me go.'

'Calm down, I didn't mean to hurt you.'

I tried to break free and pleaded with him to let me go, but his grip remained tight on my hand. He rubbed his skinny body against mine. I felt him protruding in his trousers. This is all a game to him. Of course, it is, he's just a boy. He tried to kiss me, but I turned my face away.

He persisted.

'Let me go.'

He ignored me. 'I missed you,' he whispered.

'Too bad,' I said, staring at his face.

My heart softened, and I pressed my mouth against his. My brain yelled, but my heart, my stupid heart.

Oh, Diary, what I have done? I'm such a shit! After we made love, I laid in my darkened bedroom staring into space, disappointed with myself. I had given in. I wanted to sleep and never wake up. I'm back where I started. Our matrimonial bed invaded by our lust. I wanted to perish. This is all my fault. I'm the mature one here, the one who is supposed to make sensible decisions.

Michael started to stroke my hair, his warm body pressed against mine. I wanted to fuck him again.

Is there such a thing as being addicted to a person?

The effect Michael has on me is beyond my control, only twenty-one, but his power is too strong. I washed all traces of him from my body. I stepped out of the shower, dried myself, and reached for the moisturizer. Something was odd. Richard's aftershave wasn't in the same place as it was this afternoon. I remember it was definitely on the left when I cleaned the bathroom, like it always is. How did it move from left to the right? Did Michael use it, perhaps? But, he didn't use the bathroom, or maybe he did when I was asleep? I placed the aftershave back in its rightful place. I think I must be losing the plot.

I washed the bedclothes for the second time, along with the floor, and cleared away the broken wine bottle. I opened all the windows. I have to get rid of the smell of us.

23rd May
Evening,
Diary,
I called Richard on Skype.
'How is New York?' I asked cheerfully.
'Chaotic, how is my favorite girl?' he asked.
Talking to him behind a screen was weird. He looked grey and tired. His job is having too much strain on him. I am a terrible wife, but I worry about his health.
'I'm good, how are you? Are you taking your medication?'
'Yes, tell me how you're going to spend your day?'
'Nothing much, watch TV, get some work done.'
'You should go for a walk in the park.'
'Alone?'
'You have to get used to doing things by yourself.'
What an odd thing to say.

Michael wanted me to go over to see him today, so I obliged. The flat was a little messy, with an empty pizza box on the coffee table, and saxophones on the sofa. Michael was dressed in tight black trousers and a yellow shirt. As I entered the room, I ran my fingertip over his bottom lip, as I did so many times before, and stared intensely into his eyes.

I am in love.

The travesty of loving someone so young. It's laughable, we have no future. I can't deny him his youth. He sees me as a sport, the insipid drunk wife, a hobby.

'Here I am, where you wanted me,' I said to him.
'It's simple. If you want something you reach out and grab it,' he replied.
'If all of us reasoned the way you do, we'd be in so much trouble.'
'Why?'
'So you wanted me, is that what you're saying?'
'You wouldn't be here if I didn't.'

So, because he's beautiful and talented, it gives him the right to dismiss women like rags as he did with me, and now I'm summoned again, do I have any say in this?

'I see,' I said.

He sat on the sofa and crossed his legs. He studied me like I was an exotic creature.

'Beauty and youth are not accomplishments, Mike.'

He flipped his hair confidently. 'No, but it leads you to places.'

'Knowledge is power,' I said to him.

He didn't give me a response.

'So you think you made it this far because of your looks?' I said to him.

'No, hard work and sacrifice led me to where I am,' he said.

I don't know what his story is. He hardly ever talks about himself.

'Have you ever considered what my husband would do to you if he finds out?' I asked.

He nodded his head. 'He would kill me with his bare hands.'

'That's exactly what he'll do unless the pain killed him first.'

'Because of his heart?'

'… Yes'

'Do you love him for his weakness?'

I looked at him in horror. 'That's a horrible thing to say.'

'His money then?'

'You seem to forget I'm an accountant. I know money. I work with figures every day.' I plodded towards the window, 'I make my own money. I certainly don't need his.'

'What is it then?'

'My husband is a serious man. In his world, there's little room for error. He's also ambitious. I admire him for that, but he can be tough. Once, we were at a friend's dinner party, and there was a teenage boy who couldn't figure out what he wanted to do with his life. The boy was fifteen. Even I wasn't quite sure what I wanted to do at his age. Anyway, Richard lectured the boy. Telling him that he knew what he wanted to do at nine years old. Go to Cambridge, put on a suit, be an important man, work in a powerful firm, travel the world, and see an opera at *Teatro Alla Scala*. I jumped in and joked, or be a ballerina, a clown, or a fireman. He was not happy with me. It was funny for a nine-year-old boy to dream about stuff like that but, he did know.'

'I don't see how a man like him can please a woman like you,' Michael said.

I smiled. 'I was such a different girl back then. When you start to look back, you realize your life is so different from the one you dreamed about, do you know what I mean?'

I looked over at him. 'Of course, you don't.'

'Why do you keep saying that, like it's a threat?'

'What?'

'I am young.'

I reached for another cigarette, 'I need a drink.'

'You're getting none here, how is your drinking by the way?'

'Don't be a twat, my drinking is fine.'
'Yeah right...'
He leaned forward. 'You're ruffling too many feathers.'
'What is that supposed to mean?'
'I heard you were asking around about that night.'
I remained composed. 'Because I still don't have all the answers, and the more I find out, the more baffling it gets.'
'So you went to Andy?' he said.
He sounded irritated, a bit like when Richard talks to me like I'm a twit for forgetting to "switch off the bloody light, again.'
'Can you tell me what the fuck you're doing going round to my friends, and asking them questions?'
'I see, Andy told you.'
'We're like brothers. He told me how you showed up at the club wearing a short dress, asking about that night. Give it a rest will you,' he said.
'What bothers you the most? That I went to talk to your friend wearing a short dress, or me asking him about that night?'
'Both!' he shouted.
I turned away from him. 'If you're upset, it means you're hiding something.'
'I've got nothing to hide...' he sighed, 'Andy's not a sweet guy. He's unpredictable and a hot head.'
'Are you describing your friend or yourself?'
He glared at me. 'Just don't go to him again okay?'
'Why not?'
'Because I'm telling you.'
'That's not enough. I need a valid answer.'
He kicked the coffee table with his foot. I didn't like his attitude. Why did Andy have to go and brag, why couldn't he be quiet?
'I've told you what happened. How many times are we going to have this conversation?'
'Until the truth comes out.' I snapped.
'What truth? Why don't you believe me?'
'Because something is missing. I need to find out. I believe you're all telling me half the story.'
'I assure you we're not.'
'Right, now I have your assurance. Did I get into a fight with Sam's girlfriend?'
'Sam doesn't have a girlfriend.'
'Ex-girlfriend.'
He sighed 'yes... you did.'

'Why didn't you tell me before? You can't decide things for me, I have a say in this too.'

'It was best not knowing.'

'So you were telling me half the story. You lied.'

'I didn't lie, I kept it from you.'

'It's the same thing.'

'It's not the same. You lie to your husband to come here because he can't fuck you properly.'

I shook my head. 'I don't like you anymore, you've changed, or perhaps I was so dazzled I failed to see you, for who you truly are.'

He lowered his head in dismay and then stared right at me. I wanted to hurt him, the same way he hurts me.

'Why are you doing this?'

'Because I don't like what I've become when I'm around you. You obviously came back to me to feel good about yourself. Do I stroke your ego?'

'No, I know what I look like. I don't need you or anyone to tell me.'

'Arrogant, pompous, spoiled brat.'

'I'm tired of going round in circles,' he said, putting his hands over his head.

'You're tired? I'm sick, when I'm not sick, I'm tired, when I'm not tired, I'm fed up. Did you tell your friends about us?' I asked.

He removed his hand from his head. 'No, I didn't. Do you think I'm stupid enough to tell my friends I'm seeing a married woman? I thought we were going to make up for lost time, not wasting our time with pointless arguments?'

I undid the knot of my dress. 'Here, go ahead.'

'I want to talk,' he said.

'Don't talk, talk is dangerous, it makes things happen, it makes them real.'

'What are you talking about?'

I sat on the sofa and glanced at the saxophones. 'May I?'

He nodded. I ran my finger along the golden saxophone, 'what's the difference between the two?'

'One is an alto, the other is a tenor. The tenor is larger, and the alto is higher and brighter.'

'Which do you use the most?'

'Alto…'

'Mm...'

'What's wrong with you?'

I went over to the window and looked out. 'It's a lonely neighborhood without the music. I used to wait, anxiously. It helped me to relax, it excited me. I wanted to strip naked to your music while painting pictures in my head of who was playing. Thinking to myself, how can someone create something so wonderful? And I'm here with him right now, exposing myself in a way, I never have done before.'

'Would you like me to play for you?'

'Later, now I want you to come here.'

I spent the afternoon there, as the city rose and fell around us. He played the sax for me, while I sat on the floor listening and smoking, the music filling me with ecstasy.

When he finished serenading me, he lifted me up onto his shoulders and spun me around until I was dizzy. He laid me down on the floor and ran his hand over my belly. He took the cigarette away from my hand.

'You need to quit this shit,' he said, stubbing the cigarette into an ashtray, 'I turned twenty-two.'

'Oh when?'

'May 24th.'

'Oh honey, happy belated birthday.' I kissed him on the lips, 'I should get you something.'

'No don't, getting back with you was a gift.'

I ran my hand through his hair. 'Did you dye it?'

'Yes.'

'But it was so beautiful, it was like gold, why?'

He curled his bottom lip. 'I wanted a change. Why, don't you like it?'

'Of course, I like it, sweetheart.'

I didn't want the afternoon to end, I longed to be there forever, but it would never happen. I put my clothes on as he laid on the bed watching me.

'This part I hate,' he said.

'Which part?' I asked.

'You putting your clothes back on. It means you're leaving, and going back to your life.'

I cupped his face. 'Oh honey, I'm yours.'

'Does he touch you?' he asked.

I put on my shoes and almost toppled over; taken aback by this act of jealousy.

Michael watched me rapidly. 'You still share a bed with him?'

'He'd find it odd if I don't.'

He clenched his jaw not liking my response. What did he want to me to say?

'Does he suspect?' Michael asked.

I never saw him like this. 'He's too buried in his work.'

He turned his face away, and I gently placed my hand on his cheek and made him look at me. I kissed him on the lips. He grabbed my hand to stop me from going. He looked like an angel, romantic, but dangerous. God, I could leave it all for him, abandon everything I own, Richard, my whole life. Michael is worth the risk. I would like to plant a bomb into my life and watch it explode, all for him. Feverish is this desire, a disaster waiting to happen.

26th May
Evening,
Diary,

Just got another of those damn letters but this time it wasn't just a nasty remark, but puzzling, and serious. I've read it over and over to make sure it's not my imagination.

Use your head, Sophie, what do you really know about him?

Him. Who's him? Michael? This person knows about my affair? Is it his friends? I felt like I was having an out-of-body experience. I marched up the street clutching the letter. The voices and noises in the street merged around me, and my heart hammered against my chest. As I turned the corner into Evelyne's street and stared up at the red block building, I felt someone push me, or maybe I lost my footing, I don't know, but I stumbled into the middle of the road. A car was approaching and blasted its horn.

The driver poked his head out of the window.

'Are you fucking insane! I nearly killed you, get off the fucking road,' he screamed, his face going purple.

Heads turned. I didn't want a scene. I stepped aside as the Range Rover speeded away. I placed a hand on my chest and steadied my breath. People went on with their business, too wrapped up in their bubbles to care. The note wasn't in my hand anymore.

I frantically searched the ground, I must have dropped it with the shock of seeing the Range Rover coming my way. My eyes darted across the street, and there was Sam, leaning against a pole, inhaling cigarette smoke. I hurried my pace, bumping into someone. I caught Sam grinning at me.

Did Sam push me? I'm not sure, it happened so fast, I can't make any accusations without knowing.

.

27th May
Evening,
Diary,

I didn't mention anything to Michael, about the notes, the car, or Sam lingering in the street. Why I should tell him when all I get is half answers, uncertainty, and lies. For the first time, I'm starting to believe I'm in danger. Someone wants to hurt me. I should go to the police, I must. Nobody would conjecture a drunk. I'm being punished for all the wrong I'm doing. I'm a bad person. I'm trying to recall when I was last a good person, and I can't.

Comic books and clothes were spread across the floor, and there was a large cupboard box full of LPs in the corner. The flat screamed at me to *get out of here you are too old for this*. I didn't get out. The more, I know I can't have him, that he can never be mine, the more I desire him. He was on the floor, wearing the red teddy jacket and a top hat, smoking a joint and reading from a back of an old book. *Tom Tom Club - Genius of Love* was on. I remember my mother playing this song, and dancing and singing along with it. She used to make me dance with her. We were so happy back then. She would spin me around, and I'd squeal with laughter and such happiness. Such joy! I want those years back. The years of innocence when a kiss wasn't a prologue to sex. I miss the simplicity.

'The other night, you said you used to be such a different girl to the person you are now. What did you mean by it?' Michael asked, pressing his body against mine.

'When you're young, you don't think of the consequences, or about responsibilities.'

'Were you wild?'

'No, I was lost, I got bullied a lot.'

'Why?'

'Because of my wide face.'

'I think it's perfect, for me at least,' he said.

'That's sweet... I got a mix of grades, a few A's, B's, and a few C's. My mum didn't want to hear of a C in anything, but I was good at maths. I also did my ACCA, a tedious course, and then I met Richard.'

'Where did you meet him?'

'At a friend's dinner party.'

'Did you like him right away?'

'Why do you want to know?'

'I'm interested.'

'He thought I was a pretty little thing and fussed on the way I looked. It made me feel good. I liked him because I could have a decent conversation with him about finance and politics. But as he's older than me, his knowledge is a lot broader than mine. We have struggled with the age gap, at times, like when I'd say to Richard I'm going out clubbing with the girls, he doesn't like it…' I paused, 'are you sure you want to hear about this?'

'I enjoy listening.'

'Richard is a sort of man who wants to do the right thing, he doesn't tolerate any form of scandal. He has a high-powered job that carries responsibilities so, he expects me to meet them. He didn't want me to go to clubs. I couldn't see why he wanted to prevent me from having harmless fun, I was twenty-four after all. So one time, I went out behind his back. He found out and accused me of being rebellious. He knew the risk of having a relationship with someone that young.'

'Was he married before?'

'No, but he was engaged to a woman named Penny.'

'What happened to her?'

'She died of breast cancer, so Richard withheld himself from getting attached until he met me. I must have left an impression on him or something.'

'Did you have other men before him?'

'I had a relationship for three years when I was your age. I've always been that kind of girl…'

'What kind of girl?'

'The relationship kind. After I broke from my ex-boyfriend. I went out, partied, and dated.'

'Did you like it?'

'What?'

'Dating?'

'… No… then I met Richard, and he dragged me away from all of that, caveman style.'

'He's boring.'

'He's not boring, he's an intelligent man. I felt safe around him. Protected.'

'You realize, you're referring to him in past tense?'

'Am I?'

'Like he's no longer part of your life.'

I stroked his cheek. 'I don't mean it that way.'

'Have you ever pictured what your life would be like without him?'

'No…'

'So despite everything, you love him?'

This was a difficult question to answer. I didn't want to explain my feelings for my husband to my lover, it felt wrong and unfair

He sat up. 'You don't have to answer.'

I pulled him to me and kissed him hard on the lips. Can I leave it all? It's despicable to consider it. Sophie Knight, wife of Richard Knight, files for a divorce to be with her much younger lover. She was having an affair apparently with a musician, can you imagine? That would give Richard's friends something to gossip about, to add a bit of excitement in their miserable lives. They would throw a dinner party to celebrate, I'm sure. Richard, defeated, would hide because he wouldn't be able to put up with the scandal. I try to fantasize about a life with Michael, but to my dismay, all I see is a fog and blackness.

'My parents are divorced,' he said

'I'm sorry,' I said.

'It was a mess...'

'Do you remember it?'

'Only a little, only what my mum has told me.'

'What do your parents do?'

'My mum's a seamstress. My dad's a TV presenter in Sweden. What about yours?'

'My mum was a dancer back in her day. My dad is a telecommunications director. Any brothers or sisters?'

'Two brothers. I'm the eldest, you?'

'I'm an only child. Your brothers are in Sweden?'

'Yes.'

'I miss my mother.'

'Why? Don't you speak often?'

I shake my head. 'We fell out when I started dating Richard.'

'Why?'

'Oh, she couldn't understand why I'd marry someone almost twenty years my senior. She wanted me to be with someone my own age. It was strange because mums are usually thrilled when daughters marry into success. Not my mother, though. She didn't like him, and thought he was an uptight snob.'

'You still married him despite your mother's disapproval.'

'I love him what can I say.'

Silence.

'The last time, I saw her, was at Christmas...' I trail off as I thought of my mom. How happy we were, how close we were. I could talk to her about anything. When I got my heart broken for the first time, I was sixteen. Harry was his name. I went to school with him. It was an innocent relationship, no sex, just kissing and snuggles. I loved how it felt, the first touch, the first glance; everything was new exciting and magical. He dumped me because he didn't want to be with me anymore. I went home crying. My mom made me popcorn and put on my favorite movie *My Fair Lady*.

'Do you speak to your parents?' I asked him, snapping myself back to the present.

'Yes, mum begs me to come home every day,' he replied. I smiled. 'What about your father, do you speak to him?' he asked.

I shook my head. 'He didn't approve either.'

I laid flat on the bed, Michael lifted the sheet. 'I'm all red and sore look what you did to me.'

'You're sore? You have some nerve.'

'Have you thought of leaving him?'

I stared at him shocked. 'Leave him, why?'

'You lost so much to be with him, no wonder why you drink.'

'Are you suggesting I should leave Richard for you?'

'Leave him because you want to, not for someone,' he said coldly.

I jumped off the bed, reached for my underwear, and put them on.

'What?' he said.

'Nothing.'

'You are upset about something.'

'You are such a ridiculous boy.'

'Why?'

I put on my blouse. 'Because in two years I'll be forty and you'll be twenty-four. You remain young, while I get older, have you considered that? Given your fantastic looks, it obvious, you will trade me for someone younger and prettier because nobody wants to fuck grandma's cunt!' I shouted.

'You think, I want you only for your body?'

'We're having a sexual relationship, of course you do.'

He kept staring at me disapprovingly.

'Don't you?'

'No, I don't see you as an object, but a woman that should be owned.'

I sighed. 'You don't have any idea what you're talking about.' I put on my trousers, 'I should be going.'

'Come on Sophie, why don't you spend the night?'

'What?'

'Nothing is waiting for you at that apartment.' He took my hand, 'don't be mad, stay with me.'

'Not today.'

'When?'

'I don't know.'

I traveled back home by tube and thought about the conversation with Michael. I can't believe what I'm telling Michael, things I haven't said to anyone. He's become more than a lover, he's also a friend. It's dangerous to expose myself like this. Giving him weapons to use, to seduce me into leaving my husband. Can I leave the life I've built with Richard? Watch my marriage and my reputation crumble? It's better Michael doesn't know some things. I won't mention the miscarriages, or about not being able to have children. Michael never asked anything regarding the subject. I'm glad he hasn't. Sometimes, I worry he could get me pregnant.

I opened my bag and hunted for my key. My muscles tensed. I'm a woman of habit and always place the key in the left pocket of my bag. My key was in the right pocket, but I'm sure I put it on the left. I froze as I noticed Sam walking over to me, dressed in odd scraps of clothing, a leopard-skin jacket, a red shirt, leather trousers, and a hat. He ambled past me and stared straight at me. We said nothing, but it totally freaked me out. Twice in one week, creeping through the neighborhood. What does he want? I won't believe the gibberish Andy and Michael said to me. If I got into a fight with his non-existent girlfriend, then why did they wait so long to tell me? Anyone can get into a drunken argument, it's not a taboo.

There's more, and Sam has something to do with it. They are protecting him as friends do. Did he beat me? Attack me? I shudder to think what might have happened.

I ended up watching football on TV tonight. Well actually, I just stared at the screen. I'm not a football fan. I've never understood the concept of ridiculously paid players running after a ball, while we ordinary folks struggle with debt, loans, and mortgages. I poured myself a glass of gin and tonic, then changed my mind and threw it in the sink.

29th May
Evening,
Diary,

I'm considering changing the locks, I'm so paranoid. I jump at every sound. For the first time in my life, I'm frightened of being alone. I can't wait for Richard to come home. Somebody's watching me, who knows I'm alone.

When Richard comes back, I'm going to try to find the right time to bring up the subject about us moving. I want a fresh start. He'll find it puzzling, I know he'll say, 'Why now after eleven years?' I want to move out of the city. I'm afraid of living in this apartment. I'm scared to look out of the window, to see Sam lingering on the pavement, looking up at my window. It took more than a dance and a fight to make a man behave so strangely.

3rd June
Afternoon,
Diary,

I haven't had time to write in my diary for ages, but this is what's happened...

Was in the apartment on Thursday night. I felt more alone than I've ever been.

It was about 9:45pm. I made a cup of coffee and was just contemplating the lack of food in the fridge. I almost jumped out of my skin, when I heard a doorknob rattling. I turned around to see the knob of the front door turning. I covered my mouth with my hands to prevent myself from screaming and froze. I held my breath, afraid that whoever out there would hear it. I scanned the room for a weapon to protect myself. The world is full of weapons. I tiptoed to the kitchen as my heart beat like crazy. I grabbed the butcher's knife, and stood beside the door with my back to the wall for a short while, terrified. The rattling stopped. I don't know how I managed to summon the courage, but finally, I unlocked the door and went into the corridor. My neighbor Mr. Smith and his little girl, Lisa, stood at their front door, he seemed to be having trouble finding his key.

'Good evening,' he said.

'Good evening,' I replied.

The little girl waved at me, and I waved back. As I was about the shut the door, the little girl said, 'You have a letter on the floor.'

I smiled at her, and picked it up, locking the door behind me. I tore the letter open.

Sophie,

You're playing a dangerous game.

By this time, I was shaking all over. I just stared at the words until they blurred. My breath came out in ragged gasps, as I watched raindrops burst against the windows.

What does the note mean? Does someone know about the affair? Is it a warning to stop all the questioning, because the truth is terrible and incriminating? Who delivered the letter and why were they trying to get into the apartment? I felt like I was losing the plot. I broke down at the kitchen table. I couldn't take it anymore. I dialed the police. I wanted to be sick.

'Someone tried to break into my apartment,' I exclaimed.

'Is anything stolen?'

'No, they didn't actually break in, but they tried to.'

'Is this a police matter?'

It was a total waste of time. The police don't take matters like this seriously unless you end up dead in a ditch somewhere. The discussion went on for a few minutes, and then she finally said she'd send somebody round.

I chained smoked, went around every window, making sure they were locked - as if someone was going to scale six floors in Notting Hill. I didn't switch on the TV or music. I wanted to hear everything. An hour later, the bell rang, I went to the intercom. Two-uniformed police officers stood on the pavement. I buzzed them in, and they came up to the apartment. They greeted me and took off their caps. I showed them the letter, and one of the officers stepped forward to read it.

'Have you had other letters like these before?' he asked.

'Yes.'

'Do you have them?'

I excused myself and went to get the only other note I've kept.

'I've had others, but I threw them away. I thought it was just a prank a first.'

'How many?'

'I don't remember, maybe five or six.'

'Have you any idea who they could be from?'

I shook my head. 'Well-'

'You say someone tried to get in?'

'Yes.'

'Can you describe what happened?'

'Yes, the doorknob was turned, repetitively?'

'Yes.'

I wanted to mention the key being misplaced, but I didn't say anything. I didn't want to complicate things. He rambled to the door, checked, and sighed as if he was doing something trivial.

The other officer turned to me, and said, 'Can you think of anybody who might send you this? An old friend, a co-worker, somebody who knows you, that sort of thing?'

I took a deep breath. 'Knows me?'

'Anyone with a grudge, or any practical jokers, who might do this for a laugh?'

'A laugh?'

'Some people have a twisted sense of humor,' he paused, 'whoever sent you this note, didn't commit a crime. There's no sign of forced entry.'

I couldn't believe it. They nodded at each other and put on their caps. One of the officers turned to me and said, 'If something serious happens, then call us.' He really stressed the word *serious*.

Yeah, when I end up, mugged, raped or dead, I'll call, I was tempted to say, but I bit my tongue.

They turned to go.

'Wait, aren't you going to take the letters with you?'

'Keep them. Put them in a drawer somewhere safe.'

'Aren't you going to take a statement?'

'If you're in any more trouble, we will do that. All right? Now get some sleep, we have work to do.'

Once they left, I gawped through the window and watched as their car pulled away. I couldn't stay in the apartment alone, so I gathered some belongings, mainly toiletries and a change of clothing, and packed them into my oversized work bag.

I cautiously opened the front door and scurried out like a criminal escaping a crime scene. Everyone I walked past felt like a threat. My heart pumped furiously against my chest. I've been scared before but never like that.

I hailed a taxi and gave the driver the address that now has become too associated with my life.

I called Michael from the taxi, but he didn't pick up. Arrived at his apartment, and I told the driver to wait just in case Michael wasn't there, and he wasn't. So I got the taxi driver to take me back to Notting Hill, to the club, hoping he was there.

The club wasn't busy. I spotted Michael at the bar, so I went over to him and placed my hand on his shoulder. He turned around. OMG, it wasn't him. I felt so embarrassed and removed my hand. He looked like him so much from the back, same body type, tall, lean, same hair color, and length. He flashed his green eyes at me. He really did look like Michael, or like it could he be one of his brothers.

'I'm sorry, I mistook you for someone else,' I said.

'No problem,' the young man said.

Michael appeared, 'Sophie, What are you doing here?'

The man stood between us, his eyes went from me to Michael, 'I tried to call you.' I said in a shaky voice.

'I've not got my phone on me.'

'Oh,' I said, feeling uncomfortable standing in between the two of them.

'This is my friend Matti, he's passing through from Sweden.'

'Hello,' I said to Matti.

He gave me a friendly smile, 'Hi,'

'This is my friend, Sophie,' Michael added.

The resemblance was unmistakable. If it weren't for the eyes, you'd think this is the same person. I stared at the tall, beautiful blonds, 'I'm sorry, but are you two related?'

They looked at each other. 'No,' Michael said.

'We're old friends,' Matti said.

'I see… would either of you like a drink?' I said.

'No, thanks,' they both chimed at the same time.

I ordered a double whiskey on the rocks. 'So how long have you two known each other?' Matti asked.

'A while,' Michael replied.

My hands were trembling so much I could hardly hold the glass. Michael noticed.

'So you're staying?' I asked Matti. I couldn't get over it. They had to be related.

'No, I'm heading to New York,' Matti said.

'How exciting.'

I rubbed my sweaty hand against my jeans, and reached for the glass. This time my hand had more control.

'Matti plays guitar, he's going to play with a band there,' Michael said.

'Ah.' I took a sip from my whiskey.

Michael frowned at me. I knew what he was thinking.

'Anyway, I should be going,' Matti said.

'I'm not intruding, am I?'

'Not at all, I was going anyway,' Matti said, 'It was a pleasure meeting you.' He offered me his hand, and we shook hands and, Michael watched in an observing manner, 'you're beautiful' he continued.

I blushed. 'Oh… thank you.'

Matti glanced at Michael. 'Take care of this one, he's special. I want him to be happy.'

I raised my eyebrow at Michael, what was that supposed to mean? After Matti left, I grabbed Michael's hand in desperation. 'I need to talk to you.'

'I figured you wouldn't come unannounced if you didn't,' he scolded.

'Can we go somewhere private?'

'What is it?'

'I'm scared, strange things have been happening.'

'Like what things?' he said impatiently.

I slouched on an empty stool, and he came closer. 'I think someone is following me,' I told him.

'Why would someone want to follow you?' he asked.

'I don't know.'

Michael studied my face. 'Have you been drinking?'

'I'm not drunk.' I said defensively.

'I'm only saying because I care,' he said, looking at me tenderly.

I sat at the bar and watched him play. I ordered another drink, and my tension started to ease. After he finished playing his solo, he pointed at me and dedicated the piece of music to me. What a sweet gesture. I have never had a musician dedicate a song to me before.

After he finished his set, we left the club together.

'So what's been going on?'

'Oh god, I-'

'Are you all right?'

Tears fell down my cheeks. He dropped his saxophone case on the pavement and wrapped his arms around me. I cried on his chest for a while, and he wiped away my tears with his thumb.

'Can I stay with you for the weekend?'

'Do you have to ask?'

Once inside his flat, he led me to the sofa. 'Why don't you tell me what's wrong?' he insisted.

'Can I get a drink, first?'

'No, you will not get a fucking drink,' he barked.

I began to cry, his blue eyes penetrating mine. He placed his hand on my shoulders. 'You need to stop drinking. You're all over the place.'

'I don't need any lectures especially from a twenty-two-year-old.' I snapped.

'Fine, have it your way.'

'Someone tried to get into my apartment I think,' I said.

Michael stared at me with apparent seriousness. 'What! What do you mean someone tried to get in?'

He started pacing up and down the room. 'Did you call the police?'

'Yes.'

'And?'

'They didn't do anything, as there was no sign of forced entry.'

'For fuck's sake.' he yelled.

I kept staring at him. 'Were you… '

He gazed down at me, looking angry. 'Was I what?'
'Never mind...'
He sat beside me and consoled me. 'I'm scared.'
'It's okay, you're safe now, don't go back there,' he said.
'Thank you.'

Woke up dull-headed, and not sure where I was, and then it all came flooding back to me. Michael greeted me with a mug of coffee and said good morning. Waking up in this flat and seeing him first thing felt strange. I didn't belong in there. How ridiculous the whole thing was. He sat on the bed and watched me, I removed the sheet from my body, picked up my underwear and t-shirt from the floor, and put them on, eager to cover my nakedness from him.

'I have nothing to wear,' I announced.

He blinked at me as if I said something out of the ordinary, 'What for?' he asked.

'To work, Mike, I need clothes for work. I forgot to pack something... proper.'

'Why?' he asked.

'I have to go to work.' I reasoned with him, 'I can't stay in bed all day.'

'Why can't you?' he argued.

'I must go to work.'

'Why?'

'Because I have duties and responsibilities.'

He frowned.

'Oh fuck it,' I said, looking around the room searching for my bag, 'where is my phone?'

'What for?'

'I'm going to call them.' I knew the firm would manage without me for one day, after all, they didn't fall apart when Charles forced me to take leave.

I found my phone, but the battery was dead.

'Can I use your phone?'

He handed me a cordless phone.

'There,' I said after I hung up.

He suggested we go out for lunch. I was skeptical about it, but I agreed, anyway. I couldn't stay in bed with him all day. He took me to a restaurant.

'What are we doing here?' I asked him.

He gave me the most innocent look. 'What does it look like we're doing? We're having lunch.'

Inside the restaurant, I scanned the place to see if there was anyone familiar. Richard knows many people, and many people know who I am, even though I don't know them. I kept imagining Richard walking in any minute, even though he's not the kind of man who would come to Camden for a bite to eat. Anyway, he's in New York. Acid rose up to my stomach, and my skin prickled when I pictured a colleague or Charles walking in, but I was safe. I hid behind the menu and studied it, unable to decide. A cold hand slid inside the back of my trousers and felt my bottom. I jumped, and my knees hit the table. A knife fell on the floor, and a few patrons glanced over at us. Michael laughed.

'Don't do that.' I hissed at him.

'Come on, loosen up,' he said.

'No public display of affection, I'm not your girlfriend.'

'You know what your problem is?' Michael said.

I studied the menu. 'What.'

'You want it all, the guy you screw, me, and him, the guy you go home to.'

I closed the menu and placed it on the table. 'All said is I don't want public display of affection. We're having lunch but for god's sake, don't start a fight.'

'I'm not, I'm saying it how it is.'

The waiter came over to our table. I've never had been so happy to see a waiter in my life. Before he opened his mouth, I started to give him my order, 'Ah yes, a bottle of Merlot, please.'

He shot me a stern glance. He ordered a bottle of water and a glass of orange juice.

'Merlot, seriously?' Michael said after the waiter left, 'you need help.'

'Oh come on, relax, I need a drink.'

He searched my face in silence. 'I'm going to drag you to rehab myself if necessary.'

'Oh stop it. You sound like my husband, why not join forces you two?'

He was not happy with this remark. 'You're comparing me to him, now?'

'I don't want another husband, I have one already. Order for me, will you? I can't decide,' I said.

He shook his head in disbelief. 'You've got to be kidding me.'

The waiter arrived with our drinks. He opened the wine and asked me if I liked to try it. I told him to pour it in. As I took a sip, the wine began to speak to me. By no means am I'm a wine connoisseur, but I just love to drink it, gallons of it. Michael shook his head at me and watched me with a careful eye.

'I can't do this anymore, sleeping with two people at the same time.' I brushed my hair away, 'too many strange things are happening too.'

Michael glared at me, assuming I was going to dump him. 'What are you going to do?'

'I don't know.'

I felt panic wash over me, and gulped on my wine. His annoyance vibrated between us.

'Are you going to leave him?' he asked.

'Hmm…' I murmured, draining the glass.

He looked away in distaste. 'Jesus.'

'You can't come back into my life, and expect me to fuck it all up,' I said.

He returned his gaze to me. 'Two people are doing the fucking here.'

I scanned the restaurant. There was a woman with her dog, which sat on the chair like a patron while she ate her salad.

He placed his hand on mine. 'I'm sorry, I got carried away. Forgive me.'

Throughout lunch, we talked about random, unimportant stuff. Michael shared the wine with me, and after the waiter cleared the plates away, we ordered a second bottle. I was relaxed for once.

We wobbled back to the flat. His neighbor was playing pop songs, again. Michael fiddled with his pockets and dropped his keys on the floor. Both of us went to pick them up and bumped our heads. I laid flat on the dusty floor, laughing. Michael leaned over to check I was ok and picked me up from the floor. I laughed so much my stomach hurt. Once inside his flat, I pulled him against the wall.

'You have to be one of the most beautiful men I ever been with.'

'You're pretty drunk, you know that?' he said.

'I'm fine,' I said, biting his bottom lip.

And I was drunk. I felt light-headed, and my cheeks were burning. I don't remember what gibberish I said to him, but I pushed him onto the sofa and climbed on top of him. I took off my top, then ripped off his shirt, and ran my hands over his chest.

'Such a fox, hot, hot, hot. I'd leave it all for you.'

Looking back, I wince with humiliation at the things that come out of my mouth when I'm in his presence. I need to discipline myself.

I noted a metallic taste in my mouth, and the reality of what my life with Michael would be like if I left Richard to be with him. Lunches, arguing about things, getting drunk, and having intense sex. Is this what I'm considering leaving my life for? Is it worth the risk? Is it enough? It's silly, it's not real. It's a fantasy, an illusion. Nothing but carnal lust. At least, I could be honest with him. I don't have to be ashamed, because he knows who I am. This realization brought despair, but I didn't cry, not in front of him. I could display my shame, but not my vulnerability.

We didn't do much for the rest of the evening, I rested my head on his lap, and we watched the telly while I smoked. Later, we rolled a joint, than munchies kicked in. I felt young again. We devoured what we could find, even each other.

On Saturday, we went to St Martin's Park. I watched a mom pushing a buggy. She sat down on a bench and held her baby, and I thought to myself, what I'd give to be in her place.

'Do you want children?' I asked him.

'Not really.'

'Why?'

He frowned. 'I don't think I'm good with kids.'

'Oh…' I replied. I leaned my head on his shoulder, 'has it ever been like this for you?'

'What?'

'Had you ever felt anything like this?' I asked.

'No, what about you?'

'No.'

'Are you scared?' he asked.

I ran my hand through my hair. 'It dies down, everything does.'

'How I feel about you would never die down,' he said.

At the weekend, my feelings became more intense, alarmed, and frightened. What if I did something stupid, like confess everything to Richard when I was drunk? When will the strangeness stop - the notes, Sam creeping about my neighborhood, someone trying to break into my apartment? I thought about the apartment, and how lonely it must be. Did the neighbors notice I wasn't there? I thought of going there to check on things but couldn't face it.

On Sunday, we stayed in. Michael had to work that evening and insisted I go with him. The subject came up again of Richard and my marriage. Frankly, his jealousy is becoming annoying and boring, but it terrifies me, what will stop him from going straight to Richard? I don't think he would do it in person, but there are many ways for the affair to come out in the open.

He was sitting on the sofa with his legs across, dressed in black trousers, and a sleeveless top.

Michael is mature for his age, but it's beginning to show how unreasonable, immature, and how difficult he is to manage. The truth is, people are unmanageable, unreliable, and unpredictable. I've seen it enough in my job.

'Oh what the hell…' he said, 'you did it with me, what makes me think you won't do it again with someone else?'

'Hey, Don't sit all pretty, as if you're blameless, you were with me when it happened, you're not innocent.'

It hurts me that he assumes I'd cheat on him too. If I do leave Richard for him, it won't last, he's too young to carry such a burden. Maybe he wants to brag about it, and stroke his own ego... *I am so irresistible that a wife would leave her husband for me.* Until the guilt gets the better of him.

'I know, but I don't want to have to guess when you're coming to see me again,' he said.

'We can end it right now. It's the logical thing to do,' I said.

He gave me a sad look, 'why?'

I lifted my hand to show him my wedding ring. 'Because of this. It would be hard at first, but you're so young, you'll forget me. I won't, but time makes things better. We can still be friends, we can still see each other, but not in this fashion.'

What was I saying? If I see him, I'd be in his bed, so fast it would make my head spin. The best way to do this is to be brutal, cut all ties, and never see him again.

'I don't want to be your friend,' he said crossly, like a child whose mum refused to buy him candy.

'And you think we can go on like this for ten, twenty years without getting caught?'

'I don't know what to think anymore.'

I shook my head and paced up and down. There was a grimace on his face. I didn't like the way he looked at me one bit. I lit a cigarette and sunk into the chair. I am in love and a drowning woman. I have been with Richard for so long, I grew up with him, he taught me so much. Never pictured my life without him. Just thinking about it kills me, but I *did* lose a lot for him. I don't speak to my parents, can't have children with him, and I *still* have time for a baby. I got up from the chair and took my mobile out of my bag. Michael's eyes widened.

'What are you doing?' he asked, alarmed.

'I'm going to call Richard.'

He got up from the sofa. 'And tell him what? You are going to leave him for me while he's in New York.'

'Are we going to do this? No more meetings in this apartment, no hiding, you and me together in broad daylight. If I do tell him when he gets back, are you going to be there for me?' I asked.

He dropped his eyes to the floor. 'I need more time,' he said.

'Fine... then stop with the jealousy, it's irritating, I told you from the start, I am married. You knew what you were getting yourself into.'

While he was preparing for his gig, I went to check the apartment. I took the mail up. No suspicious notes. I opened the door, the lights were on. I stood by the door, staring at my key. I swore I'd switched off the lights when I left. Or did I? I left in such a rush and in a panic, I might have forgotten to switch them off. I shut the door behind me. I placed Richard's mail on his desk and inspected each room. Everything seemed fine. I made a note of the ingredients to restock our empty fridge.

I went to the club. Michael was by the bar, but he wasn't alone,

Matti was with him. Michael didn't look happy at all. It seemed like they were arguing from their body language. I moved away to avoid being seen. Matti pointed his finger at Michael, and Michael threw up his hands in what looked like exasperation. Matti stomped away. Why on earth were they arguing?

Michael saw me and came over.

'What took you so long?' he asked, grabbing my hand.

'I told you I went to check the apartment.'

'Is everything okay?'

'It looks fine. I'll be sleeping there tonight.'

'Are you sure?'

'Yes, I need clothes for work.'

'Whatever suits you,' he said.

'Are you upset about something?'

He studied my face, and I wondered if he knew that I saw his outburst with Matti. 'No, why?' I replied.

'You look upset.'

'I'm not upset... I'm tired.'

After I watched him play, he insisted on walking with me to the apartment. When we reached the door, he pulled me to the wall and kissed me so passionately, it left me breathless.

'Mike…'

'I want to make love…'

'Oh, for God's sake.'

I took him up to the flat. I swore I'd never bring him up here again. He barely gave me time to place the keys on the hall table. He lifted me up and carried me to the bedroom.

Afterward, he told me, he was going to visit his friends at Evelyne's. I didn't know if it was true or if he was going to meet Matti and didn't want to tell me.

6th June
Afternoon,
Diary,

I hate thinking it, but I even wonder if it could be Michael. I know it's crazy. I'm questioning the man who's shown he cares deeply for me, the man I'm sleeping with, the man I'm betraying my husband for. Nothing makes sense anymore. I hate myself for thinking it. It makes little sense. Michael was at the club so it can't be him. If he wanted to come and see me, he would knock like a normal person, not fiddle with the doorknob to scare me.

7th June
Morning,
Diary,

Richard is back from his trip and greyer than usual. He bought me a pair of *Jimmy Choos*. I'm going to wear them to work tomorrow. I kissed him on the lips and stared into his eyes. I still doubt if I could risk it all. No, I can't, I need consistency, and Michael can't give any of that. I can't switch my feelings for Richard off like that.

9th June
Evening,
Diary,

Things just keep getting better, and better. God, I'm scared, I have to do something, but the police won't take me seriously.

I sat opposite Michael in a restaurant and hoped he looked like a client. This makes me laugh because I know he doesn't. He's too flamboyant, but then again, clients come in all shapes and sizes. Why am I even thinking of lies to tell, when I can say the truth? Yes, Richard, he's my lover, I love him, and there's nothing you can do about it. All Richard can do is divorce me.

'What are you thinking?' Michael asked.

'Oh, you don't want to know,' I said, playing with my finger.

'But I do want to know.'

'About the key,' I said, studying him, to see if I could catch a reaction.

He flipped his hair. 'What key?'

'The key that was misplaced in my bag.'

'Oh yeah, the key... what about it?'

'I was sure I placed it in the left pocket, not on the right.'

He arranged his hair. 'These things happen all the time.'

'Yes, but I'm not crazy.'

He sighed. 'It's easy to misplace stuff, Sophie. What's the big deal, anyway?'

'Mike!'

He signaled the waiter for the check. 'What is it?'

'Did you--' I trailed off?

'What?' He said.

There was an uncomfortable silence. The waiter placed the bill on the table. Mike's face went white.

'Oh for fuck sake, is this where we're heading?'

'What?'

'You know what.'

I paid the bill quickly before Michael caused a scene in the restaurant. I stood, and gathered my bag,

'Hey wait, I'm talking to you. Don't you dare walk away from me.' he shouted.

Once outside, he pulled my hand to stop me and rammed me against the wall.

'Do you honestly think I took your key and placed it back again?' he asked, raising his voice.

A woman in a beige coat eyed him. 'No!' I said.

'Look! I'm not going to take this shit from a broken-down alcoholic. You could have placed the key anywhere. What are you going to tell me next, I tried to get into your apartment!' he shouted.

I shut my eyes. It was foolish of me to ask him directly. Of course, he'd be upset.

'You're right, I'm sorry, it was an awful thing to say.'

He let my hand go. 'Yes, it was, you're a jerk.' He backed away, 'I want to be alone.'

'What?' I asked in a broken voice.

'It's best we stay away from each other, for a while.'

He turned to leave. 'But—'

'Don't call me, I'll call you.'

'Oh come on, don't be a baby.'

But he is a baby. I shouldn't have mentioned anything. I knew it would upset him, and now he thinks I am accusing him of stealing my key, and returning it again. He shook his hand away and stomped off.

Is it over again? I went to the general store to get the groceries. Michael was right, I do want it all, the guy I screw, and Richard. I paid and left, keeping my head low, not making eye contact with anyone. As I waited at the traffic lights, a man beside me took out a Zippo lighter and lit a cigarette. For a split second, the world stopped. The sound of the lid opening and the bright orange flame brought memories flooding back, like pages in a photo album, flipping over one by one. Each memory was a snapshot, bright and vivid. Full of detail.

Sam fires a cigarette with a Zippo, his blue eyes on me. It was dark outside, and I didn't have my coat on. I was giggling. He placed the Zippo in the back pocket of his trousers, his eyes never leaving mine.

'So here we are alone at last,' Sam said.

Heat and panic swept over me, my heart bursting out of my chest. I dropped my bags on the ground. I couldn't breathe. It was like someone was choking me.

I heard someone say, 'Are you alright, madam?'

I continue to gasp for air.

'Keep calm, and breathe deeply. Keep focusing on your breathing,' the voice said. That's all I remember, everything was a blur.

10th June
Evening,
Diary,

Didn't go to work today, Richard insisted upon it. It was the first panic attack I had. I called Richard after the panic attack and went home. He called me a doctor, who ordered me to stay in bed and rest. I felt better after a while, but it doesn't change the fact I still need answers.

It's all coming back to me little by little. I suspected Sam had something to do with that night. But what exactly? What did he do? Where did the bruises come from? Did he attack me? How did I end up outside with him? I have so many questions. Michael won't tell me, he's protecting him. How dare he lie to my face! And Andy, also covering for Sam Michael and Andy, the pair of them scheming, feeding me with lies. A fight my arse. I was in state of uncontrollable rage, and I knew who to take it out on.

I drove Richard's Mercedes over to Michael's. He doesn't use it often. Driving in London is ridiculous, anyway. Couldn't afford to waste time on tubes, taxis, or buses. I had to confront him and fast. When I arrived, I saw him bouncing down the street, his blond hair flowing behind him, accompanied by a girl, dressed in a leather jacket. I clutched the steering wheel until my knuckles turned white, so, this is how he spent his days when he wasn't with me. I parked my car in the first parking space I found, beyond caring if it was a yellow line. How many women is he seeing? I threw my cigarette on the pavement and crossed the street. By this time, they were standing outside the flat, his back to me. Is this what I considered leaving Richard for? To fuck up my life and make a total fool of myself? What a fool I am. What did I expect a man like Michael to see only me? Silly me.

I was sure they were out for a stroll, after an afternoon of steamy sex. And were on their way to resume. I couldn't bear it, imagining him giving her what he gives to me. She was beautiful, of course - long black hair, flat cheekbones, full lips, and brown eyes, and yet, somehow, he was prettier than her. I hit him on the head. He turned to face me, as I lunged forward to hit the girl. He grabbed me by the waist and lifted me off the pavement. Heads turned.

'Bitch!' she yelled.
'Leave him alone!' I yelled back.
'Whore!' She said, throwing middle fingers in the air.
'Easy,' Michael said, carrying me inside the apartment block.

'Let me go,' I demanded. He mumbled something in Swedish. Swear words maybe?

'I've had enough of you.' he hissed.

I pushed him, and moved away from him, he grappled my arm, sunk his fingers into my skin, and pressed hard. I winced. He dragged me up the stairs.

'What are you doing here? I thought I told you I'd call you,' he snapped, without looking at me.

He took me to the second floor, and with his free hand, he fiddled in his pocket.

'Of course, because it's not my day today is it?'

He pushed me against the wall. 'I don't have to explain anything to you.' he shouted in my face.

He took out his keys, opened the door, and pushed me inside. I lost my balance and fell onto the floor. He slammed the door shut and threw the keys across the room. He sighed and pushed his fringe away from his face. It fell delicately on his forehead. There was banging on the door.

'Mike! You son of a bitch open the Goddamn door.' the girl yelled.

Michael cursed as he opened the door. I stood on my feet, dusted myself, and marched over to the bedroom. The girl yelled frantically at him. Was she a girlfriend? Did he have a girlfriend all this time and didn't tell me? The bed was undressed, and the sheets were on the floor, along with condom packets, and used tissues.

'Fuck you!' the girl yelled.

The door slammed. Michael stood in the middle of the room with his hands on his hips. He turned his attention to me.

'You're stinking with alcohol. You've been drinking, haven't you?'

'No.'

'Don't lie to me. Why aren't you at work?'

'Thank God I wasn't.... I know where I stand now.'

'You're drunk.'

'I'm not drunk. What are you saying, it's all in my imagination?'

'I told you she's a friend.'

'You fucking liar. I can see the bed, you had sex with her.'

He stomped across to me. 'Me? I'm the fucking liar?' he smirked, you're pathetic you know that? You're pissed off because I had sex with a girl? You don't know the rules, Sophie. You are the one who's married not me. I've got nothing to lose.

I spent months watching you coming here, then you leave at the end. You always leave, and I'm alone. This is more than you deserve.'

He rambled past me to the kitchen, opened the fridge and stomped back in holding a bottle of wine. He unscrewed the top and took a sip from it.

'What did you expect, me to sit here waiting for you while you are at home with your husband? You can't prevent me from my youth,' he continued.

'That's it.' I yelled 'I cannot take it anymore. We're finished. It's over.'

He glared at me, and before I let him say a word, I headed towards the door. He rushed over, blocking my way.

'Out of my way, Mike.'

'Fine then,' he said, entering into my space, 'go back to your weak husband. Isn't that why you keep coming here over, and over because I give you what he can't.'

'Leave him out of this. He has nothing to do with you.'

'Go back to your boring life, to your booze, to your fucking hell.'

'Fuck you!' I said walking past him.

I clumped through the corridor, and he came after me. Why couldn't he just leave me alone? What does he want from me? He caught up with me, pulled me against the wall, and kissed me. I shoved him away.

'No, it's over.'

He took off my coat, and I pushed him. 'I love you…' he whispered, taking my mouth to his.

He'll keep on doing this until there is nothing left of me. This is never-ending. How I'm going to get out of this. This is bigger than me, and it's tearing me apart.

15th June
Afternoon,
Diary,

We stayed in with the curtains closed. We watched a movie together, in each other's arms. Richard has a terrible cough. We got into an argument because of it since he refuses to see a doctor. I think he's going to catch a cold. He complained yesterday about a headache. He's not eating like he used to, he barely touches the food.

'You should do something about that cough,' I said, once he stopped coughing.

'It's just a cough, Sophie.'

'Still, you should see a doctor.'

'I've had enough of doctors. It will pass.'

'I worry about your health more than you do.'

'For God's sake Sophie…' He stopped to cough.

I waited for him to recover, his face turned crimson.

'Are you trying to pick a fight,' he said, after his cough subsided.

'No, I worry.'

'Yeah right.'

'What is that supposed to mean?'

He coughed again.

'I'll call a doctor.'

'No!' he yelled between coughs.

'Richard!'

'I'm going to bed. I can't have you buzzing in my ear all the time,' he said, and went off to bed, still coughing.

This is the thanks I get for worrying about his health? How ungrateful. What is wrong with him? I smoke so much and even I don't even cough like that. And what were the rashes on his neck? What's wrong with him?

I went out to visit the *Blagclub*. It's been ages since I've been there. Everyone looked so dressed up heading into the club. I didn't bother to go in, I didn't think I'd find anything that might help me in there. I walked past the dry cleaners and remembered the soil on my dress. Did I leave the club with Sam and go somewhere else? No, I don't suppose we did. It happened somewhere around here. I can see it again, him standing in front of me, lighting a cigarette with a zippo, and looking at me as if he wanted to devour me.

17th June
Evening
Diary,

Richard seems to be losing his patience with me. He's snapping at every single detail. I think he has a fever but is still refusing to see a doctor.

Tried to end it with Michael today, I figured I couldn't do it in person though. So I chose the coward's way out. I opened my email browser, and with tears pouring down my face, I typed in his email address. I didn't get any further because the phone startled me. It was a client who had to make the final check on a set of accounts before I signed them off.

At lunchtime, I told Wendy to take a message if anyone called while I went out of the office for a few minutes. When I got back to the office, I tried to figure out what to write in the card I bought for Michael at the shop. There's no right way to end a relationship with someone, but this isn't a relationship, despite being in love with him. I decided not to send a card. An email will do.

Dear Michael,
This has to end, it was…

I stopped typing. It was what? Wonderful? Grand? The best and worst thing that ever happened to me? It flipped my world upside down? Technology gives people an excuse to hide behind their monitors. It gives them the confidence to say what they have to say without having to do it in person.

I should tell him in person, it's the right thing to do, but he'll be difficult. I picked up the card again and sighed, I couldn't put dear or dearest, Michael. I pictured him in my mind, so beautiful, like magic itself. I picked up the card with the kitten,

Michael,
I have to stop seeing you, and the only way to end this is to be brutal. What we are doing is wrong and dangerous, and I can't take such risks. We have to stop doing this. I have to continue my life with my husband. I'm not strong enough to live on the edge with you. It rips me apart, but there's nothing else to do. I'm sorry.
I'll always love you,
Sophie.

At 3:30pm, I went to a meeting, I wrote words such as *power*, *passion*, and *possession* on my notepad, contemplating whether I'd send the card or not.

'Are you with us, Sophie?' Charles said, scowling at me.

By 4:30, I was back at the desk. Michael called me a few times, but I ignored his calls. I don't know what to do. To send, or not to send...

20th June
Evening,
Diary,

Michael came here today, to my office. This is getting out of hand. Why can't he let me be? I thought I'd done well these past few days, not returning his calls, hoping he'd take the hint, but no. As I left work and turned around the corner, Michael started following me. He grabbed my arm and pulled me to him, his body was warm. The smell of his oaky aroma of aftershave was intoxicating and made my head hurt.

'What do you think you're doing? Are you insane?' I hissed at him

'Why aren't you answering me?'

'I've been busy.'

He furrowed his eyebrows. 'Really?'

I don't know why I said that and why I keep dragging this on. Why didn't I say *I can't see you anymore, this is taking over my life and what's left of my insanity. This is a nightmare.*

'I can't talk right now,' I said, as I attempted to walk past him.

He rammed me against the wall. 'Not until you tell me when you're coming to see me.'

'I can't come when it's convenient for you.'

'Yes, you can, you have to.'

'It's not possible, you know that.'

'I have been patient long enough. You're married, it's your problem, not mine, find the time.'

Richard was still not back when I arrived home, so I soaked in the bath for a while, trying to relax. What a mess. What giant pile of mess. How selfish Michael had become. What a big mistake. What was I thinking? The most beautiful thing I have ever seen is turning into one of my biggest regrets. I wondered if he wants me to get caught. This thought fills me with despair.

When Richard arrived home, he was coughing, again.

'Sophie.' He called.

'I'm here.' I shouted, stepping out of the bath and drying myself.

Richard barged into the bathroom. 'You're not dressed, yet?'

'I don't have a bath with my clothes on, Richard,' I said.

'You forgot didn't you?' I ignored him. He sighed checking his wristwatch, 'we have to be at the Ritz in an hour.'

Richard and his events, they're the last thing on my mind right now.

24ᵗʰ June
Afternoon
Diary,

Richard's cough has eased a little, but his skin looks yellow. He also keeps breaking out in a sweat, and there are tiny red dots on his neck. What's the matter with him? Why is he playing with his health? Doesn't he care anymore? Does he want to die? What would I do if he died? What about Michael? I considered leaving everything for him. I risked it all. Such a fantasy. What a stupid thing to do. Maybe in the next life, but not in this one.

Richard and I went to an opera last night, to see his favorite, *Madam Butterfly*. As if I don't have enough drama in my life. It was so beautiful and tragic. I ended up crying, and couldn't stop. It swam out of me, in uncontrollable sobs. Richard handed me his hanky and told me to calm down. But I didn't calm down, and I didn't care if I made a total ass of myself.

Afterward, we talked.

'What's wrong? You've been unhappy for some time, is something bothering you?'

I felt an urge to tell him everything. I wanted to ask for his help, and tell him about my dupe, but I'm weak and afraid. I can't face ending the affair and telling my husband the truth.

'Nothing, it's just it's sad she killed herself.'

Richard put his arms around me. 'Oh, honey, you're so sensitive, so romantic.'

I felt so safe to be in his arms. I yearned for him to hold me like this until the end of time.

'Go see a doctor, please.'

He sighed. 'Alright dear, I'll go and see a doctor.'

Will he, though? He probably said it to make me shut up.

30th June
Evening,
Diary,

Look at the sight of me. I'm a state. I've got bloodshot eyes, dark circles, a red nose, puffy lips, and my skin is deathly pale, although, I am naturally pale.

Went to see Michael today. His front door was ajar. He was sitting on the sofa wearing a white T-shirt and jeans, with his head tilted back, puffing on a joint. I stared at *that* body.

'You found time to see me then,' he sneered.

'No.' I shouted, slamming the door, 'I can't let you do this to me.'

The room smelled of weed and mold. He pulled me towards him on the sofa, so close there was no space between us. He's become unbearable - his stunts, the jealousy, the narcissism. I had to be strong. I could not display any more weakness.

'I can't do this anymore,' I said.

'I knew it.'

'I have to stop seeing you. I can't take it anymore.'

I was surprised at how the words flew out of my mouth.

'You don't fancy me anymore?' he asked.

'This has nothing to do with if I fancy you, that's not the point—'

'You're going to stay with him,' he said bitterly.

'He is my husband.'

'But I thought that you…' he trailed off.

'Never mind what I thought.'

'You're such a bitch.'

I opened my mouth to protest, but instead, I allowed him to call me every name in the book. Oh, he was angry and upset. It's reasonable. I couldn't hold back my tears.

'I love you, but I can't see you anymore. Please, let's end this on good terms,' I pleaded.

He glared at me

'You love me, but you're dumping me. What's the matter with you?'

'I have no choice.'

'Yes, you do. You can leave. There is a way.'

'Don't be ridiculous, you're too young, and I'm too old. We don't have a future together.'

'I don't care.'

I stood to leave. He pulled me towards him. 'Mike!'

'Sophie... you can't do this, what about what we shared, does it not mean anything to you?'

What we shared was pure lust. I cannot listen to any more lies. The bullshit. The weird things that have happened since he came into my life. The notes, the phone calls, someone following me. I want it to stop.

'Oh yes, it was precious but—'

'Then why?'

I tried to break free, but he pulled me in even closer.

'Mike, please, let me go.'

'You want me.'

'Stop!'

He pushed me against the wall, tears falling down my face. Why was he doing this? It was at that moment I wondered if he's capable of rape?

'You still want me, I know it.'

'Mike! Please, this is not about sex!'

It came to me, like a punch on the face. Sam pulling me against a wall.

'Mike, let me go, please stop!'

Michael eased down my jeans ignoring my protests,

I recall kissing Sam on the lips, and him nuzzling my neck. I pushed Michael harder, I wanted him to let me go. My heart was pumping, and my breath came in gasps. He didn't want to let me out of out his grasp. I was trapped. I didn't know what to do, stuck between my memory of Sam, and Michael trying to have his way with me. And then it came out of me loud and clear. A scream. He backed away, wide-eyed and angry.

Silence.

Pounding on the door. Loud footsteps. The anger replacing itself with alarm. Michael went to open the door and left it ajar.

'Who's screaming?' a voice of a woman demanded.

'... It's fine—'

'Screaming is not fine, young man. In the twenty-five years, I've lived here, I've never heard anyone scream.'

I pulled up my jeans and sat on the sofa.

'Shall we call the police?' a man asked.

I pictured the tenants out of their flats looking at Michael's apartment wondering what was wrong.

'What have you done to her?'

'There's no need for the police,' Michael snapped, 'We had a disagreement. She got upset, and screamed.' He opened the door wide, and a woman in her sixties, with grey hair and thick glasses, peered over at me. I smiled at her.

'See, she's fine now,' he said to reassure her, but I could hear the annoyance in his voice.

The woman glared at him and, with a soft voice, asked me, 'are you alright, dear?'

'I'm fine. I was upset and got carried away. I didn't mean to worry anyone.'

She didn't look too convinced. 'Right. Hope this won't happen again.'

'It won't,' Michael reassured her.

Michael was about to close the door, when the woman turned to me. 'So everything is handled?' she said.

'Yes, I can handle him,' I replied.

He shut the door in her face. 'Is that what I am, something to be handled like toxic waste,' he said.

'What you tried to do me just now was revolting. It's over, I mean it. We. Are. *Done*!'

'You're making a big mistake.'

'No, I'm doing the right thing. I'm sorry.'

'You're sorry?' he growled.

'I am, yes.'

'Don't do this, you don't know what I might do.'

'Cut the bullshit.'

I opened the door to leave. The proprietor, who was still in the corridor, threw me a suspicious glance as I stormed past her.

'Sophie, please come back,' Michael pleaded.

I shut my eyes fighting the tears.

'*Sophie!*'

Got home. Richard wasn't back yet. I dumped my bag on the floor and wept like a baby.

I have done it. I am free. So why don't I feel victorious?

I also removed the SIM card from my phone. I have to be strong. I'm laying here writing this, thinking of Richard and his handsome face and charisma.

The house phone just rang. I didn't answer it. I let it ring and ring.

I keep telling myself it's over now. I have done it. I'm free from him. I have found my way home.

1st July
Evening.
Diary,

Hate feeling like this. My heart is heavy and aching, but it will pass. I'll get used to it. The notes have stopped. Maybe it was Michael sending them.

I still can't understand how Richard didn't work out what was going on. How can someone be that blind? I want to bang his head with a saucepan and say, 'wake up you old fart I was having an affair.'

I let all of my clients, my parents, work, and Sylvie know I've changed my phone number.

Richard asked me. 'What for?'

'It was time for a change.'

It's coming together now, one memory after the next. Hitting me like a wave. How could they? How could Michael do this to me, him of all people? It was a lie. What they said were all lies. The puzzle is coming into place, piece by piece. They were taking me for a fool. They were covering for Sam.

I saw them sitting in the club, the strange, tall, beautiful boys, and three dark-haired men, one blond. There were all sorts of bottles on their table. One of them was wearing sunglasses with white frames, I think it was Nicky, but I can't be too sure. Sam was talking to Michael, and then, as if he knew I was staring at them, looked over at me, and then soon after, so did Michael.

I don't recall how Sylvie and I ended up at their table. There was a commotion between the men and one of the boys. Sylvie went over to the boys table, and I followed. Sam introduced himself right away. It's all muddled from there - I can't recall any of the conversations. Sylvie went off with Nicky and left me alone with them. Evelyne came to our table, said hello and sat on Andy's lap. Michael left the table. Sam offered me a drink and went over to the bar. When he came back, we danced to a song with a sax. That's the song I keep hearing. It was from the club.

But….. I never fell.

Sam and I talked by the wall, where Evelyne must have taken her selfie. I wanted to go out to get some air, so I grabbed my bag and coat and left. Sam wanted to come with me.

I walked past a dry cleaners and leaned against the wall of a large house, and smoked. Sam joined me and lit a cigarette.

'Here we are alone at last.'

There was a peculiar smell, exactly the same as the one I keep recalling. I smiled, I didn't know what to say to such a remark. It was a blur from there - I remember we kissed. And then it happened so fast. He pushed himself inside of me.

'No,' I said.

He ignored me. I tried to push him off me, but he was stronger. He covered my mouth with his hands and took his orgasm in me. I was mortified. I had tears in my eyes, and my body trembled. I sat on the pavement inspecting the damage he did to my dress.

'How could you do that to me? You Bastard!'

'I didn't do anything to you, it was sex, only sex.'

I stumbled to my feet and slapped him. He slapped me right back, so I slapped him again. I didn't care if he hit me, or killed me even, I was so angry. The last word I heard as I fell and hit my head on the pavement was,

'Look what you made me do!'

At one point, I opened my eyes. I was on the ground. Andy and Nicky stared down at me. Sam and Mike weren't there. Someone said,

'What the fuck did you do?'

3rd July,
Afternoon,
Diary,

If I tell Richard about this, he will make sure Sam goes to prison. Richard has the means and knows some of the best lawyers in the city. I don't know what to do. Now I remember, I can go to the police and report Sam. But what do I have to prove it - a torn, soiled dress? But it is evidence. If only I had remembered all this when I still had the bruises after it had just happened. Then it would be a different story.

I can't tell Richard or go to the police. They'd bring Sam in for questioning, and then Michael, who would defend him. He would tell the police everything. I can't let Richard know what's happened. And, of course, there's my drinking. No-one would believe me.

Does Evelyne know what happened? What sort of woman would hide this from another woman? Women should help each other in matters like these. How could she allow a rapist to live with her under her roof? She can't know the truth, not the whole truth anyway. I bet they lied to her too.

The more and more I think about it, the angrier I'm getting. Sam's friends were backing him up, all lying on his behalf. How deceptive, and sinister.

Maybe Michael was using me all along, none of it was real. That's why he was so bold with me, it was an act. But for what agenda or purpose, to protect Sam? The longer I took to remember, Sam would be safe? But that doesn't make any sense, Michael would have avoided me, not seduced me.

And what about the notes? Each time I open the mail, my heart stops. I haven't had one in weeks.

I must confront him. I need to tell him I know what happened.

5th July
Evening,
Diary,

I rushed up the stairs and pounded on his door. 'Coming, I'm coming.' he shouted.

Michael opened the door. He scowled at me. 'Oh, it's, you, I thought you'd be back again.'

'Don't flatter yourself, I'm not here for *that*,' I said.

'Come in,' he said, as I barged my way in.

'Everything was a lie.'

He shut the door. 'What do you mean?'

'Cut it out! I remember everything, I know what Sam did,' I said, raising my voice, 'He hit me, he was the one who knocked me out cold, not the drinking, not the fall. You knew all along, and you didn't tell me this? How could you!'

'What do you expect me to do?'

'You can't be serious.'

'I didn't know you then.'

'Is that your excuse?'

'Hey, I'm not the one that hit you! Why are you taking this on me.' he shouted.

'How could stand there and say something like that. It's sick and disgusting. How dare you. I loved you.'

'Is that what you think? I'm a sick and disgusting person, what about you? You came along with your upper-class boredom, stinking of alcohol, chain-smoking, with your intoxicating misery, spreading your corruption,' he raised his hand, 'this is what you created.'

I shook my head. 'He took advantage of me when I was helpless.'

'Helpless? You had sex with Sam then had an affair with me, and now you're acting like a victim. What you going to say next, that he raped you? You're a drunk. Get a life!'

'That *is* what he did. He raped me. I said no.'

'You let him have sex with you, as you let me, it wasn't rape.'

'I would have left everything for you. What a big fuck up I would have made out my life. You used me.'

'No, Sam used you. With him, it was just sex, and you used him too. Isn't that how it is with sex, but with us, it was more than that, and you know it. Don't worry, you are a fuck up, and you'd have done yourself a big favor if you left. You have nothing in that marriage.'

'You used me. You took advantage of me!' I stomped towards him and pushed him against a shelf of LPs. A few fell on the floor, 'I curse the day I laid my eyes on you, I was the idiot that fell for your charms, but nobody warned me you're a fucking vampire.' I pushed him, and my hands dug into his shirt. More LPs fell off the shelf. I continued shoving him, my anger pulsing through my veins, 'do you have any idea what you've done?'

He broke himself free. 'I'm very well aware what I did… how did you put it, oh yes, it wasn't memorable enough for you. Well, it wasn't memorable enough for me to give up a friend over you either.'

'This is madness.' I yelled.

'You're the creator of this madness, I was just more than happy to play along.'

I pointed my finger at him. 'Don't you think this is over. I will report him.'

'Go ahead,' he said, crossing his arms, 'do you think they are going to believe you, a fucking drunk! Go home, Sophie, to your marriage. Don't dig a bigger hole than you already have.'

'Why? Why! 'I cried.

He sat on the floor. 'Just leave, Sophie'

'I feel sorry for you, you're only twenty-two years old, and you're capable of committing such a heinous act. I don't even want to imagine what you will do when you're older. You deserve nothing but suffering.'

'Get the fuck out of here.' he shouted.

He will not stop not until I'm defeated. He will destroy me. Motivated by rage and revenge of a jilted lover. I'm thinking twice about going to the police. If he's had gone this far already, what else would he do to me?

8th July
Afternoon
Diary,

The drinking makes things less tense. Crying has become a daily thing. I feel so betrayed, how could he look at me in the eye and lie to me, when he knew all along. I'm in a state of paralyzing fear. I feel like it's not over yet. Something else is coming, but I don't know what.

Last night, I brought up the topic of moving with Richard. He got inquisitive, maybe I shouldn't have mentioned anything.

'Are you all right?' Richard asked wiping sweat from his forehead.

He's still looking green and has lost his appetite. What's wrong with him? I thought he was going to see a doctor?

'We should move,' I said.

He looked at me surprised. 'Move where?'

'We'll find a place in the country like you always wanted.'

'But you love the city.'

'I've been living here most of my life, I won't miss it… we'll move to Cornwall, it's beautiful there. We can buy a cottage.'

He coughed. 'What about your job?'

'I can quit my job. With my qualifications, I could get a job anywhere. I'm thinking about teaching.'

'Really?'

'What do you think?'

'You've never mentioned teaching before or moving, what's this all about?'

'I've told you already,' I said.

'There must be more to it. I mean, why now after all this time?'

'Because it's time. I'm ready.'

'What's wrong, Sophie?'

'Nothing's wrong,'

'Are you in some sort of trouble?'

I wanted to cry, crawl on my hands and knees, and beg for his forgiveness, but somehow I remained composed. Why must this keep dragging on? Why can't he just spit it out? It's my fault. I'm the one who started this. If only I didn't go out at all that night.

'No, Richard, I'm not in trouble.'

'Then why are you always fucking drinking?'

'Oh Richard.'

'Don't, oh Richard me, now *you* want to move. No Sophie, we are not moving, we're staying here.'

Richard got up and went to his office, and slammed the door.

'Everything is fucking no with you.' I shouted at the top of my lungs.

It's my fault. I played along with Michael. In the club, he didn't say a word. How shy and demure he was. The signs were there. How well he orchestrated everything. My drinking was his opportunity.

15th July
Midnight
Diary,

Sylvie is here in the apartment to keep an eye on me. I don't know where Richard is. I woke up in the shower with water cascading onto my clothes. Sylvie was in front of me smoking, I opened my mouth to speak, but she shook her head to stop me.

'Don't talk. Don't think about anything. It's been a shocking day,' she whispered.

'Where's Richard?'

'He was here, but he left'

'What do you mean *was and* left, where is he?'

She sighed without giving me a reply.

'Is he angry?'

'Angry is mild compared to how he's feeling. Let's not worry about that.'

And then what happened came back to me like a wave. 'Oh god.' I burst into tears.

'Come, let me help you up and take you to bed.'

She wrapped a large, fluffy blanket around me. 'Why are you here?'

'Richard called me.'

'Oh…Where's Richard?' I asked again.

'He's not here,' she said taking out my pajamas from the top drawer, 'Everything will be explained, but not tonight.'

I burst into tears. She frowned and got up. 'I'll be in the other bedroom if you need anything.'

This is what happened…

'How are you on the Wilson accounts?' Charles asked me.

'It will be ready by Friday,' I said.

'Would it be possible to finish them by tomorrow?' Charles asked, peering at me beneath his thick glasses.

'I'll do my best.'

Charles smiled, or more like his lips stretched. I'd have to pay him to smile, the pompous ass.

'Sophie?' Charles said.

'Yes?'

'Work on Wilson starts right away.' He said fiddling with his papers.

'But I have other—'

'This one is more important.'

'Right, of course.'

'Thanks.'

'Are you all right?' he asked.

I thought it was strange why he asked.

'Yes, why?'

'You seem rather... preoccupied this week, that's all."

I left the boardroom. My heart pounded against my chest. As I walked through the corridor, I heard whispering. 'Is this supposed to be a joke?' People looked up at me from over their desks and computer screens and looked away. And then came more whispers, 'oh my god.' and 'no way.' and 'what the f-'

The intern covered her mouth with her hands and looked at her computer screen. Wendy took her eyes away from her screen and looked at me, lips pressed together. I closed the door to my office and leaned against it. I could hardly breathe. I reached for the plastic bottle in my bag and took a swig of gin. The office phone rang, I picked it up. 'Yes?'

'Sophie, I want you to come to my office right away,' Charles said.

He sounded angry and hassled.

I thought it was odd, Wendy always connected me to Charles. He never called me directly. I presumed it was about the Wilson accounts again.

'Charles, I'm going to start the Wilson accounts right now,' I said.

'This is not about Wilson accounts.'

'What is this about?'

'You know what this is about.'

The line went dead, how was I supposed to know what he wanted to talk to me about? I opened the door, and all heads turned in my direction. As I paced through the corridor, I heard more whispering and giggling too. Everything rushed through my mind.

'There she is.'

'She's coming, shhh.'

I marched to Charles's assistant's desk.

'Charles wants to see me,' I said to her

She pointed at his door, and didn't say a word.

I knocked and opened the door. Charles stood beside his desk with his hand in his trousers pocket.

'Shut the door,' he said, without offering me to sit down.

His face was red, almost purple. 'Why would you do something like this?'

Did I lose someone's file again? Did I do the trial balance wrong? Couldn't he tell me instead of leaving me in suspense?

How was I supposed to answer his questions when I didn't know what I'd done?

'I don't know what you're talking about,' I said.

'You don't know what I'm talking about.' he turned his laptop to face me, pressed a button, and a slide show started with a series of photos.

My feet were paralyzed. I couldn't move, the world blurred. 'I don't know what that is.'

'You don't? Take a closer look.'

I couldn't believe what I was seeing. At first, I thought it was a joke, a cruel prank someone had done for a laugh - a woman who looked like me, posing in a set of photographs. But it *was* me, in a series of discriminating images. I felt hot all over. I stared at the screen as the pictures slid past one by one. I couldn't watch any more. 'It's all over for you, you know that?' Charles asked.

'It's not me,' I said, with tears streaming down my face.

'Not you.' Charles shouted, pausing the photo of me in all fours 'I'm sure as hell it is *you*.'

I covered my mouth, I wanted to be sick. Tears fell down my cheeks, imagining who had sent the photos. It was his bedroom. His face wasn't showing, although in one photo there was a mess of blond hair. Did he record each meeting? Did he set up a timer to take pictures of me at my most vulnerable?

I felt myself shrinking, getting smaller, and smaller, consumed with shame. I wanted the floor to swallow me up and take me away. How could Michael do this to me? Did he want to destroy my marriage? This was between him and me, and now the affair is everyone's business.

'It's all over...' Charles said.

'W-w-w-who sent them?' I whispered, staring back at the screen.

'Who sent it? *You* did,' Charles said.

I was horrified, 'I didn't send them.'

'No?'

He pressed a button on the keyboard. His email browser came on. 'Look! That is your fucking email. You sent them to everybody, *everybody* in the whole office, to our clients. To your husband, and his company, to *everyone!*'

I shook my head in disbelief. 'My email has been hacked.'

'I don't care. This is out of my hands, the directors are going to be in touch with you soon.'

The room spun. 'It wasn't me. I swear it wasn't me!'

'I don't care, maybe you were drunk when you sent them. How the fuck would I know. Now get out of my office, this is the last thing I need right now.'

I tearfully slipped out of the office. Everyone stared at me.

'Who is this?'

'Are those real?'

'It looks like her.'

Michael sent this to everyone at work, and to Richard. The humiliation Richard must have gone through, searching for an explanation, unable to believe his wife would do something like this.

Everyone was looking at me like I was a piece of meat, a whore. I was no longer a professional. I heard a woman laughing at me, as I rushed to the bathroom. I shut the cubicle door and threw up. I vomited all over the toilet seat. What did I tell Michael? Richard doesn't tolerate any form of scandal.

Everything I told Michael, everything I shared, he's going to use it against me. My price for my honesty.

On the way back to my office, I went past the kitchen and overheard a few of the men talking about me as they made their coffees.

'She's a stunner,' said one.

'Depends what your definition of stunning is. Her face is weird, but boy has she got great legs and arse. I'd fuck her,' said another.

'She's filthy.'

'I wonder who the lucky guy is.'

'Who cares who it is? Whoever he is, he's the man.'

'I feel sorry for her husband.'

'Her parents must be so proud.'

The men laughed and high-fived one another. Their laughter faded when they saw me. They dropped their heads and proceeded with their coffee. I hurried into my office and slammed the door shut behind me. I grabbed the plastic bottle filled with gin and drowned half of it. My heart was beating so fast, I thought I was going to have a heart attack. I checked my phone, and there were several text messages and missed calls from my mother, father, and Sylvie. Bastard! He sent the photos to my family and Sylvie as well! As if this is not devastating enough. How am I going to explain this to my parents?

My father-*What is going on?*

My mother-*Are you alright?*

My Mother-*Is this a joke?*

Sylvie- *Were you having an affair? Isn't that Mike?*
My Mother-*How Dare You!*
My Father-*What have you done!*
Sylvie- *Answer me!*
My father- *How could you! Your mother is in bed crying! Answer the bloody phone!*

None from Richard.

I dropped the phone on the floor. What if he sent these photos all over the internet? What if he has already? I considered what legal action I could take, and let out a cry of despair, pushing everything off my desk. Wendy opened the door and frowned at the broken laptop and papers strewn across the floor.

'Err... Mr. Williams wants to see you.' She said and shut the door.

Mr. Williams is the CEO of the firm. I stomped out of my office, taking deep breaths. Everything is slipping away, I'm finished. My marriage and career over. My reputation ruined. Everyone was judging me, as though nobody fucked in there. Everyone was a saint, except me, the drunken whore. After they get on with their day, they head to the pub, have a pint or two, and then afterward, behind closed doors, they fuck. Everyone fucks, it's natural. But, not everyone has photos taken without their consent for the whole world to see and has an affair, that's the difference. I breathed heavily as I marched back into the corridor.

'Here she comes,' someone said as I made my way to Mr. Williams's office.

He was speaking to someone on the phone.

'Yes, she's here, I call you later,' he said, and hung up, 'please sit down.'

'I'd rather stand,' I said, walking towards the window.

'The email you sent from the company's account, is disgusting.' he began.

'You have no idea what I'm going through,' I said to him.

There was a slight hesitation from him. 'You're right, I don't know.'

'So we are clear, I did not send that email. He hacked my account.'

'The *he*, you're referring to is the blond one in the photos?'

'Yes.'

'Mrs. Knight, what you do in your personal life is none of my business, but those photos were sent to your clients. Your clients have been calling, asking why their accountant sent them those photos. Can you imagine our embarrassment? You represent us.'

'So, you're firing me.'

'I'm sorry.'

'No, you're not sorry. I'll go and get my things.'

I'm sorry, but Mrs. Knight is out of the office, I'll put you through with...'

So, the word had already come out. I no longer worked there before it got to me first. The energy was sucked out of me. I could hardly breathe, it was like someone had their hands on my throat, gripping tighter, and tighter. Everything went dark.

When I came back around, faces stared down at me.

'Easy there, you fainted for a minute,' Charles said.

'Shall we get a doctor?' someone asked.

'No! No doctors, I'm fine,' I said, placing my hand on my forehead.

'Call her a cab to escort her home,' Charles ordered to someone.

'Leave me be. You don't give a damn about me.'

Charles lifted his hands as if to surrender. Someone offered a hand, but I slapped it away.

'Get away from me.' I shouted.

In the office, I put my broken laptop in a box, emptied my drawers of personal items, and, left my documents and workings behind. I picked up my phone from the floor. There were more text messages and missed calls from my parents and Sylvie. I didn't read any of them. Nothing from Richard. I collected the box and bag into my arms and walked out of my office, trying to be as composed as possible. Heads turned as I clomped out. *Don't look at anyone* I said to myself *don't look, ignore them, let them wonder*. I could almost hear Michael's victory, addressing the city.

Once outside, people hurried past me. At least out there, I didn't have to put up with people staring and making remarks. Out there, nobody knew about my humiliation. What I had done. Everyone had their problems, a meeting, a divorce, holidays to book, shopping that needs attention, a lover to meet. I hobbled two blocks, dropped the box on the pavement, and slammed my hands on the brick wall.

'*Fuck! Fuck! Fuck!*' my spit flew onto the wall, saliva dripping from my mouth.

A few people stopped to look at the corporate woman with a box by her feet losing her cool, swearing like an insane person.

I flipped my hair, picked the box up, and stomped down the street.

I didn't go home right away, knowing what waited for me there. I didn't want to face it, not yet. I wondered what Richard was doing, what my parents must have thought. Their confusion, their hearts ripped apart seeing their daughter in such fashion. Mum and Dad raised me to be well behaved, to be kind to people, disciplined, and grateful for what I have. Those photos are the opposite of what they taught me. There I was, their little girl with a much younger man.

I need to call a lawyer and see what legal actions I could take, but I don't want to deal with it right now. It's a devastating shock. In a matter of mere minutes, Michael has ruined my life. How did he manage to take those photos? He must have hidden a camera somewhere, set up a timer, and installed an app to capture our intimate moments. Who knows? What a despicable thing to do.

I went into the first pub I spotted and ordered a large house gin. I sat in the corner with the box by my side. I drained the gin, ordered another, and told the barman to keep them coming. I didn't know how long I stayed there, but it must have been for hours. The rush hour crowd gathered on the street, and in the pub. People going for a drink after work. I got a text from Sylvie.

Where are you?

I switched off my mobile and sipped on my drink. The room spun, and my vision blurred. That's all I remember.

16th July
Afternoon,
Diary,

As Sylvie told me, I got blind drunk, caused a scene at the pub, and yelled at the patrons asking them what they were looking at. I was so drunk I didn't open the door, I walked straight into it, and fell flat on my back. I have no memory of this. I don't recall Richard coming to pick me up either.

This morning, I checked my mobile and found my inbox bombarded with text messages. I searched the call history, and there it was... Michael's number. I called Mike! What did I tell him?

'Sylvie.' I shouted.

Sylvie stomped into the bedroom.

'What is it?'

'I called Mike... I called him, why?'

She sighed, trying to be patient with me. Sylvie is as angry and confused as everyone else is, but she's a friend when in desperate need of one.

'You've really burned your bridges haven't you?'

'Oh, what I have done?'

'It's when the world comes crumbling in, that's when we see ourselves as we actually are.'

'Oh please, tell me, what I did?'

'The barman told Richard you were shouting at someone on the phone. He said, and I quote: 'Listen, you son of a bitch...' was all he heard, you shouting drunken obscenities...' She ran her hand through her hair in frustration, dropped her hands to her side and glared at me, 'I can't believe you would do something like this!'

'Sylvie, you have to believe me. I did not send those photos.'

'This isn't just about the photos! You don't have any idea the hell I've been through these past twenty-four hours. I was at the shop, boxes everywhere, new stock to take out and merchandise. I nipped out for a fag to catch up on my emails. I nearly choked seeing those photos of my best friend rammed by some bloke. If that wasn't bad enough, I had to face a distraught husband asking me, if I knew about his wife's infidelity. You put me in a bad position, you must have known about those photos though?'

'No, I didn't even know they existed until yesterday.' I cried, 'he hacked my email.'

'Can you explain what you were thinking? How could you do that to Richard? He doesn't deserve this, he's a good man.'

'Mike knew about my drinking. I didn't feel any shame when I was around him. I could be myself with him, it's the only time in my life I felt I could be honest about who I am.'

'And you couldn't be honest with Richard or with me, but felt you could be honest with some kid? What on earth were you thinking?'

'I wanted him.'

'You. Wanted. Him,' she said, pacing up and down in the room, 'it takes a gorgeous young man, and everything goes out the windows, to let him do whatever he desires. Where is your sense of dignity, anyway? How could you degrade yourself?'

'Don't stand there and judge me, it's my body, not yours and certainly not his… I didn't think he would humiliate me like this. I don't expect you to understand.'

'Oh, how can you sit there and tell me that? I do understand perfectly well—just as I understood what my ex did. You put your marriage at risk for great sex.'

'The effect he had on me, how could I be so blind—'

'I don't want to listen to your infuriation concerning Mike, he cost you everything. You have to forget about him and focus on you and on your marriage.'

'I'm scared Sylvie I'm scared shitless. I don't know what he's going to do next.'

'He's done enough damage, as it is, there's nothing else he could do.'

Is it, though? He's after me, and I'm scared he won't stop until he sees me demolished completely.

She sat on the bed. 'When did it start?'

'After that night…'

She scowled at me. 'You've been having an affair with Mike all this time.'

'I was in over my head.'

'When I came for lunch, is that when it started?'

'The day after.'

'So it was him you were texting?'

'Yes.'

'Oh my God.'

'It was Jody that triggered me to go to him.'

'Who?'

'Jody, Richard's friend.'

'That miserable cow? What did she do?'

'She said I am useless because I didn't bear any children, only miscarriages.'

'That's a horrible thing to think, let alone say, but you having an affair doesn't justify that. You can't blame other people, Sop.'

'I know what happened that night. I didn't black out... I was attacked.'

'Attacked? Who attacked you?'

'Sam!'

'Sam attacked you?'

'In a way... I had sex with him.'

'You had sex with Sam? Jesus Christ, Sophie!'

'It's not as you think. At first, I didn't know what was happening, it happened so fast. I told him to stop, but he kept on going. Afterward, I slapped him, and he knocked me cold.'

'You should go to the police.'

'And do what?'

'Report him, this is serious. Does Richard know?'

I shook my head and sobbed on her chest. 'Where is Richard?'

'I haven't heard from him, I think he's with his lawyer.'

My heart sunk, he's hasn't faced me yet, and he's already at his lawyer's.

Sylvie stared at me. 'He's trying to see what legal actions he can take to make those photos disappear.'

'Not to file for divorce?'

Before Sylvie could answer me, the front door slammed shut. Sylvie left the room. I stayed on the bed unable to move.

'Richard, I don't know what to say...' Sylvie said, 'is there anything you need?'

'No, you've done enough, thank you. You can go home now. I can take it from here.'

Richard didn't come into the bedroom.

2:00am

Can't sleep. My eyes are bloodshot. I've got blemishes on my face, and my hair is brittle. I'm the creator of this mess.

I could hear *Moonlight Sonata* playing on the stereo in the living room. I went downstairs to make a cup of coffee. I had to get out of bed eventually and face Richard. He had the TV on silent and was watching a video clip he took a year ago when we were on holiday in Spain. The clip was of me wearing a red polka dot playsuit, running down the sandy beach, jumping around, and hands up in the air. I was so vibrant, young, and happy. What a difference a year makes. I ran back to him, stopped, mid-way, and did a cartwheel. Richard cheered on me, I laughed hard, my hands on my belly. I was carefree. It was as if I was watching another woman who looked like me, but wasn't me. I'm no longer a person but a thing. Since when did I allow myself to become this way? I have drifted into alcoholism and infidelity. Insubstantial, unreal, not quite there, a ghost. The song made the situation much worse. Tears fell down my cheeks. I wiped them away and turned off the stereo.

'Did you think you could go on and on?' Richard whispered, wiping the tears from his eyes.

'No,' I replied, dragging my feet to the kitchen, 'I didn't think that… it's over now.'

Richard's hand clutched the glass. I feared it would smash in his hands. He got up and followed me into the kitchen. I put the kettle on.

'Well ain't that a relief, let's open a bottle of champagne and celebrate, shall we?' He slammed the glass on the table, 'how could you do this to me?' Richard stared at me intensely. I removed the kettle and took out a wine glass from the cupboard. 'Well? What do you have to say for yourself?' he continued.

'… I just…'

'What?' he shouted. I turned my back to him and poured red wine into the glass. Richard stomped towards me 'what.'

'… I don't know.' I shouted.

'Do you have any idea what you've done? Can you even grasp what those photos did to us? It's all over, you know that, don't you? We are *finished*. Everything we have, our careers, our reputation all of it. Gone. You can't even imagine what you put me through, I'd rather lie, in the hospital bed than go through what I went through. I had to explain myself to my superiors, colleagues who respect me, and look up to me, why my wife sent an email with photos of herself with another man. Do you have any idea what that made me look like? I was laughed at, mocked. You made me look like a fool.' he roared.

'I didn't send that email.'

'I don't care who sent it, the damage is done. Not only have you taken yourself down, but you've taken me down with you. I spent this morning with my solicitors trying to find a way to make this matter disappear. Answer this for me, what were you thinking?'

'… I wanted him…'

His face turned red with rage. 'Do you think you're the only one who desires someone who's young? All of us do! But we deal with it!' He grabbed for a glass and threw it in the sink. It shattered.

I had nothing to say for myself.

He went on. 'I thought you were happy, I thought we were happy. I admit I wasn't bloody fabulous, but I was here, It's as though I'm married to a teenager, I never know what's on your mind. You're always distant. Were you unhappy?'

'… It happened.'

'Things like this don't happen by themselves, you make them happen. I don't know you anymore. If you wanted to destroy everything and humiliate me in the process, why didn't you do it with someone your own age?'

'So it's the age that bothers you.'

'Everything about it bothers me.' he yelled, grabbing my shoulder 'is that what you wanted, sex?' He shook me as if he wanted to snap the demon that possessed me to do something so horrible.

'It wasn't about sex.'

He let me go. 'He's twenty-two. What could you do with someone so young, if not for sex?'

Richard dropped his hand to his side.

'When we went to that restaurant, you were already sleeping with him?'

'No, he ended it.'

'I see, so it was going on before that. Then what?'

'You don't want to know.'

'Yes, I do damn it. I deserve that at least.'

'He came back to me when you were in New York.'

'And you took him up here, *here* in this apartment in *our bed*.'

Tears smeared down my cheeks. 'He followed me up here, I didn't invite him.'

'How many times did you bring him here?'

I stared down at the floor.

'Answer me!' he screamed, making me jump.

'Twice.'

'What on God's green earth were you thinking? He's. A. Child!'

'I can't stand this, if it were you who had an affair with a twenty-something girl, you would get a pat on the back, but if a woman does it, she's crucified.'

'He is a child.' he shouted, grabbing his hair, 'do you love him?'

'… I did once…'

'For Christ's sake!' he pointed his finger at me, 'I'm beyond done with the drinking and the smoking, you are going to rehab, I'll drag you by the hair myself if you don't go. I'm sick of you always drinking, I didn't think it was that bad, but now it's clear.'

I sat on the chair. He took the glass of wine from me. 'Starting from tonight.' he said.

We went quiet.

'Why?' he asked in a broken voice, with tears falling down his cheeks. 'Why?'

I crossed my hands and dropped my head to the floor. 'I don't know why.'

'Then find out!' he spat.

Our opera is in its final act, it's out in the open, the affair and my drinking problem. Richard slept on the sofa after eleven years of marriage.

Oh, Michael, you have a face of an angel, but you're not, you're a drama queen, you want flowers and parades, and now you have it. You're not a face from heaven. You stand on the stage as if you are God making slaves of women, and in an instant, you saw this heart of mine and transformed into my deepest desires. To Sam, you are a friend. To me, you were a lover, and you devoured all of us. You're a snake, a monster. You're a hazard, a predator, a piranha, and destroyer of lives. You're danger itself. I can picture you right now, locked away in your flat like a bird of prey in a gilded cage. You want to go after me. Fine, I deserve it, but sending those photos to my work, and to Richard's, was a step too far. I only did what I thought was right. You don't care, but I do. Oh Michael, you conquered me, were the emperor of my desires, and now you are the ruler of my life. Your mission is to demolish me and take Richard along with it. You are the earthquake that shook my ground, and I am the victim of that wreckage. I hope you are pleased with yourself, you are running my life.

17th July
Evening,
Diary,

Richard doesn't even want to look at me, not that I blame him. I have been avoiding him for good reasons. He locked himself in his study once. It was supposed to be a nursery for the two babies we didn't have.

I heard Richard cough, and arguing on the phone with someone, his lawyers, I presume.

Richard came into the kitchen while I was cooking; he's the kind of man that makes his importance known, pompous, and proud. But right now, he looks so small and defeated. To his colleagues, and to me, Richard was the man with authority. He demanded respect, but now he's an object to mock and ridicule. His face, hard, and annoyed.

'Sophie, if you were unhappy, why didn't you tell me?'

'I told you I wasn't happy.'

'But something triggered it, I'm racking my brains here trying to find out why. Was it the miscarriages? Because we didn't have a child? Because I refused counseling and to adopt? It has to be one of them at least,' he said.

I lit a cigarette and made my way to the window. 'Please stop.'

'Were you hoping he'd get you pregnant?' he shouted.

I heard myself laugh *ha ha ha*, 'I wish you could hear yourself, Richard, how ridiculous you sound.'

'If I see him, this boy, I'll kill him with my bare hands. He took you away from me. He stole you from me, and you let him.'

'There's going to be no killing of anyone,' I said, moving away from the window.

'I'll kill you too,' he said.

I have always been the pretty wife Richard showed off to his friends, the prize, the trophy. I always hated that about him. It's sexist and overbearing. Every time we went to a dinner party or an event, the other wives raised their eyebrows. I knew what they were thinking, that doll of a wife married him for his money. It's not the money, it was never about that, they seemed to forget I have my own career. Something else I have to battle with every day, being a woman with a career-trying to prove to myself in a male-dominated world.

'He's a great looking chap, isn't he?' he said.

'Don't do this, Richard. His beauty and body had nothing to do with it.'

'His looks and body have everything to do with this!' he said, 'oh yes, it does. I see it now, why you're always preoccupied and miles away, it wasn't work, it was him. It was all about him. That boy.'

'Yes, but he's a twenty-two-year-old boy.'

'My world, my passion had been my work, I took pride in what I did, and you are my world. I thought I was your world and passion too, but I was wrong. For you, it's this Swedish musician, this Michael. You put him on a pedestal -nobody deserves to be there, not even me, but you placed him in there, and it's cost you everything. You were prepared to risk it all for him. He's worth it, you must have thought—'

'Richard, please—'

'Let me bloody finish, I deserve to speak. You've taken everything from me. I will have this moment, you will give me this. He's your world, your passion.' His gaze passed through me as if I were invisible.

I shook my head in disbelief.

He sighed. 'You made me look like a fool. If it were another man, he would have thrown you out in the street by now, but I am not that kind of man. I think it's best until I decide what I'm going to do with this…' he paused, 'you find a place to stay, you can stay with Sylvie, your parents, or with him. Live in a cardboard box for all I care. I'm going to give you a week until you figure it out but, I don't want you here. Looking at you is painful enough but bearing your presence would be intolerable, do you understand?'

'Yes…'

'Good.'

19th July
Afternoon,
Diary,

Looking back at the pages I have written, the changes have been dramatic since the beginning of the year. I had the job, the apartment, and the husband, and now I have nothing. Now, I know what it feels like to lose what I own and love. All because of Michael. However, nobody forced me to jump into bed with him.

Richard has the upper hand, and now he's twisting the knife. As if I don't feel bad enough. I don't need to listen to his remarks and disapprovals, or his *you did this, now you'll have to suffer the consequences of your actions,* face. I'm the tart who humiliated him with a younger man.

20th July
Afternoon
Diary,

With everything that has been going on, I haven't had the time to reply to any of the texts or emails. It was the last thing on my mind, I haven't even bothered to look for a place to stay.

Nobody believes me. Everyone thinks I got drunk, and sent the photos. How could I, when I wasn't even aware of their existence? If Michael had told me he wanted to take pictures of me, I would have refused. I opened the first photo of me on my knees and then built up enough courage to go through them all. Most of them were taken when I spent the weekend at his place. Is that why he wanted me to spend the night? Maybe it was him, playing with my doorknob to frighten me, knowing I'd go straight to him. The photos are a gesture of his hate and hate breeds like bacteria.

Richard still hasn't gone to the doctor, no matter how many times I've told him, and now, with all that's happened, it's the last thing on his mind. He's slept on the armchair in his study for two nights in a row.

The sound of the buzzer raged through the apartment, and Richard went to the door, coughing and mumbling to himself. I buried my head under the pillow.

'She's asleep,' Richard said.

'The hell with you, you will not dictate when I will see my own daughter. You've kept us apart long enough.'

It was my mother. I didn't want to see her, the wounds were still fresh and my shame too raw.

'I'm not stopping you, Pat,' He sighed, 'It's just that she's resting.'

'Out of my way, Richard, if you let her visit more often none of this would have happened.'

'How is this my fault, damn it. I've never kept her from visiting you, she's a grown woman and can do whatever she wants, and she proved it. How dare you?' he roared at my mother, 'how dare you blame me for your daughter's infidelity. Are you trying to tell me, it's my fault she jumped in bed with another man? Is that what you are trying to tell me?' he yelled.

The yelling, the shouting, the accusations, I can't take any more.

'I made sure she had a life fit for a queen. I treated your daughter with the utmost respect. And what did I get in return?'

'Respect? Oh, please Richard, you hardly listened to her, have you considered what those miscarriages might have done to her? She suggested counseling, and you refused. She suggested adoption, and you refused. You call that respect? Didn't you even stop for one second to think how all of this had affected her, didn't you think something was wrong? Did you? It's always about putting up a good front with you, always in denial. Maybe if you listened, if you had stopped being so selfish and compromised with her, she wouldn't have gone and sought comfort from him in the first place.'

'Did you come here to torment me, is that it? You've always resented me. To hell with it Pat, damn you to hell.'

'Look, I'm not justifying her behavior. I understand you're upset.'

'Of course, I am bloody upset.'

I got out of bed and went into the hallway. Richard looked at me, and then at my mom. Her eyes shone with tears, and she had dark circles under her eyes. It breaks my heart to see her like this. This is all my doing. I hurt the people I love and care about, in exchange for my selfish desire. Dad wasn't with her. Maybe he is too disgusted to see me, yet.

'Mom…'

'Sophie…'

I inherited my mother's looks and wide face, her hair is slightly lighter than mine. We have the same eyes, but she's slightly shorter than I am.

'I'll let you two talk,' Richard said, and left.

Despite the puffy eyes and sallow skin, she was dressed impeccably in a black blouse and navy blue pencil skirt. I wished I could see her in much happier times. I could barely look at her in the eye.

'Would you like some tea?' I asked.

'Tea would be nice,' she said.

I put the kettle on and took out two mugs from the cupboards. I didn't know where to start.

'What you did, it's…' Mum trailed off.

'I didn't know it would…'

Her eyes narrowed. 'You didn't know what? That it would hurt us? It didn't occur to you how this would make me feel, seeing my daughter, my only child, in that fashion. Didn't you think about how it would make me feel? How your father must have felt? I didn't get out of the bed for days.'

Did I think about how my parents would feel? Yes, I did, but I didn't know they would find out like this either. My mum took out a tissue from her bag and blew her nose. The kettle boiled, and I made tea for both of us.

'I'm sorry.'

'This is not how I raised my child, to jump in bed with another man when the going gets tough. To see you in those photos. What were you thinking?'

I sat on the chair, ignited a cigarette avoiding eye contact 'I was… lonely.'

Her eyes grew so wide, like they were going to pop out of their sockets, 'You and Richard have been having problems for years. You were more than happy to ignore them, both of you. It's because of the miscarriages.'

'Mom please.'

'It's good to talk sometimes.'

'What do you want me to say? I got pregnant twice, but I didn't become a mother.'

'So you went off and had an affair?'

'No, I didn't plan to have an affair,' I said as tears fell down my cheeks.

'Did you send those photos?' Mum asked.

'No, I didn't know they existed,' I replied, mashing the cigarette on the ashtray and kindled another.

Mum scowled at me. 'So he sent them?'

'That's what I suspect.'

'And what legal action are you going to take?'

'Richard is taking care of it.'

'Is he now?'

'Mom, please stop blaming Richard, it's not his fault, it's mine, okay.'

'I would like to say he's not to blame, but he should have taken you more seriously, instead of keeping up appearances. He's such a phony.'

Mum took a sip of her tea. "Richard wants me out by the end of the week.'

'So he's kicking you out like an old dog,' Mum said.

'Can you blame him?'

A pause. 'No.'

'Where you're going to live?'

'I'll find a place. I have money.'

She didn't offer me to stay with her. The only place I want to be right now is at my parents, in my old bedroom with its single bed, the stuffed toys, and the dollhouse. Although she didn't say to me up front, I sensed she was telling me *you're on your own*.

23rd July
Evening,
Diary,

Sylvie told me I could stay with her until I figure out my next move. She also told me we could talk about the affair. To be honest, I don't want to go through trivial details of my relationship with Michael with her. I want to forget it ever happened.

Along with the assault, I want to erase it all from my mind.

I haven't seen Sam snooping around my neighborhood recently. It seems only Evelyne and Andy are living in the apartment now. Richard still looks green and ill but doesn't want to do anything about it.

'I don't care anymore. I'm sickened by what you did, and you're killing me slowly,' he said.

I didn't press the subject anymore. What can I say after my husband tells me something like that? The truth of the matter is, I am killing him slowly, and it tears me apart. Richard isn't home a lot, he leaves early and comes back home late. The apartment has become an empty hotel. Richard and I are two strangers that pass by without acknowledging one another. The ghost apartment. Everything is cold and white.

I'm waiting for him to say… I want a divorce.

25th July
Evening,
Diary,

I don't know where to start. Today was a nightmare come to life. It was past noon, and Richard still wasn't up. It was unlike him to stay in bed so late. I thought it was odd, but I spent a bit of time cleaning up the kitchen, it was the least I could do. I looked at our wedding photo in the living room. In October, it would have been our twelfth wedding anniversary, but there won't be any celebrations this year. I carried the photo with me to the guest bedroom and packed it along with my belongings. My life packed in an oversized handbag. It's amazing how many things I need, but I don't use everything I own. I scanned the apartment taking in all the memories.

There was nothing left to do but to inform Richard. I didn't think he'd mind if I went without telling him, but it seemed the decent thing to do.

I knocked on his door.

No response.

I knocked again.

Nothing.

I entered the darkened room and saw Richard laying there. The hairs on the back of my neck stood on end, and a cold sweat swept over me.

'Richard?'

Silence answered me back. I opened the curtains and turned around.

'Richard, I don't mean to disturb you, but- '

I froze, Richard was lying on the bed, motionless. His chest wasn't rising and falling, and there was a curious stiffness about how his shoulders rested on the pillow.

'Richard?' the sound of my own voice made me shiver.

I gasped. The color had gone from his face, and his lifeless eyes stared back at me. It was as if he could see me, but couldn't blink. I touched his hand, it was stone cold. There was a brownish liquid on the pillow.

Richard is dead. Everything rushed through my mind at once. What did he die of? How long has he been gone? Did he call out, but I didn't hear him? Question after question.

There was an empty glass of water on the bedside table. I remained bewildered, incapable of grasping the suddenness of his death. He died all alone. It felt like the world had stopped. Like nothing was real, but I knew I couldn't just stay there. I had to do something. I went over to the door and took another look at him. His eyes seemed to stare back at me. And then all the emotions, anxiety, and fear took possession of me. I somehow managed to call his GP. I don't know how, because I could barely grip the phone, I was shaking that much. As the doctor's receptionist answered, I heard myself scream.

'My husband is dead.'

Dr. Frank Williams is in his fifties and a good friend of Richard. He greeted me with a hug, and I rested my head on his shoulders and cried.

'Did you inform your family or friends to be with you?' he asked.

I shook my head. 'I suggest you do it, where is he?'

'In the master bedroom.'

Without saying a word, he marched through the bedroom. I sat on the sofa and smoked and wept.

I can't get the image of Richard out of my head. I've killed him. I caused this, his heart was too weak to handle such stress. He died of a broken heart. I could feel my heart beating in my breast like a metronome. Frank hurried out of the bedroom, without saying a word, and grabbed the phone.

I stood up. 'Is something wrong?'

I stared at him teary-eyed.

'Yes, I need someone to come here right away,' he said into the receiver.

'Sophie, you should sit down,' he instructed after he hung up.

'What's wrong?'

I covered my mouth with my hands to prevent myself from screaming. Was Richard still alive? For a moment, there was a surge of relief, my husband was going to be alright.

'I should inform you, I'm not certain about the cause of death, but it's not a heart attack, there's vomit on the sheets.'

'I don't understand.'

'And that means I can't issue a death certificate. It's out of my hands. The police are on their way.'

It's like I'm living in a bad dream and can't wake up. The ambulance arrived, followed by the police. Frank answered a few questions and left. Another well-dressed police officer entered the scene. He introduced himself as detective Thomas Blake. I'm under so much stress. I can't believe Richard is dead. Detective Blake wanted me to go down to the station. I don't understand.

If Richard didn't die of a heart attack, what caused his death? Why was vomit on the sheets?

At the police station, a female officer came into the questioning room and placed a mug of coffee in front of me. She looked more like a model than a police officer. Blake introduced her as his partner, Miranda Gibbins. I asked if I could smoke, Blake nodded.

'Mrs. Knight, you're the one who found your husband?' he asked.

'Yes, I thought it was odd he slept so late. I went to check up on him and…' I replied, twisting the tissue in my hand.

'What did you do after that?'

'Richard had problems with his heart. He was a sick man, so I called his GP right away.'

'Were there any signs of his sickness, recently?'

'Yes, coughing, loss of appetite, and his skin became sallow.'

'You were in the apartment all day, today?'

'Yes.'

'And last night, did you stay in?'

'Yes.'

'Do you remember what time it was when you last saw your husband alive?'

'Around… eleven thirty, he left the study and went to bed.'

'Did anything seem odd to you about your husband?'

'As I said he was not feeling well lately, he seemed rather confused and sleepy.'

'Since you were aware of his sickness, why you didn't call a doctor?' he asked.

'He got angry with me when I brought up the subject,' I said, wiping the tears from my eyes with the tissue.

'And you never called him a doctor despite his refusal?' Miranda asked gently.

'No.'

'You didn't hear or see anything suspicious or out of the ordinary?'

'No…'

'Your husband was on medication, wasn't he?'

'Yes, he took pills for his heart,' I said.

'How long you've been married?'

'Eleven years.'

'Can you think of anyone who might want to harm your husband?'

I shook my head. 'No.'

'Mrs. Knight, there's a bag in the guest bedroom. It has your belongings in it, were you planning to go somewhere?'

I didn't know how to explain it without sounding suspicious.

'I was going to stay with a friend.'

'You and Mr. Knight were having problems?' Miranda asked.

'Yes.'

'I see.' she said.

There was something in Blake's expression I didn't like. 'And what are the problems you were having?'

I had no choice but to tell them the truth.

'I was having an affair, and Richard found out.'

Miranda raised her eyebrows at me. 'And the name of your lover?'

'Michael Frisk.'

'Frisk, it's not English surname,' Blake said.

'No, he's Swedish,' I replied.

'How long were you having this affair?' she asked.

'Five months.'

'It's been bought to my attention that your husband inherited a large sum of money last year after his mother died, right?' Blake said.

'Yes, he came from a wealthy family,' I said.

How did they find this out so quickly? And why this was even relevant?

'Was he insured?' Miranda asked.

'Yes.'

'Who is the beneficiary?'

'I am.'

'Sole beneficiary?' Blake asked.

They think I killed my husband for money, so I could access all of his money and run off with my lover. My body trembled as my world was falling apart. With a shaking hand, I picked up another cigarette. Miranda fired it up for me.

'Are you suggesting I killed my husband?' I asked, 'how dare you.' I said in outrage, 'I want a lawyer.'

'We're trying to help you,' Blake said.

'Am I free to go?'

'Yes.'

I was let go after that. The apartment is a crime scene so I can't go back there. I called Sylvie and she came to pick me up. I dissolved into tears. She wrapped her arms around me and consoled me, telling me everything was going to be okay. I keep thinking Blake will come back any minute with a warrant of my arrest.

27th July,
Afternoon,
Diary,

I sat in Sylvie's living room with my parents. Sylvie brought a tray with tea and placed it on the coffee table. She took a seat beside me and took my hand.

'The police think he was murdered. How is it even possible?' my mom asked.

'That's what they lead me to believe,' I replied.

'I can't believe it, who could have done this?' Mum helped herself to a cup of tea.

'I don't know, Mum, but the police think it's me,' I said.

'Oh dear god.' Mum blurted.

'Have you hired a solicitor yet?' Dad asked.

'I'm looking for one, do you know of anyone?'

Mum and Dad looked at each other. 'Yes, I do.' Dad replied. He took his mobile from his pocket. 'Don't talk to the police. Whatever you say they can hold it as evidence.'

The lawyer arrived shortly after. His name was Jonathan Hayes.

'Whatever you do,' he said, 'don't speak to the police without me present. You have the right remain silent and don't nod or shake your head. No signs of body language.'

I went to the police station for more questioning. This time accompanied by Jonathan but it didn't reassure me. The police, or at least the detective, think I did it.

The same questions seemed to go over and over. Asking me to repeat stories about Richard and Michael. It feels obscene.

Michael must have been interviewed by Blake and told him about my drinking, which made me look even worse. Mike, you and your big mouth, you won't stop until you see me rot.

'Mrs. Knight, we got the results from the autopsy. Your husband didn't die of natural causes, he died of sodium hypochlorite poisoning. Your husband was murdered,' Blake said.

I buried my face in my hands while Jonathan looked at the report. Miranda kept looking at me. Observing. Studying me.

'What's that?' I asked.

'Your husband was poisoned,' Miranda said.

Sodium hypochlorite. The room spun, how on earth could Richard have been murdered.

'It's not possible,' I said, with tears spilling down my eyes.

I suddenly felt his eyes studying mine for signs. They thought I did it. Me, the prime suspect in a murder investigation.

It's natural they think I did it, the wife or the husband is always the prime suspect. I began to sweat. I glanced at Jonathan, and he gave me a subtle nod.

'I was receiving notes.'

Miranda leaned forward. 'What kind of notes?'

'I called the police, and they came out to visit me, but the police officer didn't make a statement. They thought the notes were a prank. We also got mysterious phone calls. The silent type.'

'Were the notes targeted to you and your husband?'

'To me.'

'Have you kept them?'

'I kept two of them.'

Blake looked at Miranda with some kind of mutual understanding between them. She nodded and left the room.

'Was your husband aware of your drinking?' Blake asked.

'He made remarks.'

'And your lover knew?'

'Knew what?'

'About your drinking?'

'Yes.'

'And not so long ago you had a quarrel with Michael about photographs you had sent yourself?'

'I suggest you withdraw. No evidence indicates my client had the photographs,' Jonathan said, 'Mr. Knight was working with his lawyers, you can contact them.'

'We are working on that but there is no evidence Michael sent the photos, and hacking into someone's emails is a crime.' Blake said.

I couldn't believe this. 'What are you going to ask her next, that my client sent the notes to herself and called herself?' Jonathan asked Blake.

'I haven't said that, Mr. Hayes.'

'My client had been attacked, and someone sent her those notes,' Jonathan said.

'What happened?' Blake asked.

I told Blake what Sam did to me, the misplaced key, and everything else. After I finished, Blake leaned forward at his desk and gave me a stern look.

'Wait, you're telling me Mike's friend… this Sam, hit you after a drunken one night stand and you had an affair with Mike, and now you are accusing Mike of hacking into your email. Meanwhile, one of his friends was sending you notes and making anonymous calls?'

How must I look in Blake's eyes, a drunk who claims to have been assaulted by a bloke, has an affair with his friend, and a husband who winds up poisoned to death, after finding out about her affair. He must think I'm the biggest whore in town.

'I didn't know at the time because I had no recollection of what happened. I have my dress in my closet, it's soiled, and it's also torn from the shoulder, you can have a look if you like.'

'Why didn't you report it sooner?' Blake asked.

'I just told you, I couldn't remember at the time. I had memory loss after it happened. I did make a report after I received one of those notes, but the police didn't take me seriously.' I said, exasperated.

'I will look into this,' he said.

It was clear, he was convinced I had killed Richard. 'Please do,' I said.

He sighed and shook his head. 'Mrs. Knight, let's say Michael had sent those photos, why would he do that?'

'Because I ended the affair. He's bitter and wants to humiliate me and cause problems with my husband, that's why. And what about the key I found misplaced in my bag?'

'Keys get misplaced all the time, you could have misplaced it yourself.'

'I am not crazy, I'm positive I placed it in the right pocket.'

'Back to your affair... Michael said you were planning to leave your husband to be with him?'

'No, I loved my husband, the affair was a mistake.'

'But Michael said otherwise, and I quote reading from his notes, "she had become impossible, her drinking was out of control. She has deep emotional issues. She told me constantly she'd leave her husband so we could be together. I tried to break it off, but she wouldn't have it."'

I glanced at Jonathan with my mouth gaped open. 'I suggest you stop with this line of questioning. My client is telling the truth.'

Blake sighed. 'Fine. We're done here.'

Out of the police station, Jonathan told me he's going to prepare me for further questioning. We need to go through everything that happened and start to gather evidence. This has made me alarmed, though Jonathan assured me not to be, I can't help it.

30th July
Afternoon,
Diary,

I sit alone, petrified. I can't help feeling I'm next. I'm trying to think of someone who would want to wish Richard harm? Richard didn't have enemies, or at least not the kind that would want him dead. I'm so helpless, I can't go anywhere. Richard died in the apartment, and only I was there. It makes me a prime suspect.

Who could have done this? I peered out of the window. They are watching me, including the journalists who keep stalking outside Sylvie's apartment trying to photograph me. I can't turn on the TV without seeing my face. They think I did it too. The drunken wife and cheater. I look like an asshole to the public, the most hated woman in Britain, and I didn't even do anything. There was a headline on a local talk show hosted by Olivia Gilmore, a famous TV personality, which said:

Did she? Or Didn't she?

She showed a clip of Michael walking down the street dressed in black trousers, a T-shirt of Bridget Bardot, a red blazer, and sunglasses. He was ignoring the questions from reporters, the next headline said

Blond Bombshell Michael Frisk Sophie's Knight former lover.

He walked over to the car that was waiting for him, with his head down.

'What made you have an affair with Mrs. Knight knowing she was married?' A journalist asked.

As he stepped into the car, he answered, 'I fancied her.'

I bet he loved being called a bombshell by Olivia Gilmore. I couldn't bear to watch, she hasn't ever met me. Who is she to make judgments? I am innocent. I didn't kill Richard.

I'm drowning, I've never felt this alone in my life. I can't answer any more questions from my lawyer or the police. It's like I'm in a movie I don't want to be in. How am I going to prove my innocence?

3rd August
Evening,

Poison, the woman's weapon, also known as the coward's weapon. Everything is slipping away, I'm writing this on a few pieces of paper I asked for in the police station. I am in custody charged with Richard's murder. Blake came with the warrant for my arrest. I'm waiting for Jonathan to do something. The police found bleach in the kitchen cupboard under the sink. The bottle was almost empty. I couldn't believe my ears. I don't keep washing products under the sink. I put them near the washing machine. Along with the bleach were plastic tubes and a turkey baster. One of them was used. Both had my fingerprints, and Richard's DNA was on the turkey baster. My diary was taken from me and placed in an evidence bag. I'm glad they have it, they'll find out the truth now.

Another interview took place, which took forever. They also found sodium hypochlorite in Richard's aftershave. I pleaded with them, I am innocent, but it was of no use. They are not going to believe me, why should they? I'm the woman with a drinking problem who cheated on her husband. In their eyes, I'm a liar. They want the facts, the evidence, but they don't understand, it was planted there. I'm being framed. When Blake told me the aftershave contained poison, it all came to me. I recall finding the aftershave misplaced after Michael had been in the apartment.

'In your diary entry, you wrote that you found the aftershave misplaced?'

'Yes, along with my key.'

Then it came to me, like someone punched me on the face.

'It can't be,' I said, 'impossible!'

But it is possible and makes perfect sense. The puzzle is coming together, I have been so blind. The aftershave and the key were misplaced, it was *Mike*. He had planned it all along. If only I had realized?

He played us like his puppets on a string. The saddest part is that Richard is dead. Michael killed Richard and framed me for his murder. I see it now. Why didn't Michael go after me, why did Richard have to suffer, an innocent man? How could someone do something like this? He wanted to ruin my life, and he succeeded.

An affair and murder are similar. You'll need three tools to be successful:

The right person—me the drunk, an excellent candidate to have a relationship with, and to frame for murder.

Opportunity—my drinking.

Motive—his jealous rage.

Who was sending those notes? I have no proof, because Michael covered his tracks so well. My hands are trembling from not having a drink. The horror is sinking in. I'm going to prison for a long time.

5th August
Morning,

The judge refused bail, so I am here, in custody, like a criminal. Jonathan prepared me for what's coming.

'Do you think I killed him?' I asked Jonathan.

He paused for a while. 'The first rule of being a solicitor is what you think doesn't matter.'

'It matters to me,' I said.

'No, but it's not me we have to convince, it's the jury.'

My life, my freedom, and my innocence depend on the jury's verdict. I sit here recalling my old life before the affair, how serene it was. Jonathan told me, we have to gather witnesses for the case. I asked if Michael will testify. He said he might. He is going to crush me in the courtroom, and I'll have to sit there and take it.

10th August
Evening,

My husband is dead, my career is finished, and my life is over. All that's left is for me to die. I have nothing to live for anymore. A man who looks like an angel has cost me everything. Nothing can save me from that fate now. I could get a minimum of thirty years for something I didn't do.

Things are moving quickly as I move closer to my fate. Today, was my first day on trial. I was taken by a police van where I was escorted inside with my hands in cuffs like a criminal. The flashbulbs of the paparazzi surrounded me, as I was led through a dark corridor. We went into a courtroom. I have never been inside one before. I watched the jury as they filed in, all different in age, gender, and ethnicity. Those people would decide my future. And today was my first chance to try to convince them of my innocence.

The room moved when the judge walked in, he was an elderly man wearing a robe and a wig. He climbed the steps to an altar.

I can't write often, it will only be a matter of time before I have to stop. I'm so scared. I can't bear prison, let alone to be there for something I didn't do. I don't talk to any of the inmates in there, not even the woman I share the room with. She's in for selling drugs, and I've heard them whisper to one another *The Husband Killer*.

The prosecutor addressed the jury. 'Ladies and gentlemen of the jury, you'll hear ironclad proof of Mrs. Knight's guilt and evidence from the night of 25th of July. Sophie Knight poisoned her husband Richard Knight.'

Ms. Taylor is a snotty woman around my age, with long blonde hair, brown eyes, and flat cheekbones.

They put forward versions about how I plotted to kill my husband. Ms. Taylor's theory is I've been poisoning Richard's aftershave. That I had a lot to drink that night, killed him. My story was going to sound colorful, but I had to give it my all. I will not sit in a cell for the next twenty or so years, I'd hire a private investigator if necessary. I will come out as a free woman and prove Michael did it.

The judge nodded, and the barrister addressed the jury. They all looked at me with curiosity.

Sylvie turned up to testify. She was tastefully dressed in a designer grey suit.

'Ms. Edwards, how long have you known the defendant?' Ms. Taylor asked.

'Fifteen years.'

'So you're good friends?'

'Yes, we're close.'

'And you didn't know she has a drinking problem?'

'Objection!' Jonathan said.

The Judge addressed Sylvie. 'Sustained, answer the question.'

'Well... she did drink here and there, but it didn't occur to me she had a drinking problem.'

'And she stayed with you when she and her husband were having problems?'

'Yes.'

'Did you know she was having an affair?'

'I found out through an email.'

'So, you didn't know about that before?'

She shook her head. 'No.'

'So, you're not that close then?'

'Yes, we are.'

'How would you describe Mrs. Knight's marriage?'

'Stable, she took care of Richard when he got sick, she's nurturing and loving.'

'If her marriage was stable, why would she have an affair?'

'I don't know.'

'Do you believe Sophie knight murdered her husband?'

'No.'

20th August
Evening,

Michael loves every bit of this, I couldn't bear it to see him sit there and lie to the jury. Especially, when he told the court about my drinking.

'She always asked me to give her a drink,' Michael said.

'Did you give her any?' Ms. Taylor asked.

'No, she used to go to the pub down the road from where I live.'

'How did you know this?'

'I went there to get her myself.'

'I see… and you ended the affair, right?'

'Yes.'

'How did she take it?'

'Not well.'

'Did she got angry, threaten you? Showed signs of violent behavior?'

'She was angry but didn't threaten me, no.'

'What happened then?'

'I didn't see her for a month or so… then, I saw her and….'

'And what?'

He lowered his eyes. Oh, he was good.

'And what? You had sex?' she asked.

'Yes.'

'I see…did she mention her husband to you?' Ms. Taylor asked, pacing down the courtroom.

'Yes.'

She turned to him. 'What did she say?'

'That she was unhappy, that she wanted to leave him. She *hated* him.'

I wanted to take off my shoes, throw them at him, and yell 'liar!' I glanced at Jonathan who listened intently without objecting to what the persecutor was asking Michael.

'Hate, that's a strong word.'

'That's what she said.'

'And she was going to leave her husband to be with you?'

'Yes,' he said.

There were whispers from the court. The judge banged his gavel.

'No further questions,' she said.

'You didn't seem to mind she was married, you still went after her, didn't you?' Jonathan asked, standing up and buttoning up his blazer.

'Well, I liked her,' Michael replied.

'And why not? Mrs. Knight is a stunning woman. But, you kept making advances even when she told you many times she wasn't interested.'

'Objection!'

'Overruled... answer the question,' the judge said.

'That's not th
e impression she gave me,' Michael said.

'All of this happened after the night Sophie had suffered from memory loss. Was she with you and your friends the night before?'

'Yes, she was.'

Jonathan turned to the court. 'Item eighteen, ladies and gentleman, is the dress Sophie wore that night she had her memory loss.'

The dress have been forensically examined. I had high hopes the forensics would find traces of DNA on it but to my dismay, nothing.

Jonathan advanced to the table, 'are you aware she kept a diary?'

Mike's face remained composed. 'No, I wasn't.'

Jonathan paced around the courtroom. 'Yes ladies and gentleman of the jury, Mrs. Knight kept a diary. Item twenty-one. I'm going to read some passages from the diary for the jury.'

He turned to the jury. 'The diary has *you* written all over it.' He turned to Michael who sat there frozen.

'Objection how is this relevant to Mrs. Knight killing her husband?' Ms. Taylor asked.

'Sustained,' the judge said.

'She kept every record of every encounter she had with you.' Jonathan told Michael.

He read from the diary. 'You ran to her in the street, and you told her, and I quote,' "You never said you're happily married." Did you or didn't you say those exact same words to my client?'

'I did, yes. As I said, I was attracted to her.'

'So much you left her a note at her mailbox, didn't you? Item twenty-three,' he said. Michael squirmed. Jonathan showed the note to him, 'Isn't this your handwriting?'

He peeked at the note and wrinkled his nose with disgust. 'Yes.'

'What was your intention?'

'I liked her company.'

'You barely knew Mrs. Knight, and you enjoyed her company? On the other hand, you had a friend to protect? Is that why you seduced Mrs. Knight? Is that why you sent her notes?'

'Objection Argumentative!'

'I'll allow it,' the judge replied.

Mike's face turned white. 'What notes? I didn't send her any notes.'

Jonathan reached for the notes. 'You weren't aware the notes existed? Item sixteen.'

'No, I wasn't.'

'You didn't write her notes' Jonathan said.

'No, I did not.'

Jonathan went to table, gathered the note, and walked over to Mike. 'Can you read the note to the jury?'

'*You're making a huge mistake. Look around you, and you'll find the truth.*' Michael read it in a composed manner.

'Doesn't that note look familiar to you?' Jonathan asked, pacing up and down.

'No.'

'Did you also repeatedly call her house? And did you pushed her into an oncoming car?'

'Objection.'

'Who sent them? Your friends? Is that why you hacked her email and sent discriminating photographs to her colleagues and family, to humiliate her?'

'Objection. What is the point of this?'

'Get to the point,' the judge said.

'Did you threaten her? Mrs. Knight was receiving notes that upset her. Did you send them to her to scare her?'

'No, I did not. I never sent her any notes, and no I didn't make any phone calls to her house, how could I? I didn't have her home number.'

I scanned the courtroom and did a double take, Andy was there at the back listening to Mike, shaking his head with disbelief. Did he come with Mike? Does he know I didn't do it?

25th August
Afternoon,

Today Jonathan told me the police are getting anonymous phone calls asking for Blake. The callers told him I didn't kill my husband, and that if they look more closely, the truth is there. Blake isn't the kind to let something like this be ignored. However, he's more than happy to ignore everything I told him. In his eyes, I'm a drunk, and a fantasist even. Who's making the anonymous calls?

I lost my job, my license, and my reputation. I have nothing to live for. Even if, by a sort of miracle, I am proven innocent, there'll always be the suspicion. Did she, or didn't she?

My neighbor, Mr. Smith's testimony, helped a little.

'You saw Mrs. Knight and her lover go to her apartment?'

'Yes, she opened the door, and they walked in,' Mr. Smith said.

'What was your reaction?' Ms. Taylor asked.

'I was shocked, but it was none of my business.'

'Were you aware Mrs. Knight and her husband were having problems?'

'No, they seemed fine to me. That's why I found it odd to see her with another man.'

'Did you hear them argue, shout?'

'No, nothing of that sort, they are decent people. If they argued they made sure they weren't being heard.'

'Were you aware Sophie has a drinking problem?'

'I saw her in the neighborhood buying wine, and sometimes she seemed off.'

'In what way off?'

'Unsteady walks, slurring in her speech.'

'Did you hear anything odd the night Mr. Knight was killed?'

'No, I didn't.'

'Were you surprised she killed her husband?'

'Yes, most surprised. Sophie always seemed loving and nurturing to her husband, she took care of him.'

'No further questions.'

30th August
Afternoon,

It was my turn to testify today, and I knew what was coming. Jonathan told me to stay calm. The strange thing was, I felt calm. This is the most horrifying experience of my life, and I am calm.

'Mrs. Knight, you heard the testimony presented to this court and your explanation is someone killed your husband?' Ms. Taylor asked.

'That's correct.'

'Well let's consider the possibilities. Did a ghost murder your husband?'

'Objection!' Jonathan said.

'Aliens perhaps?'

'Objection! Is Ms. Taylor questioning the witness or making a closing argument?'

'Withdrawn,' she said.

'I told you what happened,' I said.

'Yes, you told us you were asleep. Maybe you were sleepwalking when you killed him. Or perhaps drunk?'

'Objection!'

Tears fell down my cheeks. 'I loved my husband, and I didn't kill him.'

'Is that why you were having an affair? Is that your undying love for your husband, Mrs. Knight? And now you blame your lover when he was seen in a club full of people, the same person you blamed for hacking the emails you sent yourself?'

'I did not kill my husband! You have to believe me!'

I sat there humiliated, and defeated. My Mum was crying, and Andy was in the back listening. I can't understand why he's at the court hearings. Why do I have the impression Andy knows I didn't do it? Why doesn't he come forward and help me? He won't, they are like brothers, that's what Michael said. They're protecting Sam. The police are still looking for him. Is Andy willing to carry such burden to defend his friend who assaulted a woman, and killed the husband of that very woman? I don't think he can. I wonder what Michael will do? He's killed once, perhaps he'd kill again.

Michael won't tolerate going to prison, and what they do to pretty boys like him. He'd kill himself instead of going through that. Andy looked at me with a puzzling expression, like he knows something more, and was telling me, *you don't deserve this*. He knows I didn't do it. Andy nodded before walking out. I have the feeling something terrible is about to happen, I don't know what, but I can feel it, and I can't do anything to stop it from happening.

10th September
Evening

Jonathan told me the night Richard died, Michael was in the club, and alibis confirmed it. How is that possible? How can someone be at the same place at once? Precision is a fundamental key. How did he do it? It takes a lot of effort to plan something like this.

Jonathan stood in the courtroom and began to tell the jury,

'It all began the night Mr. and Mrs. Knight bumped into Michael in the restaurant. When Michael saw Richard in person, he started to become envious of him. Until then the man was non-existent.'

Jonathan paced up and down the room.

'Michael knew Mr. Knight had heart problems and was on medication, because Sophie told him so.' Jonathan addressed the room. 'He set out a plan that involved poison, the weapon of choice for wives to get rid of their husbands. It's a classic, old-fashioned way to commit a crime. Which poison though? All of them are lethal. He decided the poison would be *sodium hypochlorite,* most commonly found in household bleach. The most accessible poison found in hardware stores. If you look at item fifteen, that is the bottle of bleach found in Sophie's cupboard under in the sink. She did not keep any washing products there so where did it come from? There is another matter to consider, item twenty, the turkey basters. There was no record of Sophie buying or owning any. Why should she?'

Jonathan faced the jury. 'To commit the perfect crime, it requires discipline and patience. Michael bought the bleach, and rather than carrying a bottle to her flat he carried it inside item twenty-the plastic tubes, safely hidden in the breast pocket of his blazer. He went to Evelyne's more frequently, passing through Sophie's neighborhood, hoping he'd catch her on her way in or out. On the afternoon before Richard's death, the opportunity presented itself. In her diary, item twenty-one, Sophie wrote about how she ran into Michael near her apartment that afternoon. He followed her there, they argued and had make-up sex. She fell asleep, and I propose to the jury, that Michael got out of the bed, took the tube of bleach with him to the bathroom and removed item seventeen, that is Richard's aftershave.

Then came the key, Sophie had found it misplaced in her bag. In her diary, she wrote.' Jonathan paused for a brief moment and studied the jury, holding their attention as my dairy was passed around. 'Michael could have made a copy and placed the key back, only he made a slight mistake. He placed it in the wrong pocket,' Jonathan explained, 'In her diary entries she wrote that Michael came to her apartment for the second time with the excuse that he wanted to make love to her.' Another slight pause, 'when Sophie ended the affair, it sent his jealousy into a downward spiral.'

As Jonathan explained all of this to jury, I wondered what Michael thought when I ended the affair.

Sophie took the pleasure, my passion, my love, my body, my dignity, and my pride. She took and took until she left me with nothing, and when she had her fill, she tossed me aside like garbage to join the line of rejected, unwanted, inconvenient lovers. Did she actually think she would hurt me and win? No fucking way, she doesn't get to win.

Jonathan's voice brought me back to the present. 'First, he let the affair get into the open by hacking into her email and sending those photos. He made sure everything she loved and owned crumbled. Now, the night of the murder, Richard spent most of the day in his study and then went to bed. By then, the bleach had done severe damage. Nausea hit Richard like a punch. Meanwhile, Sophie drank a bottle of wine in front of the TV, switched off the lights, and went to sleep. Michael entered the flat using the set of keys that he'd had copied. The supplies were in his pocket. He located the master bedroom, dipped the turkey basters into the bleach and forced it into Richard's mouth. With Richard's heart condition, one dose was enough to kill him. He continued until the bleach was finished. He would have felt agonizing pain, with the bleach tearing up his esophagus, and the rest of his organs, and died a slow and painful death,' Jonathan said.

I imagined Michael looking into the eyes of a dead man, of him coming into my room and gently pressing the turkey baster against my finger long enough to leave a fingerprint, and doing the same again with the bottle of bleach. Jonathan's voice brought me back to attention.

'He planted the bleach, the tubes, and turkey basters under the sink and fled the scene.'

How did it feel to be a murderer? Killing an innocent man, he had no quarrel with. To have Richard's murder tied around his neck for the rest of his life. I still can't establish how he had alibis. Did he force them? All of them? No, there's an explanation. It's right there in front of me, only I'm missing it.

15th September
Evening

Waiting has become a big part of my life. Staring at walls has become my main pastime. The whole experience has put me off drinking. Michael is roaming in the streets living his life, while I am here. How did it lead to this? I told Michael where we stood from the beginning. I thought I was clear, but no matter how many times I told him, he didn't really believe me. He thought I'd leave it all for him.

I've done bad things this year but not enough to go to prison for. Michael wants to punish me, to humiliate me, to see me rot. Nothing will give him more pleasure than to see me go to prison. Andy has been to the courtroom twice. Maybe he was there the whole time, but I didn't see him. Was it Andy sending me the notes? My instinct tells me he knows I'm innocent. He knows Michael did it. I can't do anything, nobody will believe me. Can't Andy testify as a witness?

20th September
Night

Jonathan came to see me this afternoon to deliver some terrible news. As he began to tell me, I saw his lips moving, but the moment didn't seem real.

'It can't be...no...it must be a mistake.'

'No, it's no mistake, Sophie.'

He placed a newspaper in front of me, a photo of me, then another picture of the flat.

Fire in Camden.

The headline read. Two people dead, five injured. I stared at the headline without reading the article, the words smudged from my vision. All I heard were background noises and voices. Jonathan placed his hand on my shoulder.

'Are you all right?'

When will this nightmare end?

'Sophie?'

I just want to lie down, close my eyes, and wake up when it's all over. Will it ever be over?

21st September
Afternoon,

I sat in the room looking at the tiny window. The sun is out, that's all I know. I've got the newspaper lying on the bed beside me, and I still can't believe it. I've read it several times now, reminding myself it's real. The bodies found in Michael's flat are still unidentified. Jonathan told me he'd let me know when there's more news.

Is Michael dead? Sam? Andy? My mind is racing. I can't relax. I'm so tired, haven't had a proper sleep in months. I feel dirty, haggard, and weak. *A fire.* The flat burned to ashes. Did he start the fire? I don't believe it's an accident, even though the newspaper said it might be an electrical fault.

Maybe Michael is involved and made it look like an accident. How many lives is he going to ruin to save his own skin? Mike's not dead, not in a million years. I feel so helpless, if only they had listened, then none of this would have happened. Nobody wants to listen to a drunk.

24th September
Afternoon

Jonathan came to visit me today. He placed a few newspapers on the table in front of me. The bodies have been identified - and they say they are Michael and Antti Hekkila's, formerly known by his stage name as just Andy. Michael is dead. No, he can't be dead! It's impossible! He also told me the police had found incriminating stuff about Andy, and that the police are questioning Evelyne.

'Are you listening to me, Sophie?' Jonathan asked.

'I'm sorry, it's a terrible shock, it makes no sense. I told you Michael killed Richard, and now he's framed Andy for it? Can't they see?'

'Sophie, Michael called the police before the fire and said, 'you're sending the wrong person to prison, it wasn't Sophie, it was Andy. I've been stabbed, please come. There was a struggle. Both bodies had stab wounds.'

At Evelyne's apartment, Andy had a room that nobody was allowed into, he carried the key everywhere with him. The police found it on the body. In the room, the police found guitars, cocaine, money, and marijuana. Apart from that, they found tubes, bleach, turkey basters, photographs of me, a photograph of Richard, and black French knickers. Evelyne said they are not hers, and the police suspect they are mine. How did Andy manage to get my panties? And if that wasn't devastating enough, they found a key, but it didn't match any locks at Evelyne's apartment. Blake tried it on my apartment, and it worked.

'Andy must have been the one sending you those notes, and who tried to push you and everything else,' Jonathan said.

I shook my head, Andy had nothing to do with this. Was he a character? Yes. Full of shit? Yes. A stalker? Never.

'You know Michael might have planted everything there,' I said to Jonathan

'A drug dealer came forward. He was questioned and admitted he sold Andy the drugs.'

I couldn't listen anymore, about the lives he destroyed, and the innocent people he'd hurt. I know Mike's not dead there's something I'm missing. It's there, but I'm too confused to see it.

30th September
Evening,

Can't get it out of my head, did he do it to spare me from the terrible fate? If it weren't for that night, if I didn't leave the club with Sam, none of this would have happened.

Blake has just been here to have a word with me. Evelyne is still at the police station, she must be going through a tough time right now. The confusion, the unanswered questions, the shock, Andy didn't kill Richard, how could he? He had no reasons to, nor did he send me the notes. He's just another man dragged through the mud.

Black told me the charges against me will be dropped, and my name will be cleared. There's a new lead to the case, and I have to wait to show up to court in front of a judge, again. 'Just be happy, Mrs. Knight, soon you'll be a free woman.'

What's the point? That's what I keep asking myself. What's the point? The damage is done. It won't bring my husband back.

1st October
Morning,

This is my story. This year I started writing a diary, hopeful I'd turn my life around, but look how appalling I've behaved. It's not over yet, not until I've solved the mystery. There are questions that need answering. How did Michael frame Andy? What did indeed happen in that flat? What happened to Sam? Where is Sam? Is he dead too? Was he the one sending me the bloody notes and making those phone calls? Did he try to push me to an oncoming car? Why?

I have to find out what happened. Michael's dead. I read each snippet about the accident. Did Andy make the anonymous phone calls?

5th October
Afternoon,

Blake came to see me, to identify the underwear. They are mine all right. Michael could have taken them from my bag, he took my key, so God knows what else he took that I'm not aware of. It gives me the creeps.

I've been lying on the bed staring at the ceiling, going over our affair to look for more clues. Our relationship was a fantasy. I was in such a trance, I failed to realize until it was too late. I've been going over the night I found the key misplaced, the evening I saw Sam.

Someone tried to get into the flat and left me a note by the door. After the police came, I ran out of the flat and went straight to the enemy, who offered solace, comfort, and love when I needed it. I found Michael in the club and met his friend, Matti, the blond, who looked like him.

I saw their outburst and how upset Michael was. He was troubled that night, deep in thought. Matti said he was a musician passing through from Sweden, before going to New York? Whatever happened to him? I had totally forgotten about him, I must speak to Blake at once.

8th October
Afternoon,

'But you have to understand, perhaps Matti has something to do with this? What if the alibis about Michael being in the club weren't true? Maybe it wasn't him they saw, but Matti,' I said to Blake.

He stood across from me, with his hands sunk into his grey coat pockets.

'What crime novels have you been reading?' Blake asked.

It makes sense. Matti might have been in the club, the night Richard was murdered. The people at the club might have mistaken him for Michael.

'He looks a lot like him, the only difference is Michael has blue eyes, Matti has green eyes.'

'Had.' Blake corrected me.

'I don't believe he's dead.'

'What are you saying?'

'I have a theory…'

Blake crossed his arms. 'Let's hear it.'

I circled around the room. 'What if whoever saw Mike in the club wasn't Mike but Matti?'

'Mike performed at the club, Sophie. There's footage.'

'What about afterward? What if he sneaked out and the people there thought it was him, but it wasn't.'

Blake shook his head.

'Hear me out will you,' I snapped.

He sighed.

'In the flat, two bodies were found - Andy's and Michael's, but what if it was Matti and not Michael?'

'The identification was positive. You might find it hard to believe, but the body was of Michael Frisk - he's dead, Sophie. He died after he made the phone call to the police.'

I sighed. 'You're not listening to me detective. What if Michael was using another name?'

'Why would he hide his identity?'

'Let's say Michael is living as this lad Matti, this person from his past. Michael had something on Matti and Matti wanted to frame Michael. Maybe that's why I saw them argue that night and their friendship was just for the public…. So, Michael finds a way to get rid of him in that flat. Michael killed Matti and put his body in the flat, don't ask me how, I'm just hypothesizing. Maybe he invited him over and killed him there. While he was looking for a way to get rid of the body, Andy showed up to confront him, and told him he knew he killed Richard. That was when he decided to get rid of Andy too, and the fire was deliberate to destroy the evidence.'

Blake rubs his face, he's not getting it. 'Do you have any idea how crazy this sounds?'

'Is it, though?'

'He must be smart for a kid.'

'But that's the thing with Mike, he is relentless. He does whatever's necessary.'

'Leave the detective work to me, Sophie. The case is closed, and soon you'll be free a woman. Just put this behind you. It's not easy, but try to take care of yourself.'

'What do you mean take care of myself?'

'The drinking.'

'I haven't had a drink in months.'

'Good, stick with it. The drinking led you into this trouble in the first place.'

'Sam will know if that body you found is truly Michael's, and I bet he knows where he is.'

'We searched Evelyne's place. He left like he was in a hurry.'

I stared at him thinking *that's it?* They're going to stop looking for him? What about what he did to me?

Blake turned to leave. 'It's a good theory, I must admit, but we can't prove it.'

'Did you find saxophones?'

Blake spun around. 'What?'

I turned to him. It was the first time I saw the good detective confused.

'In Michael's flat, did you find saxophones? He owned three. One silver, one gold, and one red.'

'No, we didn't find any saxophones, we did find a guitar... what was left of it.'

I know they didn't find jack shit because he took them with him. A musician would not leave his prized possessions behind.

15th October
Morning,
Dear Diary,

I'm a free woman. Bought a new diary. I've decided that since the year is almost over, I will start afresh, but to do so, I have to move out of the city. I don't want to live in an apartment where Richard died. Since Richard had no relatives, he left everything under my name. I'm going to use the money wisely. Even if Blake doesn't believe my theory, I'm going to stick with it. Mum is helping me look after things. I missed her so much, no wonder I felt so lost all those years.

'If you were so lonely, why didn't you talk to me about it?' she said.

'I didn't want to worry you, and what with Richard and all… how things were between us…'

She placed her hand on mine. 'I'm still your mother. I would have listened and helped you. As if the miscarriages weren't enough. What you've been through is awful.'

'I know.'

'I don't see why Blake won't follow up on your theory. Richard's death needs some form of justice.'

Mum took over from me washing the cups. 'Let me do that for you, you need to rest.'

I lay in the guest bedroom. I can't sleep in the master bedroom. Mum is going to clear Richard's things as it is too hard for me. I couldn't sleep so I switched on my laptop instead. My Inbox is full of unread emails, but I'm not ready to deal with that yet. I Googled "Michael Frisk," and the stuff that came up was unbearable. The affair, the murder, the fire. How he "died" in the fire. I closed the window and typed "high schools in Sweden." I'll send emails to every school around the country if that's what it takes. This is where I'm going to start to prove I am correct.

18th October
Afternoon,
Dear Diary,

I think I know where Michael will be. I bet he's in New York. He told me he wanted to go there the night he invited me to his apartment for the first time. Matti said he was going to New York too. It's there in my old dairy. I need to tell DC Blake.

25th October
Evening
Dear Diary,

I was awoken by voices. It was mum arguing with another woman.

'I have to speak to her, it's urgent,' a pleading voice said.

'She has been through enough, why don't you people leave her alone.' Mum hissed.

I got up and checked what the excitement was. Mum stood by the front door with her hands on her hips, I took a step forward to see who she was talking to. Evelyne stared at me with bloodshot eyes, shaken.

'It's okay, mum,' I said.

Mum and Evelyne turned to me. 'Are you sure, dear?' Mum asked.

'Yes, please, Evelyne, come in,' I said.

Mum moved out of the way, and Evelyne lurched in the apartment. 'Can you leave us, Mum?' I said.

Mum left. I glanced at the wispy girl before me.

'Thank you for seeing me,' she said, 'I know this is hard after what you've been through, but I…'

I invited her to sit down and handed her a box of tissues.

She scanned the boxes in the apartment. 'Are you moving?' she asked.

'Yes.'

'I see,' she said, 'where are you moving to?'

'To my parents until I figure out my next move,' I replied.

I went to the kitchen and put the kettle on.

'Can I have one?' she said, pointing at my cigarette.

'Oh sure, here.'

I handed her my packet of cigarettes and a lighter. I finished making the tea and sat beside her making sure there was enough distance between us.

'It's so hard,' she said, puffing on her cigarette, 'I still can't believe that he's…'

She buried her face in tissues and sobbed.

'Did you have an affair with him?'

'Who?'

'Andy.'

'God, no.'

'I hated you, you know,' she said.

I stared at her.

'Not hated you, more like envied you.'

'Why?'

'You had everything, well at least in my eyes you had, the successful, handsome husband, the apartment, money, the career, and the clothes. I used to see you walk down the street with your nose up in the air as if the world was at your feet. I would never have guessed you'd turn into an alcoholic and an adulteress.'

'Did you come here to torment me?'

'Sorry, I didn't mean to sound like that... no, I came here because I thought you might understand what I'm going through. I feel so bad to have waited all this time to speak to you.'

'It's all right. I need to ask you a few questions too.'

'If you're going to ask about Sam, I don't know where he is. I already told the police this. They think I have something to do with him disappearing. He left like he was in a hurry. His things are still in my apartment. He left his guitars behind which strike me as odd because his guitars were his life.'

'Did you know what he did to me?'

She looked at me in horror. 'No, I didn't have any idea at the time. He didn't mean it, I know Sam, he's such a happy-go-lucky kind of guy. It must have been an accident.'

I let her continue, despite my urge to put her right.

'There's no excuse for assault, and if I'd known anything, I would have reported him myself. They made sure I didn't find out, but after that night they started to behave strangely.'

'In what sense strangely?'

'I had an argument with Andy that night. I left the club and went home to bed. I woke up the next day at around eight, and they were awake, Andy, Mike, and Sam. It was odd because they didn't usually wake up that early, Andy and Sam at least. Michael used to wake up early to do sit-ups, he liked to take care of himself. Sam's bedroom door was closed. I walked past his room, and they were talking in Swedish so I couldn't understand what they were saying, but your name popped up,' she paused and took a sip of her tea.

'They came out ten minutes later, Sam was deathly pale and shaken up, like he was scared and had been crying. I asked Andy...' She paused as fat tears fall down her cheeks. I passed her the box of tissues. She took a few and blew her nose, 'I asked Andy if something was the matter, and all he told me was that Sam got into a fight. I found it strange, he didn't look like he had been in a fight, no black eyes or anything like that.'

She sparked another cigarette. 'I didn't think about it again until I saw you once with Mike, you were coming out of the grocery store. You didn't see me, you were too into him to take any notice, I think. You looked in a trance. I thought now there is a woman who has everything, but she can't help mess it up. Your marriage was none of my business, but I knew it was only a matter of time before something happened between you two.'

'What made you think that?'

She puffed on her cigarette. 'I never understood the big deal with Mike, yes he was good looking, but he was too pretty for my taste. The first time Andy introduced me to him, I thought he was gay, but he got that a lot. I saw him with enough women to know he wasn't. He didn't care what people thought of him, and I liked that in him. He was quiet, private and took care of friends. He was loyal. Andy and Sam loved to party, but Mike wasn't into that, not every night at least. He was sensible, intelligent, and different. I'm not saying he was an angel, he had his demons.'

'Which were?'

'I don't know, as I said he was private, kept himself to himself. Once Andy told me that back in Sweden, he was living with a musician friend and his wife for a while, and became involved with her.'

'Wait,' I said confused, 'you're telling me that Mike was living with his friend and was having sex with his wife and this guy was okay with it?'

'That's what Andy said. So after I saw you two talking, I told him that this is not Sweden, we do things differently here. I recall telling him, "You're not going to fuck somebody else's wife and get a pat on the back from her husband." He told me it's not what I think. I think he had genuine feelings towards you. Two weeks later, he moved out, telling me he needed his privacy and thanked me for everything. He said he'd be forever grateful, that sort of crap. I didn't know you were both having sex with each other.'

She lit another cigarette. 'One afternoon I came home, and Mike was there. He pushed Sam against the wall and pulled him by his shirt. I had no idea what they were talking about, but they were speaking in their native tongue,' she paused to take a sip of her tea, 'Mike saw me and shut the door. I don't understand what you were thinking, you didn't think of the risks?'

'Of course, I did.'

'After you were arrested, me and Andy were shocked and made anonymous phone calls to the police. We knew it couldn't be you.'

'So, it was you?'

'Yes, Andy went to court to listen to your case. The night before... the fire... Andy was high on drugs. I didn't like him taking drugs in my apartment. We argued a lot about that. He kept saying, 'I won't let him get away with it.' When I asked what he was talking about it, he kept repeating the same words. And the next day....'

'When I came to your college you ran away from me. Why?'

'I knew you were skeptical. I didn't know what was going on and wanted to stay out of it. When I saw you I panicked and ran, I'm sorry.'

She began to cry again so I put my arms around her. 'Would you like more tea?'

She nodded. I cleared the cups away and put the kettle on again.

'The police kept asking me questions, and looking at me as if I had something to do with it, but I swear I didn't know,' she cried.

'Did you tell the police what you just told me?'

'Yes.'

'Why didn't you come forward to the police before and tell them I was innocent?'

'I was frightened.'

'Frightened? I was going to go to prison for something I didn't do, that is frightening.'

'I'm sorry,' she said, blowing her nose with a tissue,' I'm so sorry for everything. I was scared I...' She broke into tears again. 'I should have done something, but I didn't know what.'

'Do you think Mike killed my husband?'

There was a long pause. 'It doesn't matter what I think now, the case is closed.'

'Not to me, it isn't.'

'Please don't get angry at me, I can't take it.'

I handed her a fresh cup of tea. 'I'm not angry at you, I'm trying to get to the bottom of this. Were you sending me notes?'

She blinked at me. 'No.'

'Do you know about them?'

'Why would I? You were getting notes?'

'Yes?'

'What did they say?'

'Nasty stuff...'

'Did you know about the phone calls and someone trying to push me into the road?'

'No, Maybe it was Mike, he must have been jealous of your husband.'

'No, I saw his reaction in court. When he was asked about the notes and the phone calls.' I sat beside her, and continued, 'do you know a man called Matti, a friend of Mike's?'

She shook her head. 'No, but Mike knew many people, being a musician. Why do you ask?'

'Because I think Mike is still alive, and that body was of Matti, not of Mike. Mike was hiding his true identity.'

'That's crazy.'

'Is it?'

'People change their name all the time, it doesn't make them criminals.'

'You don't understand. What I'm telling you is, the body the police found was of the real Mike, that's why the identification was positive.'

'I don't know, all I know is that my life feels over.'

'I know, now you know how I felt. Get some rest, and be with your family.

30th October
Evening,
Dear Diary,

I visited Richard's grave today and sat beside his tombstone. I stared in disbelief at the words *Richard Knight a loving husband rest in peace*. It will be the first Christmas I'm going to spend without him.

I arranged a bouquet of daffodils into the vase on his grave.

'I'm so sorry you had to suffer because of my actions. I'm sorry I lied to you, and hid my drinking from you. I'm sorry I wasn't a good wife. I didn't mean it to turn out this way. I'm not asking you to forgive me. I just want to say what I didn't get a chance to, to hold you one last time and tell you, despite all the bad I've done, that you were the only one, and you are still the only one I ever loved. I will make this right.'

5th November
Afternoon,
Dear Diary

I'm going to live with my Mum in Hounslow for a while, and I'm searching for properties to start my life anew. A cottage in Cornwall perhaps? And maybe a career in teaching? Doesn't sound too bad to me.

I went to the police station with the book I got in the mail yesterday, from Sweden. A high school yearbook. Inside are the two great looking blonds that could pass as brothers, Mike and Matti. Under Mike's picture is the name 'Matti' and under Matti's picture it says 'Mike'. I left it for Blake so he could admit I am correct. The man I mistook for Michael that night is indeed the real Michael, and the man I was a having an affair with is Matti. Michael is dead, but Matti is alive and living in New York. Now it's up to Blake to work out the rest.

I continued with the final touches of the packing, ensuring everything was folded neatly, and labeled. I stacked the boxes into the corner of the living room. I don't know where Mum is going to put all of this. The apartment is up for sale. I can't wait until this place is sold, I don't want to ever have to step foot in it again. I closed and taped up the last box, and wrote "books" on the label. I looked around the room, which had been once so alive, decorated with furniture and fine art, and filled with laughter. It's now nothing more than a hollow shell, filled with sadness and bad memories.

The sound of the buzzer startled me. I went to the intercom to see who it was. It was a delivery for me. I thought it was strange because I hadn't ordered anything. A uniformed man from UPS handed me a large white box tied with a red ribbon, addressed to me. I signed for it, then took the box inside and placed it on the sofa. I must have spent several minutes inspecting it, not daring to open. Something felt weird, it had no return address, or note, just stamps from England. And what was with the bow? I untied the silky red ribbon and pulled it away from the box. As I opened the lid, my heart hammered against my chest. I opened the lid.

Perched inside a velvet casing was a gleaming golden alto saxophone. I jumped away from the box and circled the room, not knowing what to do. I surveyed the box and the gleaming alto golden saxophone inside.

What kind of sick message is this? So, I was right, he is alive, and he's sent me that saxophone to mock me.

I shut my eyes in despair, so that means he's still in England.

I didn't touch the saxophone. I left it in the box and called Blake. Fifteen minutes later, Blake arrived at the apartment.

'Where is it?' Blake asked.

I pointed to the sofa. Miranda turned to me. 'Did you touch it?'

I shook my head.

Blake inspected the golden saxophone without touching it. 'We need to take it to the lab for prints,' he instructed Miranda. She nodded.

'Of course,' I said.

He removed his gloves. Miranda took the box and left.

'You should leave the apartment,' Blake said.

'I'm moving today,' I said.

'Good, I got your book.'

'And?'

'We're working on it. I will get in touch with the school, this afternoon.'

'So, you believe me now?'

'I do, but to reopen a case can be difficult.'

'Not if you have strong evidence.'

Mom came in. 'What's wrong?'

Blake smiled. 'I'll see myself out.' He turned to the door and stopped, 'good luck, Sophie.'

'Thank you.'

'Honey, what's wrong?'

'We need to get out of here, I'll explain in the car.'

It was dark by the time I gathered my things and loaded them into my mother's car. Mom waited for me in the car as I locked my apartment and carried the last box with me. And then I saw him, standing by the pole. Sam. Smoking, dressed in all black and a white blazer, his eyes set on me. I dropped the box to the floor.

'Sophie, what's wrong?' Mom said.

He was holding something. It was hard to tell in the dark, but it looked like a note. Blake got out of the car. He didn't leave right away, maybe to see we left safely. My eyes went back to Sam, who hadn't noticed the detective coming his way. I watched Blake take Sam away and drove away.

10th November
Evening,
Dear Diary,

I thought that the whole ordeal was over, but it wasn't. The phone rang, and my mom picked it. 'For God's sake,' she said, and passed the phone to me, 'it's Blake.'

My brain went into overdrive wondering why he was calling. Had they found Michael? That had to be it, I figured. I swallowed and took a deep breath.

'Yes.' I said sounding business like.

'I don't know how to say this,' he said, 'I have rather unsettling news, and if you don't want to hear, I'll understand.'

'Tell me,' I snapped.

I didn't mean it to come out that way, but I just wanted him to tell me.

There was a pause.

'Sam won't speak to us.'

'Oh,' I said.

Is that supposed to be my problem? He was their concern now, not mine.

'He said he wants to talk to you.'

'What on earth does he want to say to me? Hasn't he done enough?'

'I understand if you don't—'

'Talk to me about what?' I asked.

'He didn't say.'

'Oh sod it. Just tell me when and I'll be there,' I said.

After I hung up, I dragged myself into my old bedroom with boy bands posters on the wall and dropped onto the bed. I haven't bothered to look for an apartment yet. I haven't looked because I want to get out of the city. I'm sick of it. I'm sick of everything. I can't move on if I stay here. Too many memories, too much pain. Everywhere reminds me of *him*. What does Sam want to say to me that he couldn't tell me before he was arrested? Why now? The curiosity is eating away at me.

13th November
Afternoon,
Dear Diary,

I went to the police station and Blake came to greet me.

'Take your time,' he said with an assuring smile, 'I know this is not easy for you but, through you, we can get him talking.'

'Don't thank me just yet,' I replied.

'Now, if you feel uncomfortable in any way there's going to be an officer outside the room.'

'Wait… you're not coming in there with me.'

'It won't work if I do, he wants to speak to you alone.'

'But…'

'No need to be alarmed, Sophie,' he said.

We are on a first name basis now as if we are old friends.

'You're going to be safe,' Blake said. He paused and looked at me wryly, 'just be on your guard. I come across the worst kind you can imagine. The lowest scum on earth.' I stared at him. He composed himself, 'whenever you are ready.'

Sam was already at the table when I walked in the room. It was a cold and drab, grey room, without any windows. I sat opposite him. Only a table separated us. I didn't feel safe, despite having the police-woman standing outside the door. Sam stared at me. It occurred to me how young he looked. Barely in his twenties. The black wavy fringe wasn't covering his eyes for once. I could see them, blue and clear. I scanned them to detect any coldness in them, but I could only sense warmth. It made my body shudder. He broke eye contact and leaned back against the chair.

'I'm here, so talk,' I said, crossing my arms.

He took a deep inhale of breath and lowered his eyes to the table. 'There are some things I need to explain to you. Some things you have to understand.'

'Yes, you do,' I agreed, 'you can start with the notes.'

'The notes were a warning.'

'A warning?'

'Yes, against Matti or as you know him, Mike,' he said.

We stared at each other. I shuddered with the cold, as I realized that Sam knew who the real Matti is.

'You were sending me upsetting notes, to warn me against Matti. It doesn't make much sense.'

'Now Sophie, let's not get ahead of ourselves, I'm not your enemy. I am the one who told you about the photo on Facebook.

The clues were right in front of you, but you had your head too far into your own ass to notice.'

'Why did you send me the notes? What about the phone calls?'

'That was me too.'

'How did you get my number?'

'It's not hard to get anyone's number nowadays,' he said with a sly smile.

It made me sick, 'you attacked me.'

'Now, that's where you're wrong, Sophie. I didn't do it.'

I grabbed the chair. 'I remember what you did to me.'

'But that's where you're wrong, your memory is confused. You're an alcoholic, Sophie, what you remember don't mean shit. Yes, I did dance with you, but I left shortly afterward because Andy got in a fight with some geezer.'

'No, Matti went to stop the fight, not you.'

'No, Matti was out with you.'

I let it sink for a moment what he was implying. There was silence. It only lasted for a second, but it felt like ages. 'What? No, You're lying. It was you.'

'Remember what you want, but it was Matti who did it, not me.'

I jumped out of the chair and made my way over to the door.

'I was the one who found you on the ground. Matti was shaking on the pavement. He was crying and freaking out. He took my lighter to light a joint. He was playing with it when I found him. I have seen his wrath, but I didn't think he'd go that far. So, I did what I had to do. He was my friend after all. He was like a big brother.'

I turned and glanced at him. 'Think long and hard, it's in the depths of your brain, only you won't allow it to surface, because you're afraid.'

I took a seat again. 'Why didn't tell me like a normal person? Why didn't you tell the police?' I asked.

'Well, he was my friend, and you never reported it.'

'You kept quiet because he's your friend?'

'Yes, but I wanted you to remember.'

'You think stalking me was your way of helping me?' I paused, 'Sylvie told me she saw you crying the day after what had happened.'

'I was upset... we all were for what he did.'

'And you and Andy didn't care to tell me the truth. You were awful to me.'

'Who would have believed us?'

My eyes found the floor as snippets of that awful night started to come back to me.

'No,' I said, 'It can't be.'

'You were having an affair with your attacker,' Sam said in a whisper.

'No.'

'I was sixteen when I met Matti. He was a little older. I thought he was gay at first, but I grew fond of him. We didn't have much in Sweden, we both came from low-class families, and we just clicked. Girls loved him. He wasn't interested in them in a way. The first time I saw his anger was when he started seeing this girl. Women always seemed to bring the worst out of him.' He narrowed his eyes at me, 'you brought out the worst in him.

I sat there frozen.

'Anyway,' Sam said, breaking the silence. They got into some argument. It was a silly thing not worth remembering. But he went nuts. We were on a railway line, you see. He jumped onto the rails and shouted at the girl, 'see my rage, see my rage.' He said it over and over again. A train was coming. We could hear it in the distance. I managed to calm him down, and he got off the track before the train ran him over. I know this is a lot of take in, but it wasn't me, you have to believe that.'

'Who pushed me down the road?'

Silence.

'Nobody pushed you, you stumbled. You took a wrong step. You were holding the note I sent you.'

'No, I didn't I...'

'You did. I took the note and got rid of it. Look, I wasn't jealous of you and Matti. I just wanted you to see. To stop what you were doing before it went further. Matti knew I was up to something and came to see me one night when Evelyne and Andy were out. This was two days after you saw me looking up at your window.'

'What did he say?' I asked.

'That whatever I was doing, it had to stop. That you wouldn't believe me. That I was creeping you out...'

'Someone tried to break into my apartment, was that you?'

'No, it wasn't me. I may have done some crazy shit, but that wasn't me.'

'You honestly think he loved you?' Sam asked.

'I don't know what to think anymore.'

'What's done is done. Your husband is dead. Your life is shattered. I'm going to prison and Matti well…'

An uncomfortable silence enveloped the room.

'Why did Mike and Matti switch identities? You must know why the real Matti was using Mike's name.'

'It's something they did.'

'They did for fun you mean?'

'Yeah…'

'So, Mike had nothing on Matti.'

'Not that I am aware of. Mike was in the picture longer than I was.'

I didn't believe him but I wasn't going to push it. It didn't matter anyway. I rubbed my face with my hands. 'You know where he is?' I asked.

'Yes.'

'Are you going to tell the police?'

'I am, yeah,' Sam replied.

The urge to go to the nearest pub was irresistible, but I resisted. After a brief conversation with Blake, where I told him everything Sam had told me, I left the police station. The city buzzed around me. I cried in the taxi, still shaking from the news. It felt like a blow in the gut as it swept over me. Me drinking. Sylvie laughing with Nicky. The music was so loud it felt like an intruder. And then I recalled it, as clear as day. I went to the bar to get myself a drink. Matti came over and said something, I don't remember what, but we smiled at each other, and I walked past him out of the club. He stood in front lighting a joint with a zippo.

Sam's zippo.

Thanks for reading!

Please add a review and let me know what you thought.

Reviews are helpful to authors, thank you for taking the time to support me and my work. Don't forget to share your review on social media and encourage others to read the story too!

You can also sign up for my monthly newsletter, to receive special offers, giveaways, discounts, bonus content, and updates on my new releases: Also, you will get a free short story when signing up!

https://joannewritesbooks.com

Get a free short story when joining the list

Other works by J.S Ellis

The Secret She Kept

She's dead. Why would she lie?

Days before her murder, Anthony's friend, Lottie, lent him her laptop. Curiosity getting the best of him, he clicks on a file and finds videos recorded by her in the year leading up to her death. Within those recordings, she exposes dark secrets someone will kill to keep hidden, and Lottie's toxic relationship with Anthony's long-time friend, Davian.

When Anthony's childhood friend, Davian is placed under arrest for the murder, Anthony refuses to believe he could do such a thing but Lottie was infatuated by Davian. More damning evidence piles up, Anthony wonders if it's possible a man he's known for most of his life has kept a sinister side of himself hidden.

Now, Anthony faces an impossible choice; turn the laptop over to the police and risk being accused of hindering the investigation, or try to solve the case himself. Lottie gave him the computer for a reason. There was something there she wanted him to see. Can he put the pieces of the puzzle together in time to uncover the killer?

Theodore: The Neighbour's Cat.

My roommate is a serial killer.

And I have been powerless to stop him because I... am a cat.

Don't get me wrong, Dean has never been cruel to me. He provides me with shelter, toys, and plenty of affection. But I have seen his dark side, his brutal treatment of women, and I can't bear to watch anyone else get hurt.

Jane from next door is attractive for a human, not to mention being incredibly kind. That kindness may get her killed. I've seen how Dean looks at her, I know what he's plotting. In his mind, she's his for the taking. I wasn't able to save the others, but I'm not ready to give up. One way or another, I have to figure out how to communicate to Jane that she's in danger.

Can I find a way to warn her in time? Or will she become just another name on his growing list of victims?

The Rich Man

Her boyfriend vanished, but moving on could be murder...

Acey left without a word, leaving Elena alone to pick up the pieces of her broken heart. Determined not to be crushed by his betrayal, she forces herself to get over him.

Never did she fathom the unspeakable darkness closing in...

Sinclair Diamond breezes into her life like an answered prayer. Handsome. Wealthy. Charming. As he lovingly dotes on her, Elena finds herself falling for him.

But Sinclair has unspeakable secrets all his own.

Men in black suits trailing them. Shady business dealings. The odd chain of events surrounding his first wife's death. The more Elena learns about Sinclair, the more her apprehension builds. Yet when a ghost from her past reappears, Elena is forced to face a startling truth that could cost her everything.

Can she escape the web of deceit tightening around her? Or will she be the next to mysteriously disappear?

Lost and Found Book 1

Despite being polar opposites, Phoebe and Adele's friendship has stretched on for years. One a bubbly blonde, the other raven-haired and studious. They seem to have nothing in common, yet the bond between them is unbreakable.

Or so Phoebe thought.

She never believed Adele would hide anything from her until she sees her sneaking off with her handsome neighbor. Feeling betrayed, Phoebe begins to see cracks in their friendship she never noticed before.

Then, Adele vanishes.

Fearing for Adele's safety, Phoebe searches for clues about her disappearance. However, the deeper she digs, the more she realizes she didn't know Adele as well as she thought. Yet as revelations come to light, one mystery remains. What happened to Adele? And how is her disappearance connected to the stranger next door?

Hide and Seek Book 2

Hope is waning with Phoebe no closer to finding her best friend, Adele. Her suspicions involving her neighbor, Alan, have been cleared, leaving her no other hunches to pursue.

Until the letter arrives.

A message, written in Adele's hand, paints a picture of a side of her friend's life Phoebe never knew. Renewed with optimism that she is still alive, Phoebe launches back into the investigation. Among the pages of Adele's communications Phoebe finds evidence pointing to an unlikely suspect...

And yet another connection to Alan.

He seemed so concerned about the investigation, wanting to help in any way he could. Was the man next door a genuine ally? Or working to protect the real culprit?

The Confidant

Secrets have deadly consequences.

A part of him knew she was always lying, but he could change that. He could change her.

When charismatic Zoë first sits in Jason's salon chair, he can immediately tell they have a connection. Who wouldn't? She was smart, witty, and incredibly funny, everything someone could want in a budding friendship. But soon, Jason learns there is more to Zoë than meets the eye.

When lies are uncovered and secrets exposed, Jason must decide just how far he's willing to go in the name of friendship.

How far should he go to uncover the truth? If he digs too deep, could Jason lose the very person he's trying to keep?

When it all comes crashing to the light, and someone's very life hangs in the balance, will he regret what he's done? Or will Jason wish he had only done more?

Scan the code to buy the books

Acknowledgments

I'm a daydreamer. Sometimes I don't even know where I'm going because I've got my head stuck in the clouds. Thanks to those daydreams, I've been given the ability to write stories. I've been scribbling ever since I was a child. I didn't like reading though, the love of books came later much later.

I would like to thank my caring and kind fiancé Giacomo for his endless support and cheering. For being my critique partner, and offering invaluable advice. Thank you for opening my eyes at some points. I'd like to thank my mom and dad who can't understand my love of books, and my dad for threatening to throw all of my books away. He never did. To my brother, Jonathan. To my friends. To the beta readers who took the time to read it and provided helpful feedback.

Lastly, I would like to THANK YOU for reading this book.

About the Author

J.S Ellis is a thriller author. She lives in Malta with her husband and their furbaby, Eloise. When she's not writing or reading, she's either cooking, eating cheese and chocolate, or listening to good music and enjoying a glass of wine or two.

Website https://joannewritesbooks.com
Facebook https://www.facebook.com/authorJ.SEllis/
Instagram @ author_j.sellis
Goodreads http://bit.ly/2P8a9xx
Pinterest: https://bit.ly/3iqBvrU
Amazon: https://amzn.to/30rbKSq
Bingebooks: https://bingebooks.com/author/j-s-ellis
Bookbub: https://www.bookbub.com/authors/j-s-ellis

Made in the USA
Columbia, SC
13 February 2022